PRAISE FOR OTHER BOOKS BY HJ GAUDREAU

Amazon Readers React:

Betrayal in the Louvre

Enjoyed the book very much. I like the story line and characters. ...I have been to the Louvre and I always enjoy reading books where I can see in my mind where the scenes take place

The Collingwood Legacy

...very interesting read. Has just enough history... Keeps you on the edge of your seat without excessive violence. Just a great read.

Betrayal in the Louvre

...such a good read that it was hard to put down. Finally, a gift that he could get excited about. I will be ordering his second book for his upcoming birthday!

Betrayal in the Louvre

... an action packed, fast paced, yet educational read. The author does an excellent job setting the stage for the characters and time periods in which they lived.

The Collingwood Legacy

...really interesting learning about Detroit's bootlegging era and the Purple Gang. I liked going from the past to the present times. I would highly recommend it to history and mystery buffs alike.

A two hundred year old cure for mankind's greatest threat?

A beautiful and brilliant woman's
affair leads to deadly revenge.

A simple cure for viral infections is the Holy Grail
of medical science...and worth killing for!

A message from one of history's greatest doctors
holds the key to stopping AIDS and EBOLA.

A brutal killer stalks Jim and Eve through the
dense woods of the Huron National Forest.

The third installment of the Crenshaw Thrillers
finds Jim and Eve facing life in prison for murders
they didn't commit.

Has their luck finally run out?

THE
VIRUS
CONSPIRACY

H J Gaudreau

THE
VIRUS
CONSPIRACY

DEDICATION

Readers of my first two books may well remember Jim and Eve's lovable beagle. Molly was real. This past winter we lost her after fifteen years as part of our family.

Molly's 'spot' on the stairs allowed her to monitor the whereabouts of everyone in the house. From there she kept a close eye on her boy, our son Thomas. When he came downstairs, she came downstairs. When Thomas left for college she moved her 'spot' to the corner of the family room. There she could monitor Eve in the kitchen and me in my chair. Often she would get up, walk over to me, sit down and lean on my leg for a minute or two. Then, assured that I knew she loved me, she would return to her duties monitoring the house. I know that it's silly to shed a tear over a dog, but damn...I miss her.

ACKNOWLEDGMENTS

Once again I must thank my life long companion, Eve. You've done more than you'll ever know to make this book and my life better.

Many, many thanks to Lacey O'Connor. Lacey, once again you created a masterpiece for a book cover. You're a joy to work with.

The conflicts in Iraq, Afghanistan, Vietnam, Korea, are fading from the news. To some the effects of these wars will never fade. Don't let our nation's support for these veterans, who gave more than anyone should, turn into just a bumper sticker.

Please Support:
The Wounded Warrior Project
www.woundedwarriorproject.org

THE
VIRUS
CONSPIRACY

Chapter 1

Sarah Cox lifted her heavy blonde hair from under her gown and tossed it back and upward. Still not comfortable she shifted her weight from hip to hip. This was boring and the newly covered, recently renovated burgundy velvet chair she presently occupied reminded her of sitting on a lumpy pile of towels. She glanced around the chamber. Hill Auditorium had been dressed in its finest. Blue and gold bunting hung from the balcony to her rear. The stage she currently faced had been painted blue and gold. "No, it's maize and blue," she corrected herself. Carnations, each dyed in the same tired colors lined the curved stage edge. The United States flag, the University's flag and the flags of thirty-seven other countries lined the rear of the stage. The rear wall was covered by heavy curtains, blue of course, trimmed with gold tassels. A blue velvet rope separated the first forty rows of the audience from the remainder. Those seats were now filled with soon to be graduates of the University. The herd: parents, family, guests, and other strap hangers, all sat behind the rope and in the balcony.

Slightly behind the center line of the stage sat a row of twelve high-back, dark blue mahogany arm chairs. Each chair had the University crest embroidered in the center of its leather chair back. A gold emblem was mounted to the top of each chair identifying the endowment or department it represented. The exalted ones, their resumes long ago completed, their sole purpose in life now being to hang on as long as possible stuffing cash into their bank accounts so their grandchildren could inherit a ton of money and live a gilded life, courtesy of their superior family name, had shuffled into position over an hour ago. Now, their overstuffed lounge chairs were becoming a bit too comfortable. One or two of the ancient bastards were fighting off the occasional nod; Sarah expected a heavy snore to erupt any moment.

Half circle rings, each nested in the other, one end planted in the floor to her left then soaring overhead to crash to the floor on her right lined the ceiling and gave it a classic funnel appearance. The whole having the effect of focusing attention on the large podium at the front center of the stage. The podium was festooned with flowers, all in the school colors, which by now nearly nauseated Sarah. The podium had been constructed or rolled into position, she wasn't exactly sure, and a medium built, overweight dowager stood behind. The woman's gray hair peeked from under the black mortar board mounted to her head and her nasal voice did its best to lull the 'here because we have to be' crowd to sleep.

Sarah's attention, never focused on the proceedings at the dais, had shifted from the old farts to the flags. She attempted to identify each country, failed miserably then shifted her attention to her program. Now back to the flags. The cycle repeated. She did not want to be here. Wouldn't have been here save for the fact that her Grandmother was paying the bills and Grandma wanted to see her graduate. Sarah leaned back slightly, the chair squeaked. She glanced to her left, then right along the row of equally bored and deeply indebted students. Elaine McCloud glanced back and smiled. Elaine was easily the most obnoxious ass Sarah had ever met. Elaine never failed to mention that her father was head of the cardiac care unit at Henry Ford hospital. She never failed to mention her undergraduate degree from Oxford...yeah, that one, Oxford England. She was sure you had heard of it. And, Elaine never failed to flash those big, huge, remind me of a horse, teeth. Sarah complied with the social convention, nodded and shot a quick, insincere smile back.

The speaker droned on, now she was talking about the history of medicine. Sarah's brain screamed, "No one FRIGGIN' cares." The speaker didn't hear. Dr. Kimberly Jamison, Ph.D. biochemistry, MIT; Ph.D. Medical Ethics, Yale and science adviser to the President was now discussing the challenges the new graduates would face in the coming years. Drug resistant bacteria, world travel, weapons of mass destruction and on and on. Mankind would be lucky to survive until Saturday. Now she slogged into more frequent and virulent virus attacks. Sarah thought about rolling her program into a tight shaft and jamming it up her nose, under the lamina terminalis, past the optic chiasma and deep into her thalamus. Maybe that would let her escape this torture. Sarah began thinking of sex, not sex with her boyfriend Glenn, just sex.

She leaned forward, suddenly more than a little distracted. Four seats to her left Thomas Langley sat, head in his hands and contemplated the floor. She studied him. She had liked Thomas, even flirted with him. He'd been too busy to notice her. He turned toward her, looked past her, then seemed to return to the current reality. Now he smiled at her. She smiled back, "your loss," she thought. Sarah sat back in her seat and began to imagine a cool sheet and warm body oils. Just as Glenn's hands began to explore her lower back Dr. Jamison's voice seeped into her daydream.

"...and so in the year 1819 Dr. Beaumont traveled to the Indian village. Here it seems, Dr. Beaumont was forced to treat a viral outbreak with herbs and other pharmaceuticals of the period." Sarah rolled her eyes. Was she really going to tell that tired story?

Jamison droned on, "We don't know the veracity of this story, we don't know which herbs and other drugs he used. But we are fairly certain the outbreak mentioned was a virus in the order of Orthomyxoviridae. Some even believe it was avian influenza." Hadn't this woman attended any of the basic courses in virology? The story was impossible, it was...well just that, a story. Sarah shook her head. Drink a potion, cure the flu. The whole thing was impossible, stupid and this old woman was naïve to the extreme.

"Sadly, our level of expertise, our level of understanding and our ability to treat viral outbreaks is little improved from the primitive methods of Dr. Beaumont. You are faced with that same problem, to comfort the victims of viral infections, to treat, cure and defeat these terrible, and increasingly dangerous diseases. That, ladies and gentlemen is the medical challenge of the new century, to develop antiviral drugs as potent, safe and effective as penicillin."

There were two halves to the whole with Sarah. Born of an upper middle crust family she wasn't afraid to spend an evening in some biker bar and even the occasional night with someone she picked up there. The other side was cunning, analytical, driven and immensely intelligent. Now she began to wonder, did Beaumont really cure avian flu? Had it really been in the United States as far back as 1819? Impossible. She tilted her head to the right, her unconscious thinking position. Bird flu back then, that would be amazing. Avian flu was a killer and, given the inevitable mutations, could become a plague as deadly as the Black Plague of the Middle Ages. But to cure it. To stop the deadly virus in its tracks. Had Beaumont cured it? The old bat giving the speech seemed to think he did. That didn't quite line up with her first year history of medicine class now did it? But, to do that, to stop the virus cold, that would be worth some money. Sarah began to dream about being rich, not doctor rich. Not a four bedroom house on a lake with a boat and vacation to Europe or a beach during the winter rich. No, rich like the men on the top floor of the Renaissance Center. Rich enough to own the lake, the beach, and the airplane that took her to Europe's finest ski slopes and warmest beaches.

Suddenly the graduates all stood and Sarah was staring at someone's ass. She jumped to her feet, turned and shuffled down the aisle. Doctor what's-her-name handed Sarah a rolled up piece of blank white paper with blue and gold ribbons tied around the scroll. The real thing would come in the mail in another "two to three weeks". That did it. She could now pen the letters 'M.D.' after her name. Soon Sarah was engulfed in a sea of hugging parents, students, boyfriends, girlfriends and finally, her Grandmother. Then, inevitably, the damned stupid pictures.

Chapter 2

The Au Sable River swept sharply to the left, curving around a small grove of paper birch trees and whittled away at the bank opposite from where Jim now stood. The ground was tall here, the river swift and cold. This area was special, it even had a name: The Holy Waters. So named because of its beauty, peacefulness and the abundance of rainbow, brook and brown trout in impressive sizes. Fly fishermen from around the world listed this stretch of river as among the most beautiful and best. This stretch, this river bend in an endless series of bends, was Jim's favorite.

The river's current had undercut the bank exposing clusters of tree roots as the water washed the ground away, pushing the bank back into the forest. The roots seemed to drip from the sandy soil, desperate attempts at finding footing from the doomed survivors on the embankment above. Their stablemate, a medium sized Jack Pine had been the first to go. The tree had collapsed into the water, destroying the smallish Kirtland's Warbler nest in its arms. The tree now lay bent downstream, its green needles and curving cones long washed away. The empty nest now brown and ragged hung suspended in the dead branches above the water. The force of the water was doing its best to carry away the corpse and hide the crime forever.

A dark seam creased the water, extending from the dead trunk at a sharp angle to the river's edge into the middle of the fast flowing stream. It marked a change in water depth and speed. And, it presented a target and a home. Behind the seam a small eddy, a calm pool, where the current was blocked stood out in contrast to the water in front. The seam itself was the focus of the current which rebounded from the log, changed direction and resumed its trip. Anything floating along the surface or bouncing along the pebbled bottom was directed to this one long transition zone. And here was the perfect home for the trout that inhabited this magnificent river. As if by magic a quiet splash, a sip, and the bull's eye rings of a feeding brown trout expanded outward from the seam.

Jim Crenshaw, retired Air Force Colonel, one time aerospace executive, and now full time farmer worked his way into position to cast to the rising fish. Carefully stepping around a large boulder he eyed the current. A quick glance behind to ensure his back cast would not snag in the trees and he began the cast. Jim's line snaked out behind, straightened, then paused. With a controlled forward push of his arm the rod loaded, bending like an English longbow, then straightened. The action sent his fly line to the target ten feet upstream from the fish. The line settled, his hand tied Adams dry fly dropping silently to the water. Jim allowed a short drift, lifted the rod tip, then flicked his wrist and threw a small amount of slack in the line. This upstream bend, known as a "mend" allowed his fly to drift at the speed of the current. Carefully he studied the fly, then, "No...No, no, no...awww DAMN!" Jim's line bowed down stream. One end attached to his fly rod, the other to a fly firmly embedded in an unseen branch.

Jim's shoulders slumped. Now the great question. Could he pull the fly free or flick it off the snag? That might be just subtle enough to keep the trout from diving for cover. Or, should he break off the fly and hope the fish stuck around as he tied on another? Or maybe surrender to the gods of the river. He'd wade across the stream, retrieve his fly then head back to camp for lunch. Frustrated, Jim gathered the slack of his line, raised the rod tip and, like a horseman's whip brought the rod down. The line immediately formed a loop that rolled toward the fly. The snag popped out of the water, but the fly didn't come loose. Jim sighed. He went through the process again. No luck. The Adams was firmly attached to an unseen limb lurking beneath the water. Another sigh and, after a moment's hesitation he decided to retrieve the fly.

Slowly Jim waded across the river. Each foot placement required careful thought. To fall here could be trouble, more than one fly fisherman had drowned in two feet of river, overpowered by the force of the current and unlucky. If he went under there was always a chance of hitting his head on a rock. His waders could flood and he might be swept under a log or his gear snag on an unseen branch trapping him underwater, leaving him helpless. Jim reached the far side of the river, found the pesky branch and freed the Adams. As he prepared for the return trip across the river the tinkle of a small bell sounded from the direction of Jim's camp. His wife's "bear bell," a small bell clipped to the back of her hat, sang in the distance. His eyes followed the sound and finally he spotted a blaze of hunter's orange moving along the side of the river. After a minute his wife, Eve, pushed aside a small bush, spotted Jim and called, "You ready for some lunch?"

"Yeah, I guess. I'm getting frustrated. You know, they say fly fishing is relaxing. Today it's not. I'm finding every snag on this river. I've missed two good fish, lost four flies and just snagged again."

Eve grinned, "Hummm...I'd be frustrated too. Well, if fishing and camping isn't relaxing you could always call your buddies at Martin Aerospace and get your old job back," Eve knew Jim's stomach would flip at the thought of giving up the farm and going back to the aerospace world.

"On the other hand, I did land one nice one. About an eighteen or twenty inch brook trout. Besides, who would do our plowing and harvesting? And you know what they say: A bad day..."

"Yeah, a bad day fishing is better than a good day at

work, I know," Eve laughed as she finished one of Jim's favorite sayings.

"I'll be right there," Jim called and Eve began looking for a place to sit while she waited for her husband.

Jim began his trek back across the river, again carefully picking his way between the rocks on the river bottom. He was in the middle of the stream, standing in knee deep water when he heard Eve's surprised yell. Her shout snapped Jim's head up and he quickly checked the surrounding area for bears or other danger. Then he spotted Eve standing at the edge of the river, her left arm pointing at the shoreline. He smiled, "Hon, there's no poisonous snakes in Michigan...well, one but it's pretty rare."

"Who said anything about snakes?" Eve voice was humorless. "There's a hand. A person's hand right there."

Eve's serious look and voice chilled him and he did his best to hurry across the river. Finally Jim reached the shore. As quickly as he could Jim climbed the steep bank, laid his fly rod on the ground and joined his wife. "A hand? Are you sure? Where?"

She pointed. "That looks like a complete hand Jim, right there." She shook her finger at what appeared to be a perfectly intact skeletal right hand. "I think we've found a dead body."

"Let's not get ahead of ourselves...I can't really tell from here, maybe that's some sort of animal." Jim bent to get a better view but Eve was pointing into a hole washed out by last spring's high water. He climbed a few feet down the bank then dropped to his knees and reached into the opening.

"What are you doing?" Eve's excited voice rang in his ear but Jim didn't reply.

Carefully he began to move branches and sticks away from what, he had to admit, certainly appeared to be the bones of a right hand.

"Jim, you're not supposed to do that. We'd better get the police. They'll be mad if you disturb a crime scene."

He didn't look up. "I'm just clearing a few leaves to get a better view. I want to be sure this is a human hand before we go calling the cops." He slowly lifted a branch and set it aside. "We're a long way out in the woods…" Jim moved a leaf. "…if we bring them out here and this turns out to be a dead raccoon…" he moved another branch, "…we'll look pretty stupid. And, they'll be more than just mad at us." Jim hadn't taken his eyes off his work as he spoke. He moved another leaf and sat back on his haunches. Turning his face up to Eve he said, "But, I think it's safe to say we'd better call the cops. Hon, you're right. This is human."

Chapter 3

Trooper Cheryl MacIntire was the first on scene. "On scene" being a misnomer as the scene was actually some two miles away. In fact, she was standing in the Mio Ranger Station parking lot. Cheryl noted the ranger's old Ford Explorer and a newer, mud covered Jeep Grand Cherokee. She quickly pulled a small notebook from her chest pocket and wrote down the license plate number of the Cherokee. Then she shifted her attention to the small building which served as the ranger's station. It took only a moment and Cheryl spotted movement behind the window. She didn't immediately begin walking in that direction. Instead, Cheryl continued to survey the surrounding area. The ranger apparently was a busy man, the parking lot was littered with cigarette butts, plastic bottle caps and the occasional fast food wrapper.

Cheryl shook her head in disgust then glanced skyward. Some clouds but no rain in them. She thanked her lucky stars, she knew this was going to be a hike in the woods. To be on the safe side she went to the trunk of her cruiser and pulled out a jacket and changed to her old boots.

Officer MacIntire had been on the Michigan State Police force for the past four years, having been hired after two years with the Detroit city police force. A graduate of Michigan State University, with a degree in criminal justice, she was young, pretty and a good cop. Cheryl opened the door to the building. A large man, wearing blue jeans and a Michigan Department of Natural Resources regulation green shirt, white beard and green watch cap sat behind a Formica topped counter. Dan Hubble, the local ranger, stood, reached over the counter top and offered his hand. "Hi Cheryl, good to see ya," he said. "Sorry to bother ya but I think we got something ya might want to take a look at."

Cheryl shook the ranger's hand and took a quick glance around the building. Dan Hubble was not one of her favorite people. He wasn't a bad sort, just a bit of a whiner. "They," whoever "they" were, had kept Dan from the fame and fortune he was due. To Dan the government was corrupt, the President a traitor, the Congress a modern re-creation of Sodom. His politics had gotten old, she hoped he wouldn't launch into another tired diatribe today.

A small counter with a glass front separated the room into halves. It was filled with things a hiker might have forgotten: bug spray, compass, plastic poncho, health food bars, pocket knives and other trinkets. Being a ranger also involved being a store clerk. A desk braced the back wall, a rear exit hid in the corner. Along the wall to her right, and behind the counter rested a vinyl couch. A man and woman sat on the couch, the man was just getting to his feet. "I'm Jim Crenshaw, this is my wife, Eve," he said and extended his hand.

Cheryl shook hands all around. Dan motioned to a metal folding chair then held out a cup of coffee. "Sorry we had to bring you out here Cheryl."

"No worries Dan, it's been a few weeks since I stopped. I needed to get in here anyway." She turned to Jim and Eve. "I understand you two had an exciting camping trip."

"You could say that," Eve replied. "But to tell the truth, I would have been happier with some fresh trout, a few bird sightings and a cold beer."

Cheryl laughed. "Yeah, probably would have been a better weekend. So, let me get your statement and then we'll go check this out."

Thirty minutes later Jim and Eve signed a two page document describing exactly where they had camped, how long they had been there, where and what they had found. Then the couple climbed into their Jeep and led Trooper MacIntier and

Ranger Hubble south on McKinley Road to a two track trail which ran into the forest. A mile down the trail they parked.

"From here we walk," Jim called.

Sometime later the four approached Jim and Eve's camp. Cheryl took out her handheld GPS, looked at the screen, then wrote down the coordinates. Twenty minutes later they had located the spot where Eve had found the skeletal hand. Again the GPS coordinates were noted.

Cheryl did a quick survey of the area. She didn't find any obvious signs of human activity other than Jim and Eve's footprints. Satisfied she slowly eased down the bank until her eyes were level with the bones protruding from the soft earth. She pulled her flashlight from her belt and carefully examined the find. Occasionally Cheryl would lean forward and blow some dirt away from some part of the find. Several minutes passed. Jim looked at Eve and shrugged. Ranger Hubble finally broke the silence. "Well, wha'cha see?"

Without looking up she said, "Something is different here. At first I thought, 'Maybe a Halloween toy'. But now I don't think so." She stood and looked at Ranger Hubble, "I don't know Dan, but this doesn't seem right."

"What'ya mean?" he asked.

She stood and carefully moved several feet downstream from the bones. Then she began climbing up the bank. Jim reached out to take her hand, but she refused the offer and grabbed a root. Jim glanced at Eve. Cheryl said, "Something very odd about that. It's definitely a hand, but it's all entangled in the roots of the tree. Like it's been there an awful long time." She shook her head, "I'm calling Lansing, it's definitely human. I'm betting this is going to get a lot of attention, maybe a missing person or some old dead case."

Four hours later a Ford F350 equipped with a mobile laboratory and pulling a dark blue trailer with four all terrain vehicles turned into the Ranger station parking lot. A Michigan

State Police emblem with the words "Crime Scene Investigation" boldly stenciled in gold stood out on each side of the cargo box. The truck stopped and two young men wearing blue coveralls with State Police emblems on the back got out. The driver adjusted the long dark hair flowing from his blue baseball hat then went to the rear of the truck. His partner went to the Ranger Station to check in.

The truck was followed by three state police cruisers. A tall, muscular man with short red hair drove the lead cruiser. He parked near the mobile crime lab, unfolded himself from his cruiser, pulled his hat's visor low and surveyed the area. Ranger Hubble opened the door to the station and the tall man quickly spotted the uniform shirt. "I'm Sergeant Jim Meyer, understand you've got a mystery," he said to Hubble.

Hubble came off the porch and shook hands. "C'mon inside, I'll catch you up."

Once inside the little building Dan introduced Jim and Eve. They quickly began to explain their involvement. MacIntier briefed Meyer on her actions from the morning and offered to lead the new arrivals to the site. An hour later they were deep in the woods attempting to follow the direct course Cheryl's GPS laid out to the bones. After climbing over the third fallen tree Jim whispered to Eve, "Would have been a lot easier to take the trail like we told them." Eve grinned and nodded in reply.

Eventually arriving at the site they began looking for the bones Eve had spotted earlier that morning. It didn't take long before Jim called, "Right here," and could be seen pointing at the river bank.

Meyer asked Jim and Eve to stay away from the area then directed a yellow police tape perimeter be established some fifty feet in all directions from the actual site of the bones. When the site was reasonably secure he established a grid and soon he and the three troopers were searching the area for any additional bones or evidence. The crime scene technicians began their work as this was being done.

The work went slowly. One trooper blundered onto a bee hive in a hollow tree. Fortunately the air was cool and the bees just buzzed. Sergeant Meyer told him if he found another hive he was buying the whole post a round. After an hour of searching, with summer shadows growing long Meyer gathered his team. "I got nothing, how 'bout you guys."

"I've got bubkus," Cheryl announced. The others all agreed.

"You guys find anything?" Meyer called down the bank to the two technicians.

"We gotta talk Sergeant Meyer," one called back as he scrambled up the bank. His partner glanced in Meyer's general direction then began packing their equipment.

"So talk," Meyer said as the man approached.

"Well sir, if this was a murder you ain't catching the killer."

Meyer bristled, "Why's that?"

"'Cause if it was a murder it happened a long, long time ago."

"How long?"

"Beats me. Never saw anything like this before."

"What? What the hell do you mean 'beats me'? I thought you guys were the experts!" Meyer could see this case going to the dogs in a hurry.

"Sergeant Meyer, I'm telling you this is different. We're going to need a specialist."

The three troopers had gathered beside their Sergeant. Meyer's confusion was growing. "A specialist? Wha'da ya mean 'a specialist'? I thought you were a specialist."

"No man, this is different. I think we're going to need to call some university or something like that. I can't tell the age of these bones, but I'm telling ya, they're old, very old."

"How old?" MacIntier asked as the other troopers edged in to hear this.

"Like I said, I can't tell. But I'm going to guess a long time, like a hundred years or more," the technician replied. "I think so anyway, but someone with better equipment then the crap we've got is going to have to get this back to their lab to really test that. I could be big time wrong. Maybe the minerals from around here leeched into the bones very quickly and make it look old. Or something else very weird happened. I'm not the expert on that kinda stuff. I'm kinda surprised field mice, bears and things, forest animals ya know, or something like that didn't eat these bones a long time ago. I'm guessing that's what happened to the rest of the body."

"So why not these?" MacIntier asked.

"Well, again, it's a guess..." he paused for a moment. "I think this hand was separated by animals from the body then buried. I think it's here now because the ground is different and right here exceptionally dry. The river has just eroded the bank to the site."

Meyer didn't like that answer. He searched for a response, but couldn't find one. Finally he said, "Okay, fair enough. Mr. Hubble, we're going to have to cordon off your forest here until we know this isn't a crime scene."

The ranger smiled, "Sergeant Meyer, you can do that, it ain't going to work though. See ya got people coming down the river right there on canoes all the time. You'd have to end the season for three canoe liveries up stream. They couldn't afford that. Then you've got the fly fishermen that fish the river right there, they would be mad and they wouldn't pay attention to a sign in the woods anyway. This is a flies only stretch of water and they love it. And, you know as well as I do, there's more than a few nut jobs living around here that would want to get on the site just because you told them they couldn't. Plus, you've got all kinds of animals that roam through here."

"So what the hell do we do? Let people traipse all over a crime scene? Not going to happen," Meyer shot back.

"If it were me, I'd get whoever you want to get out here right away and keep this on the down low," Dan replied evenly.

Chapter 4

Sarah Cox's new Cadillac CTS-V Coupe grabbed the road hard as she accelerated through a sharp left hand curve on Grand Rapid's Laraway Lake Drive. Reaching Cascade Road she braked once, glanced left, then right and zipped past the stop sign at forty miles an hour. She could have a driver and ride to work in the back doing paperwork. In fact, she thought, she probably should, she certainly needed the extra office time. But she loved to go fast and she loved that curve and she loved this car.

In moments the dark red coupe sped past Watermark Country Club and found the entry ramp to I-96. Here she was forced to slow as the morning traffic began to gather. Gritting her teeth, she cursed the traffic then reminded herself that it was a hundred times worse in Chicago or New York or Los Angeles and small traffic jams were better than big traffic jams. Sarah settled into the boring fifty mile an hour portion of her commute and turned on National Public Radio to catch the news. No one agreed on anything, the arguments didn't change anyone's mind and in the end they all seemed very pleased to have been on the radio. It was always the same. She switched the radio off. Twenty minutes later she entered the small parking garage under her building and braked in the spot marked: "CEO – Sarah Cox". The marker sported a Viral BioTech company logo.

Life had been good to Sarah. She had completed her residency at Chicago's Mt. Sinai, then a fellowship at the University of Texas in virology, followed by a short time at the Center For Disease Control in Atlanta. From there Sarah had been lured to Metapalm Pharmaceuticals, a small start-up company located in Chicago that had exploded on the scene shortly after Sarah had started at the CDC.

Thomas Langley, a brilliant doctor turned biochemist, founder of the company and former classmate had developed several new drugs in the treatment of post-polio syndrome. He quickly parlayed these early successes into a modestly successful pharmaceutical company. Then he met an old medical school classmate, Sarah Cox. Thomas immediately began courting her with promises of money, stock options and her own laboratory. After six months of wine, dinners, shows and eventually shared hotel rooms she'd made the move. Thomas was wonderful and she moved into his top floor condo in downtown Chicago. Sarah started as chief scientist and soon displaced the executive vice-president in charge of research. It was a dream job.

Metapalm pioneered the use of herbs and organics to treat disease. Together Thomas and Sarah grew the company beyond anything Thomas could do on his own. Key to Metapalm's success had been the willingness to collect samples from under explored, ignored and forgotten sources. The strategy had worked and Metapalm had scored big with several new drugs.

That was a good gig she thought, and it had been a lot of fun both professionally and personally. She'd spent months in the amazon jungles, diving coral reefs in Australia and had even explored the bottom of Lake Michigan collecting actinomycetes from the bottom dwelling creatures and plants there. She'd made a ton of money, gotta love stock options, and her bank accounts had steadily grown. But it all came unraveled on her fourth trip to the Amazon. She'd met a British scientist named Malcom something.

She blamed the affair on his accent, the work and the jungle. In truth, she just wanted to move on, Metapalm and Thomas had become something different. She had struggled to put the feeling into words, eventually settling on "an impediment". Thomas and Metapalm were an impediment. Her departure was hastened by the discovery that Thomas also had an affair, several of them.

She considered her indiscretion to be just that. A one time "woops, won't happen again" sort of deal. Thomas on the other hand was a serial philanderer. The discovery had prompted Sarah to take stock of her life. The excitement of growing a company for someone else had faded. Sarah dreamed of joining the ranks of the, if not super, then "better than you", rich and she couldn't do it working for someone else. It had been time to remove the impediment. Seven years after signing with Metapalm she announced she was leaving.

Sarah's leaving came at a curious time. She had pushed Metapalm from antibiotic drugs into antiviral research. The company made great progress against several different viral diseases and fully expected to introduce several new drugs. Her announcement sent shock waves through the venture capital and drug research worlds. The announcement also sent shock waves through her boss and presumed future husband, Metapalm president Thomas Langley. Langley had fallen into a deep depression, abandoned his company and began drifting around the Caribbean on a thirty-eight foot sailboat. It took thirteen months for the company board to track him down, haul him back to Chicago, dry him out, stuff him full of anti-depressants and get him back in his lab.

Unknown to Langley, or the rest of the world, Sarah had bolted with more than a few trade secrets stuffed into her back pocket. The most enriching being the test formula for a drug which would combat several types of the herpes virus. A short time later her new company, Viral BioTech had a major home run and herpes was rapidly becoming a disease of the past.

The first meeting of the day was with Alex Tolovek, once the owner of his own accounting firm, now Viral

BioTech's Chief Financial Officer. Sarah sat on a gun metal gray leather couch in front of a large teak coffee table with inlaid African slate. The CFO sat next to her and laid a three ring binder open on the table. Alex was a thinish man of modest height, bald with a full mustache which had once been brown, but now was turning to gray. He was quiet, unassuming. Tolovek had provided a transition plan and funding sources for Sarah as she had contemplated leaving Metapalm. Two years later, and six months after bringing the anti-herpes drug Molovox to market, she had found herself needing top tier accounting and financial advice. That was when Sarah convinced Alex to sell his company and join hers.

"Morning Sarah, I've got some good news; we're going to be able to keep the lights on another month." It was a line that had once been a bit iffy, and now served to remind them both how far they had come. She smiled and laid her hand on his. "Where are we at Alex?" she said. Tolovek didn't smile, "Sarah, we're starting to have some problems," and he began running through the details.

Ten minutes later he came to what he considered to be the critical issue of the day. "Bottom line, for the year we're showing a profit in the neighborhood of fourteen million. For us, for any company this size, not bad. We've grown steadily. Our anti-herpes drugs have driven revenue and our stock price is now over twenty bucks a share. We're in good shape, current revenue supports that price. Normally, I'd be excited about that, but look here." He pulled another chart from his binder. "We need to hit a home run. Otherwise we're short of new product. We won't be able to sustain our current revenues."

She examined the product development chart. "We'll be okay Alex."

He shook his head, "We can't ignore this Sarah. We've started to incur some major expenses, we're covering those. It's the future expenses that are building much faster than I had previously projected. We're into our contingency funds. I've funded those accounts from past retained earnings, but once current expenditures exceed revenue we're going to have problems fast. The anti-flu tests are going to drive that further. The tests are failing. We need to kill the project."

Her head snapped up, "We can't kill that. Anti-flu drugs may lead to a broad spectrum anti-viral drug. That's the future of this company!" Sarah's specialty and her passion was the hunt for a virus killing drug. He had hit a soft spot.

"Sarah the cost is killing us. The tests we're running are draining cash at an unsustainable rate. We can't keep this up."

"We've got to keep this up, we're close."

"I don't care how close Sarah, this isn't horseshoes, this is grenades. We're going to kill ourselves if we keep this up. And if that's not bad enough there's more."

She glared at him, "What else?"

"We're going to need that money, even bigger bills are coming. We have to settle on the Praximtine case, that's going to cost us in the neighborhood of ten million." He studied her reaction to that number.

"How much cash did we put in the legal risk pool?" she asked.

"Twelve."

"Okay, we're covered. What else?"

"The biggest hit is the loss of patent protection on Zanatoval and Matatoval."

"We invented the damn things! I thought our patents were going to be extended?" Sarah had conveniently forgotten exactly how she had invented the anti-herpes drugs.

"I spoke to Roger last night. It hasn't been announced yet, but we're going to lose. The judge wouldn't extend them."

"I thought that extension was a lock?"

"Someone at Metapalm got to the judge. We lose

30

patent protection in fourteen months. Once that happens anyone can make the generic and our revenue is going to collapse. Zanatoval and Matatoval make up half our revenue and sixty percent of profits. We lose those with nothing to take their place and we're hosed, share prices will drop into single digits. We lose millions. You lose millions."

Sarah folded her hands into a tent and leaned her chin on her fingers, vaguely studying the chart in front of her. "Anything we can do? Different judge maybe?"

"That opportunity is gone Sarah. Which puts us back to the original problem..."

Sarah's eyes rotated upward and met his, "It's not that bad, we'll find...?"

He cut her off, "We don't have anything in the pipeline. Current new product testing is going badly. At this rate we'll be lucky to morph into a compounding pharmacy."

"Alex, if we're able to get the anti-flu drugs through testing..."

"Sarah, I don't get this. What is the market? Flu? Who cares about flu? Why are we spending millions on something already addressed? Anyone can go out and get a vaccine for the flu. When we're done what do we have to sell? Something someone else invented years and years ago?"

She smiled. Alex thought that she actually looked interested for the first time today. "Influenza is caused by a virus, not a microbe. Penicillin doesn't touch a virus."

"Yeah, I got that, but what's the market?"

"Vaccines are weakened or dead viruses. Introduce them to the body and the body builds a resistance. But if the resistance isn't established before the real deal shows up there is no way to kill the virus. Right now, if someone fails to get the vaccine and gets the flu the only treatment option is to treat the symptoms. There is nothing that kills the influenza virus."

"Okay, so what? When we're done people can skip their

vaccine?"

"No Alex, the influenza virus is a tough nut to crack. It keeps changing. But it's a very typical, almost common virus."

"So?"

She liked Alex Tolovek, but sometimes wondered if he could or would ever grasp the bigger picture. "Alex, modern medicine can treat bacterial infections, but it can't treat viral infections. Right now we do our best with viral specific drugs, but the results are mixed. Look at AIDS. The mortality rate has decreased significantly because we're attacking the virus and suppressing the symptoms. But, no one is claiming AIDs is cured. The reason? Because it's not. We're not curing these people because we aren't killing the virus."

"And what does that have to do with the flu?"

"It's the virus. Think about killing the virus. What the medical community needs is a penicillin for viruses. We're not working on just a flu drug, we're working on the first step of a broad spectrum anti-viral drug."

"Sarah, it's just costing us too much money." His frustration was mounting, she clearly wasn't seeing the big picture.

"If we're able to formulate an anti-viral which addresses a large number of individual viruses, is safe, harmless.... Alex, if we do that, we'll make more money and be more famous than Fleming, Salk and Pasture all rolled into one."

"Sarah, maybe it's time that we..."

She cut him off. "Okay, I've got it. What's next?" Sarah suppressed her next comment, which she knew wouldn't be complimentary.

Alex decided he'd pressed on killing the anti-flu drugs too hard. Maybe she'd understand once he finished with the rest of his charts. "Let's look at other current projects."

Ten minutes later Alex had finished his summary.

Before he could return to the topic of cash flow she had closed her binder and walked to her desk. "Thank you Alex."

Tolovek studied her, then picked up his briefing books and walked to the office door. Putting his hand on the knob he turned. "We need another home run Sarah."

"And what if it's delayed?" she answered.

"Maybe our tests are too...well, maybe we're being too hard on ourselves?"

"What?"

"Well, maybe if the tests showed a bit more encouraging results. A climb in our stock price right now would give us a little..."

She cut him off, "You know we can't fake results. It would come out in the end and then the entire company would not only be gone, but we'd all be in jail."

She watched the door softly close behind him, then found an aspirin bottle and poured four of the white pills into her hand. It was going to be a long, hard and probably frustrating day. Crushing a button on her PC she sat back and watched the screen flash to life. It took a moment for the anti-virus software to run. If only there were an anti-virus for the body. She paused, then typed in her password.

"Morning Sarah," Bobbie Downing leaned in from the outer office. Bobbie was a newly hired molecular biologist. Sarah considered her to be one of the keys to the company's future growth. If she could keep her. Bobbie presented a unique problem, she was brilliant...and couldn't decide what she wanted to do when she grew up. Just twenty-nine years old she had already completed her PhD in molecular biology, then had completely reversed course and studied archaeology. She was scheduled to defend her thesis this August. Sarah considered the two doctorates to be the oddest combination she had ever heard of. Nevertheless, she liked the kid and couldn't deny her talent. So, in an attempt to ensure Bobbie stayed with the company Sarah allowed Bobbie to work part time and to select those things which interested her to work on.

"Morning Bobbie," Sarah glanced up at the doorway. Bobbie's long black hair, butter smooth skin and athletic body immediately reminded Sarah that she needed to actually go to the gym where she was a member.

"I've finished the run on the T2 samples. Can't start on the T3 for another twenty-four hours. The results are in the folder. File title is, 'T2 Test One' if you want to review." Bobbie referred to the intranet web address the company used to move data from one person or group to another.

"How's it look?" Sarah already knew the answer, Bobbie would have been jumping up and down if the test had gone well.

"Not what we'd hoped. The decay rates varied wildly and the survival rate was too high."

Sarah nodded then bent back to her computer, a sure sign she didn't want to discuss anything else with the new kid on the block.

"And, I've got a little gig from the State Police, I guess some guy found a skeleton near Mio. They're guessing it's from a hundred years ago and they need an amino acid test."

Sarah looked up, surprised. "What? You're doing what?"

"I guess we have some sort of contract with the State Police Department to do specialized chemical analysis? I don't really know, I just got a call from Paula and was told they needed the test," Bobbie explained referring to Paula Pelitier, chief scientist at BioTech. "I guess no one else around here has done one. Apparently the cops only call us when their lab can't handle the workload. Paula said they called us last night and we needed to send someone to Mio this afternoon."

"Oh, huh...don't...I didn't know that contract was still in

effect. We haven't done a police job in over a year." Sarah sat back in her chair, interested. "So, how does amino acids and dating a bone relate?"

Bobbie thought for a moment, she needed to be careful. It was a fairly simple ratio analysis, and her boss was a medical doctor. She didn't want to make the explanation sound as simple as it really was and imply her boss was stupid.

"As you know, all amino acids are stored in the body in two different configurations. The "D" and the "L" sides. So we test for..."

"Wait, what is a 'configuration'?"

"You really want to know?" Bobbie could see her short lived career coming to an end.

"Wouldn't ask if I didn't," Sarah shot back, becoming annoyed.

"What we're really talking about is the configuration of the dextrorotatory and levorotatory forms of glyceraldehyde. We identify the left and right sides of the configuration by the letters D and L for dexter and laevus.

"Okay, got it, sorry I asked," Sarah hated these young kids.

"So, when an animal, or person, dies, the amino acids in the "L" side start to equalize with the "D" side. We then simply analyze the ratio of "L" to "D" and it gives us a pretty accurate date of death.

Well, okay, I'll take your word for it. Go ahead, you might have fun," she attempted to return to her computer then frowned. She certainly didn't need her scientists working for the police, she needed them here. Frustrated she called, "Bobbie!"

The young woman was already two steps into the outer office. She quickly turned and leaned into the CEO's office. "Yes ma'am?"

"Where the hell is Mio?"

"About three or four hours north. Sort of here," she pointed at the back of her hand, the universal, readymade Michigan map.

"North east of Clare?"

"More to the east, but yeah, I guess."

"Well, look, get this done as soon as possible. I need you here."

"Will do, never know this might be something we can use in our systemic scleroderma work," Bobbie replied, completely missing Sarah's grimace.

Sarah waited until Bobbie had left the outer office, then asked her secretary to close the office door. Returning to her desk chair she ran her hands over the leather arms. She thought about the company finances for a bit; this wasn't what she had expected when she'd started this mess. A moment later she pulled a bottle of one hundred year old scotch from her bottom desk drawer and poured a half tumbler full. "Hair of the dog," she said to her reflection in the computer screen and drained the glass.

Chapter 5

Bobbie Downing returned to her office happy. She was new and only a part time employee. She only worked two or three days a week at Viral BioTech, but was paid handsomely. She was about to finish a second doctorate degree and she knew they wanted her here full time. Her life was perfect, the only thing missing was a husband but she knew that would come in time.

Viral BioTech, and especially her current boss Paula Pelitier, wasn't pressing very hard for her to sign on, they were being very low key about their recruitment. But she knew how badly they wanted her and it felt good. And, she knew the commitment came with a big pay raise. There was only one problem, she didn't know if she wanted to spend the rest of her life in a white lab coat or working in the field exploring the mysteries of the past. It was a decision for the future-Bobbie, not one for the today-Bobbie. It could wait until the PhD was awarded. Maybe, with luck, she could combine the two. It was an interesting thought and she had indulged it while returning from Sarah's office, but now she needed to finish preparing the T3 test samples for tomorrow. She went to the equipment closet and began removing the various items needed.

Forty-five minutes later she was satisfied there was nothing more to be done. After one last look at her notes she hurried to her locker in the basement gym. She stuffed hiking boots, a change of clothes, a handful of power bars and an assortment of hand tools into a large, bright green backpack. She then grabbed her jacket and slipped out of the back of the building. Moments later Bobbie had climbed into her bright yellow soft top Jeep Wrangler and begun the three and a half hour drive to the Mio Ranger Station. Construction on I-69 slowed Bobbie a bit. She didn't arrive at the Ranger Station until mid-afternoon.

Trooper MacIntier had just finished backing a green ATV off the utility trailer attached to an older model State Police SUV when she heard a vehicle slow then turn into the Ranger Station parking lot. The yellow Jeep quickly dodged around a three foot tall sandwich board sign which read "No Parking" then drove around a line of bright orange parking cones. MacIntier frowned as she watched the Jeep come to rest next to a crime lab technician's F150. A young woman, wearing jeans and a Gortex jacket stepped down from the Wrangler.

Irritated, Cheryl began walking toward the vehicle. Suppressing an urge to grab the girl by the throat and pin this idiot's nose on the No Parking sign, she called, "I'm sorry ma'am, this station is closed today. You'll have to leave the parking area. We have those 'No Parking' signs and orange cones in the driveway for a reason."

"Oh, I thought I was supposed to park there?" Bobbie said.

"No, this parking lot is closed." Cheryl said tartly.

"I'll move." Bobbie did an about face and returned to her Jeep. She backed out of the parking space then drove to the road and parked the Jeep next to the ditch which ran along side. Bobbie climbed down from the Jeep then walked the fifty feet back to the parking lot. MacIntier was just about to start the ATV when she again noticed the young woman.

"Ma'am, what are you doing? I told you this station is closed!" MacIntier was considering cuffing this idiot when the young woman said, "I'm looking for a Sergeant Meyer, my name is Bobbie Downing. I'm here to make a field study and recover some bones."

"What? Are you kidding me? Why didn't you say something?" MacIntier didn't know if she should be laughing or angry. "The parking lot's closed for non-police related business."

Bobbie shrugged, "Oh...well you said...and I thought..." Her voice trailed off, then recovering Bobbie asked, "Is Sergeant Meyer around?"

"In there," Cheryl pointed at the Station, "and introduce yourself as soon as you open the door." Cheryl returned to her task of unloading the trailer and shook her head.

Bobbie opened the door to the small log sided building. Immediately two sets of eyes focused on her. "Hi, I'm Bobbie Downing," she immediately announced.

Sergeant Meyer introduced himself and Ranger Hubble, then quickly briefed her on the bones, the site topography and other pertinent facts. Bobbie took in the information then glanced at a framed park map mounted on the wall. "Where are we talking about?" she asked. Dan Hubble took a step forward and jabbed a thick finger on the map. "Here," he said. Bobbie asked a few more questions. Meyer and Hubble did their best, answering some, but could only guess at others. Eventually Bobbie was out of questions and the three found themselves staring at each other.

"Well, ah...okay. I guess you need to see the site," Meyer said.

"Yeah, I guess so, can't do much work from here," Bobbie said and smiled.

Meyer held the door for Bobbie then glanced back at Hubble. "Kids, they send me kids," he whispered. Then he closed the door and escorted Bobbie to the parking lot.

"This is Trooper MacIntier."

Cheryl smiled, "We've met."

"Let's get you set up and we'll be on our way," Meyer said then went to his own ATV.

MacIntier handed Bobbie a helmet and leather gloves and went over the operation of the ATV. Soon the three were mounting ATVs for the ride to the site.

"We'll detour to the Crenshaw's campsite on the way," Meyer yelled over the motor's rumble. "You can get some of your answers from them."

Eve was lying in a hammock strung between two trees when she heard the group approach. As the three riders dismounted Eve put down her novel and called, "Sergeant Meyer, Cheryl, how are you? We've certainly given you two a busy day!"

"Hi Eve, sorry to bother you, I'm sure this wasn't in your camping plans," Cheryl said as she shook her hand. "This is Bobbie Downing, she's an expert in bones and all things old."

Eve reached out to shake Downing's hand, "I'm Eve Crenshaw, welcome to our humble little campsite. I'm glad you're here, I need an expert, my husband is right over there."

Bobbie's face went blank, "Ahhh...I'm sorry?"

MacIntier and Meyer were beginning to chuckle. Eve pointed at her husband. "She said you were an expert in all things old, he's right there."

"I heard that!" Jim called. The group turned to see a man wearing green chest waders, a fishing vest, baseball hat and carrying a fly rod.

"Oh...oh, I get it," Bobbie said and grinned. Eve pointed to several logs set on their end. "Have a seat. Can I get you folks some hot coffee? Pot's fresh." They accepted the offer and waited for Jim to hang his waders on a line strung between two trees. Five minutes later, after a bit of small talk, Bobbie began to interview the two campers. Carefully she went over the details of the site, the weather, the water level and anything else she could think of. The Crenshaws answered her questions, provided added detail and poured more coffee.

Eventually, Bobbie said, "Well, it all seems fairly routine. I'm a bit mystified as to how this hand is so well preserved."

"Now hold on Doctor Downing, we're still not certain this is really an old skeleton. It could be a recent death. Or did I miss part of the process here. Don't you have to do some laboratory magic on this thing before we can release the site to the academics?" Sergeant Meyer asked.

"Of course, absolutely, and I don't want to sound like I'm getting ahead of the process. Obviously, we're going to have a bit of work ahead of us," Bobbie did her best not to look embarrassed. "So, the site is this way?"

"Yup, about fifty yards up river," Jim said. "If we're all ready, let's go."

Ten minutes later the group spotted a cluster of trees in the shape of the letter U that marked the spot. The area where Eve had found the bones was surrounded by yellow tape with the words, "Police Line – Do Not Cross" printed every twelve inches. Cheryl pointed out the cut in the bank where the bones had been found. Then she pointed to a wooden frame with a metal screen underneath resting on two logs used as legs. "Our lab guys did that. It's standard procedure when looking at a buried skeleton," she said.

A quick peek into the frame revealed a right hand, its bones held in place with what looked like hard, dry leather. Unable to resist, Bobbie picked it up and began turning it over in her hands.

"What do you think Doc?" Jim asked.

She glanced up, "Sir, please just call me Bobbie, doctor makes me sound old and I think of my father."

Jim grinned. "Now you're making me feel old. Call me Jim."

Bobbie grinned back. "Okay, deal." Looking back at the relic she said, "Well, to tell the truth, I can't really tell anything yet. A mummified human hand or any animal mummified in this state, given our weather, is obviously extremely rare." She turned the hand over. "I don't recall ever reading of such a thing before," she continued to examine the gruesome object lost in thought.

Finished with the hand for a moment Bobbie ducked under the tape and climbed down the wash to the site. She removed her backpack and laid a handful of tools on the ground. Then she sat on her knees and began scraping at the earth.

After several minutes Eve leaned to Jim and whispered, "Why are we all standing here watching her scrape dirt?"

Jim grinned, "Because it's history being unearthed, this stuff is cool."

Eve shook her head, "Seems just like watching someone dig to me."

At that moment Bobbie stopped, sat back on her knees, picked up a small paint brush and began cleaning a small object. Jim glanced at Eve, "Wonder what she found?"

"Find something doc?" Sergeant Meyer called.

Bobbie smiled. Then she looked up out of the wash, "I can't be certain until I get those bones back in the lab, but I'm going to guess that if the victim was murdered the killer is long gone."

"And why's that?" Meyer asked.

Bobbie held up a small oblong object. "See this? It's bone. See the decorative carving on the top? Right here you see the hole through the end and you can see the circles around the middle. Those circles are from being pushed into the open end of a tube." She handed the object up to Cheryl. She quickly examined the object then passed it to Meyer. "I think the killer is long gone because of that, and this..." Bobbie pulled a flat, round circular object from the ground and handed it to Jim.

"I'm pretty sure what you're looking at are the parts to a colonial tobacco canteen stopper."

A quick glance at the group confirmed to Jim that he wasn't the only one mystified. "A what?" he asked.

Bobbie stood, "I believe what you're looking at is a stopper, sort of like the cork in a wine bottle. In that era, pipe tobacco was often carried in a small canteen made of leather, bone, metal or sometimes even sea shells. A stopper was used to keep the tobacco from falling out. Some stoppers had a leather...well, washer for lack of a better term, which was held in place by that small bone disk. A leather cord went through the entire thing and secured it to the canteen, preventing it from being lost. I think that's what you're holding."

The group passed the two objects back and forth. Jim carefully examined each then said, "When were these used? I've never heard of a tobacco canteen."

Bobbie smiled, "That's the thing, the handmade canteens were mostly found on the frontier during the colonial era then they sort of went out of fashion. Although, to be fair, some are still around. Anyway, tobacco pouches tended to replace them as clothing changed to include more pockets on shirts and pants. The proximity to the bones, the appearance of the bones themselves all lead to a guess...but it's probably a good guess, that you've stumbled upon the skeleton of either a Native American that used a European style tobacco canteen or one of the first settlers or trappers of Michigan. This skeleton could date from the early 1800s."

Chapter 6

Sergeant Meyer held the tobacco canteen stopper away from his body, then moved it in close. "Playing the trombone Sergeant Meyer?" Jim asked with a knowing grin.

"Age catches up with all of us Jim. Maybe it's time for some glasses." He glanced at Trooper MacIntire and then focused on Bobbie Downing. "You're sure about this? Couldn't this be something else? Or, maybe this was already in the area and the bones just ended up in the same place?"

Bobbie was still kneeling in the dirt. Slowly she stood up, flexed her knees and then said, "Well, no, actually I can't say for certain. I think you're holding a canteen stopper. It could be something totally different, something that I've never seen before. I don't think it is, but there's always that chance. And, obviously I can't say with a hundred percent certainty that the bones or the stopper date from the 1800s. I haven't run the dating tests. All I'm saying is that it appears that they do, that the evidence leads to that conclusion. It would be nice to find the rest of the canteen, maybe a period button or something more definitive. But, this is all we have right now. Like I said, I have to run the tests on the bones before I can say anything for sure."

Eve put her hand to her mouth and whispered to Jim, "She sounds like a TV crime fighter."

Sergeant Meyer thought Bobbie's comments over. "Okay doc, give me something here. I'm going to either pay a ton of overtime to post a trooper and protect this site or I'm not. The department can use the money someplace else that's for sure. If I spend all the OT money guarding the site and it turns out to be a relic and not a murder vic; well, I'm in deep kimshi then too."

Bobbie Downing began to look overwhelmed. Before she could put together her thoughts Meyer burst out again, "Well, do I guard the site?"

Jim glanced at Cheryl and Eve. Trooper MacIntier was beginning to look uncomfortable. Jim leaned forward, "Sergeant Meyer, forgive my interruption but...well, the site is in the middle of the woods, right? Except for the yellow tape no one would know it's here. Why not save the overtime money and take the chance. I mean, let's face it. Unless some canoer gets out of the river right on top of this little dig there's not a lot of likelihood it will be discovered."

Meyer looked at Jim, "I know Jim, but if this is a murder scene and someone blunders around on it my ass is grass if you know what I mean."

"Understand that, but to give you a little piece of mind why not have the ranger close down the camping area where Eve and I are set up. Have him close the Ranger Station parking lot too. He could even put up some bogus sign; a flea infestation, bears sighted in the area, alien landings, something to keep people away. Problem solved."

Bobbie recovered her wits, "I'll rush the results. I'll be able to finish them in two days."

It was Meyer's turn to look overwhelmed. He didn't want to make the call, but he was the man on site so he swallowed hard, thought for a moment more then announced, "Okay, thanks folks. I'll take your advice."

Decision made Sergeant Meyer returned to his authoritative ways. Looking at Cheryl he said, "That means we're through here."

In rapid succession he turned to Bobbie, "We'll close the area until I get word on your tests, but I'm not seeing the use of posting a trooper. We'll close the ranger station and have Ranger Hubble keep campers and the like from the area."

"I'm going to want to continue working here a bit,"

Bobbie announced.

"I don't think that's a problem," he turned to MacIntire, "We'll start taking our equipment back now." Then turning back to Bobbie, Meyer said, "I'll need the ATV, but not for another hour or so. Tell you what. I'll leave that till last and give you a shout on the radio."

"That's fine, I appreciate it. But can I come out here this weekend or next week? I'd like to see what more I can find on this." Bobbie was becoming concerned that a big and potentially important find was going to be taken away from her.

"I don't think so. Right now it's a potential crime scene. If you decide this is an old settler or Indian then the site belongs to the Department of Natural Resources. The DNR boys really get protective of this sort of thing. Their people will be responsible for the site and any archaeological digs conducted here. I'm sorry Ms. Downing, but other than confirming the age of the bones, I can't really let you continue to work here."

Bobbie was crushed. This was the find of the decade she was sure. "Oh...well, I guess that makes sense. Do you think the DNR will let me in on that dig?" Bobbie could feel herself being pushed off an important discovery. The idea that she wouldn't be involved with the dig and more importantly the interpretation of its findings was not sitting well.

Sergeant Meyer knew adding an outside expert to the DNR's in-house team was a long shot. He glanced at Cheryl. She shrugged as if to say, "What harm?" He could see the genuine passion Bobbie Downing had for archaeology and the history of the state. Suddenly, for no reason he could ever explain Meyer said, "Well, I don't know. It's already late in the day, and I've got some things to do at the office tomorrow. I think I'm in court this week, then my off days are Friday and Saturday. You know Bobbie, I'll probably not get a chance to talk to those folks until next Monday."

Downing stared at Meyer for a moment, then she realized what he was saying. "Thank you Sergeant Meyer," she grinned. Meyer then passed a handheld two way radio to Bobbie. A moment later he and Trooper MacIntier began to load the crime scene equipment on their ATVs.

Jim and Eve watched the sudden burst of activity for a moment then turned to walk back to their camp. Suddenly Eve stopped, "Hey Bobbie, stop by the camp when you're finished." Bobbie smiled, agreed and quickly returned to her work. Eve glanced at Jim and together they set off for their camp, leaving Bobbie Downing alone to dig to her heart's content.

Bobbie began by cutting away the remaining roots which extended from the overhanging earth. Then, using a larger hand trowel she began removing dirt and placing it in the State Police wire screen sieve. When she was satisfied with the amount of dirt in the sieve she began to gently shake the frame until all the dirt had passed through leaving a tray full of small pebbles, sticks and, with luck, something significant.

Suddenly a noise, like someone walking across the forest floor alerted Bobbie. Certain she had been left alone she froze, listening. Someone was coming closer. She could hear their footsteps. "Hello?" she called. The footsteps stopped. Bobbie listened carefully. A minute passed, then another. The steps started again. Bobbie stood and carefully studied the woods around her. "Hello?" she called again. Two squirrels dashed up a tree just to her right. Bobbie smiled, shook her head and returned to her dig.

It was slow, hard work. She knelt on her knees for five minutes carefully filling the sieve then stood and shook the frame. Kneel, stand, kneel, stand, kneel, stand; an hour later Bobbie was tired and frustrated. Several times she swore someone was walking in the woods around her, just out of sight behind a group of pines. She knew it was just the small animals of the forest, but the sounds were alien in what should be a silent forest. After losing count of how many frames of dirt she had run through the sieve Bobbie's luck changed. As the dirt fell through the sieve Bobbie was thrilled to find what appeared to be a golden yellow straw.

Larger in diameter at one end and tapering rapidly to a slender straw, the object at first appeared to be nothing more than a yellow stick. Bobbie knew better. Walking to the river she quickly rinsed the dirt off and smiled. The large end appeared to have teeth marks, human teeth marks. Bobbie was holding a bone pipe stem.

She enjoyed her small triumph for a moment then knelt in the dirt once more. A few trowels of dirt later and she felt the tool collide with something solid. Fully expecting a large stone, but mindful of proper archaeological technique she dropped the trowel and began removing dirt with her fingers, a paintbrush and a very small artist's trowel. Forcing herself to work slowly she carefully removed the loose soil to reveal a large dark brown surface. The excitement of discovery, of seeing something not seen in perhaps a hundred or even two hundred years, swept over her. Working just a bit faster Bobbie's efforts soon revealed a hard rectangular leather box. The object was somewhat large, flat on the bottom and tapered to the top. The top was actually a flap, secured shut by two straps running from the back, across the top to two rusted buckles near the front bottom. The rear of the box had two thick straps secured to the structure with one a bit wider than the other. These two straps terminated in a frayed edge, as if they had been forcibly separated from a larger piece.

This was a mystery. She carefully turned the object over in her hands attempting to catalog it in her mind. Her attention was drawn not to the obvious, she wasn't looking at the buckles. She hadn't even thought of opening the container. Instead, she examined the two wide straps. These were sewn into the back of the box using a very heavy gauge thread;

almost as if the maker had used a sailor's awl to set the thread. At last a wide grin creased her face. The straps were intended to hold two containers, one on each side of a horse. She had discovered one side of a saddlebag.

Bobbie's smile lasted only a minute or two. The radio chimed. Sergeant Meyer's voice announced that Bobbie needed to bring the ATV back to the ranger station. Time was up. Disappointed at leaving, but thrilled with her find Bobbie carefully wrapped the objects and placed them inside her jacket. She made one last look around the site, started the ATV and began the trip back to the ranger station.

Some minutes later Bobbie found the Crenshaw's campsite. Relieved she was on the correct trail she waved and stopped. Jim was tying a fresh batch of flies for the evening's hatch on a portable fly tying bench and Eve had just begun to prepare dinner. "Mr. and Mrs. Crenshaw, I just wanted to say good-bye, I've got to give my ride back to the police."

Eve wiped her hands on a towel and walked to Bobbie's side. "It was nice meeting you Bobbie. I'm really sorry you're being run off the site. What's going to happen now?"

"I've got to get back to Grand Rapids and process the bones. That will take me a day, maybe two. Then I'll give a report to the State Police. I'm hoping to join the DNR when they dig the site."

"I thought Sergeant Meyer was giving you a few days to work here by yourself?" Jim asked.

"He did....and I would," she hesitated. Then, with an embarrassed laugh said, "But to be honest, I got a little afraid out there alone."

"Why do you have to be here alone?" Jim asked.

"Well..." Bobbie didn't want to admit that a lifetime of studying had left her only a few friends, none that she considered close enough to camp with then guard her while she spent the day digging. To make matters worse, the more she thought about it, none of her peers in the archaeology department were interested enough in Michigan's history to camp this site either. After a moment she snapped back to the present, "I guess, I mean, well...really I don't have anyone I could con into standing guard while I dug in the dirt," she said with a false laugh.

Eve glanced a knowing look at Jim. "You know Bobbie, it's summertime. We're just watching corn grow at home and I'm out of school so..."

"Any excuse I've got to go fishing in this river is fine with me," Jim interjected.

"You can camp with us and dig all you want," Eve said.

Bobbie glanced from Eve to Jim. "You really wouldn't mind?" she asked, excitement building in her voice.

"Of course not!" Jim called. "We'll have a great time."

"I'll make sure he doesn't bring his guitar," Eve whispered to Bobbie who immediately began to laugh.

"Alright, you've got a deal, and thank you so much," Bobbie exclaimed.

Ten minutes later arrangements had been made to meet two days hence at the Little Boots Country Diner near Houghton Lake then drive together to the Mio Ranger Station.

Chapter 7

The return trip to Viral BioTech's building seemed to be over in a flash. Bobbie had enjoyed the drive, the hum of the road helped her think. The skeletal hand, the artifacts, the strange mummification; it was all a wonderful mystery. A mystery that if solved would only help address the bigger mystery; who's hand, who's artifacts?

The building was dark when Bobbie Downing's yellow Jeep rolled to a stop in the employee parking lot. Bobbie carefully removed the wooden box provided by the State Police which contained the mummified hand from the back of the Jeep. She pushed the bubble wrapped saddlebag inside her backpack then placed her hiking boots with the pipe stem wrapped in tissue tucked inside and her jacket on top of the box. She then picked up the pile, balanced it on one knee, shifted her hands for a better grip and made her way to the lab's back door. Here Bobbie put the entire assembly down, then swiped her key card to unlock the building's heavy metal door. Holding the door open with her foot Bobbie again picked up her pile of treasures and swung into the building. A few moments later she was at the laboratory door. Again she swiped her key card, then entered the lab. She hung her jacket on the back of a chair, put her boots next to the door, flipped on the lights and began to remove the precious tissues. Finished with the boots she took the saddlebag from her backpack and carefully laid it and the pipe stem on her workstation desk.

Pleased with her own self control she turned her attention to the reason she had driven north in the first place. Her first task was to select an appropriate piece of tissue or bone to sample. This was a judgment call. Bobbie carefully examined the hand. She paused. "Just treat this like any other find, like an object, not a part of a person," she told herself. She slowly turned it over in her hands. She was looking for an area with the minimum amount of mineral leaching from the surrounding soil. Since this was a mummified object her task was nearly impossible. Finally, she narrowed her selections to two. A section of the leathery, mummified skin from under the wrist and a sample from one of the metacarpal bones of the fourth finger.

Next, she removed several glass slides from a cabinet on the wall, then turned on a pair of computers and an attached color printer. She removed a tray of instruments from a tall sterile white cabinet and placed it next to the wooden box. By force of habit she donned a hairnet and put a surgeon's mask over her nose and mouth. Finally, she sat down at her lab bench and began to prepare the sample. Five hours later the large machine which charted the X-ray crystallography of an object sounded an alarm.

Bobbie was sitting in an oversized desk chair, slumped forward, her head on her crossed arms fast asleep. The alarm jarred her awake with a snap of the head. It took a moment for her to remember where she was and what she was doing. Once those mysteries were solved Bobbie wiped the drool off her cheek, stood, stretched and went to the machine. Paper kerchunked out of the printer and slid into a tray. One or two sheets had fallen to the floor already. Bobbie picked the sheets off the floor then removed the remainder from the tray. When she had finished assembling the stack she quickly scanned the pages and satisfied herself that the test appeared to have run successfully.

She was anxious to begin plowing through the data, but details of her real job seemed to be leaking into her consciousness. Now her mind was fully focused on the T2, test two pending for tomorrow morning. She glanced at the clock and corrected herself, this morning. For the fourth time she inventoried the vials of serum in a small kitchen refrigerator then counted the petri dishes resting in a large incubator. A quick survey of the equipment she had assembled before she had departed for Mio and she was satisfied. All appeared ready for the big day.

Once again she studied the wall clock, that couldn't be right. She checked her cell phone, damn, it was. Bobbie picked up her jacket and backpack, glanced again at the wall clock and cursed the fact that she had to be back to work in four hours. She took one final look around the lab, then left the building.

At 7:40 the next morning, exactly four hours and ten minutes after driving out of this same parking lot Bobbie Downing's Jeep rolled back in. Bobbie, now wearing a blue and tan varsity jacket over a clean pair of blue jeans and Honolulu blue Detroit Lions tee shirt swiped her key card and entered the building. Her focus this morning was on the last round of T2 tests. When that was complete she would prepare for the upcoming T3 testing procedure. She immediately set to work reviewing the various tests, cataloging the results and preparing to conduct the next round. By noon she couldn't focus. It was when she misplaced a note she had written while peering through a microscope that she realized the only thing she'd eaten since breakfast the previous day was a power bar on the drive to Mio. Electing to take the outside pathway, Bobbie grabbed her jacket, pushed the lab door open and walked to the company cafeteria.

Fifteen minutes later she was back at her desk, spoon in hand eating a cup of yogurt and staring at the treasures she'd found the previous day. Glancing at the large institutional clock on the far wall she decided that she could spend a little time on the half saddlebag.

The first task was the most obvious. She had to open the long closed container. This was not going to be easy. The leather had been in a very unusual environment, it had dried, not rotted, in the same micro environment that had caused the flesh on the cadaver hand to mummify. The flap and the body of the saddlebag had fused together over the years, it now appeared to be one solid piece. She would need to clean, then soften the entire bag.

Crossing the lab floor Bobbie found the supply closet. A very mild baby soap was used for much of the hand washing in this laboratory. Bobby searched for a bottle of the soap and was quickly rewarded. She then recrossed the laboratory and entered a small kitchenette in the rear. Here she removed a bottle of vinegar. Pouring warm water, soap and a few dashes of vinegar in a bowl she made her cleaning solution.

She began slowly rubbing the face of the bag using the homemade solution and a series of clean towels. Gradually the encrusted sand and dirt dissolved and the leather began to appear a bit more pliable. After thirty minutes of this she was satisfied the leather was as clean as she could make it. Now she needed a few more exotic ingredients not likely to be found in this laboratory. Bobbie was nothing if not efficient and she had anticipated this problem. Pulling her jacket from the back of her desk chair she removed a small plastic bag from an inner pocket. She then put the contents on a lab table and lit a Bunsen burner. She heated and poured equal amounts of beeswax and cocoa butter into a Griffin beaker. This she heated for thirty seconds, stirred, then doubled the mixture with sweet almond oil. Now she stirred and heated the entire mixture until it was very warm. She set the mixture aside to cool and grabbed a soda from the kitchenette. When the goo had cooled enough to work with she began to massage the concoction into the leather. Noting the stress the leather endured at the buckles and the fold of the cover she paid particular attention to those areas.

By now the laboratory had filled with technicians

returning from their lunch. Several crowded around Bobbie's table examining her find. Soon her lab mates began to bombard her with questions. Finally, Bobbie was convinced to tell about her adventurers in the Mio woods and the work with the State Police. Her story seemed to gain her a measure of respect from her new colleagues. The brief moment in the spotlight faded as quickly as it had begun when Bobby announced the saddlebag would have to 'sit' and allow the cream to soak into the leather. The anticlimax soon had her new found friends drifting back to their daily duties leaving Bobbie to clean her work area and finish making notes on the bag and her efforts thus far.

Chapter 8

Alex Tolovek's office was a crowded, messy place. His desk was dominated by two large LCD monitors attached to a slightly larger than normal desktop computer. While he could display anything he chose on the two screens his default setting was a display any accountant would appreciate. On the right were the accumulated inputs of the two accounting clerks responsible for approving, tracking and logging all significant expenditures of the company. On the left was a summation of the company balance sheet. One look and Alex had a real time picture of the state of the company's finances. Alex studied the two screens. He reached out and clicked a few icons with his wireless mouse. The screen on the right dissolved, replaced with a graphic displaying expected expenditures against expected revenue. His stomach turned. Cash outlays were accelerating. Income was steady even slightly growing but a click or two of the mouse and he could project income for varying time frames. Twelve months from now wouldn't look good, a two years would be catastrophic.

He didn't need to move a mouse or click a button, he'd seen it all before. He did it anyway. A graph appeared on the screen. On the vertical axis were increments marked in millions. Millions of dollars. On the horizontal axis were hash marks extending from the origin at the lower left corner to the right edge of the screen. Each mark represented a month, thirty-six marks, three years. A blue line entered the screen at the twelve million mark. It streaked across the screen, climbing at a slow but steady pace for five months then leveling off. The line represented company revenue. It was made up mostly of their latest anti-herpes drug. The level off represented the completion of market penetration for their wonder drug. After all, only so many people had herpes.

Below the blue line a red line entered at the ten and a half million mark. This line represented company expenses. It shadowed the blue for the next five months, then its trajectory altered upward sharply. The red line shot past the blue at a seventy degree angle for another five months then reversed course and restabilized below the blue ten months in the future. The large spike reflected legal fees and payments of twenty-five million dollars, the result of a cold sore cream known as Praximtine, which cured cold sores, but left its users with shingles like symptoms for the remainder of their lives.

Tolovek studied the lines. A click of the mouse and he overlaid Viral BioTech's projected stock price on the screen. The projected prices were guesses to be sure, but they were very educated guesses and were all based on the company's historical stock price to company earnings ratios mixed with historical value judgments based on expected sales rates. The projections showed the company's stock price slowly climbing, then suddenly descending from an anticipated high of twenty-two dollars a share to under fifteen. The court cases, loss of product development, the expected settlement, each took a bit of the panache from the stock. Ultimately the sum was greater than the parts, the stock price would begin to fall.

What came next was the true disaster. He'd run the numbers through his computer many times. He'd calculated the numbers by hand. They never changed. He moved the mouse to the right. At the fourteen month point the red line decreased reflecting decreased materials and labor costs. Those costs decreased because they were not going to be making nearly as much product. That sad fact was reflected in the blue line; the floor fell from underneath it. The line turned down sharply, reached four million and stabilized. This reflected the loss of revenue expected when the patents expired on their two biggest sellers, Zanatoval and Matatoval.

He glanced at the projected stock price, it began to deteriorate from twenty five dollars a share, a reflection of the inevitable market rumors. By the fifteen month point the company's share price was projected to be under ten dollars. By the end of month sixteen it was somewhere between one and two dollars. In essence, the company, its stock and his future would be worth one twenty-fifth of what it was today.

There had to be a way out of this. There had to be a way to prop up the stock, sell his shares and move someplace warm. But there wasn't, he had done the math, worked the scenarios. They all ended the same. He was all in with Sarah. He'd once owned his own accounting firm. "AT Accounting PLC, Alex Tolovek CPA and Owner." It wasn't much, only six employees plus himself. He'd been comfortable. No wife, no children, but he'd taken the occasional vacation, had even been to England once.

Then he met Sarah. She'd flirted with him, she'd taken him to dinner, even sent him flowers. He smiled at the memory. "I'm just a macho guy," he thought. Then she'd offered him a job, he'd thought there was something more. Obviously that wasn't the case. But, it was a pitch that he couldn't refuse. She'd pay him twice what he could ever hope to make while running the little accounting firm, provide him a healthy employment contract and a share of the company. All he had to do was help finance the venture. He couldn't lose, when she'd approached him she already had a drug ready for market. It was a readymade winner. So, Alex Tolovek swallowed his pride, gave up his independence and sold his accounting firm. The money was immediately invested in Sarah. He owned twenty percent of the company. Two years later he was worth millions. At least on paper. But he was an officer of the company. The investment bank handling the initial public offering had tied each of the officers into the company for seven years. It was highly unusual, but they said pharmaceuticals were high risk. He couldn't sell his shares for another year. He shook his head, still amazed he'd agreed to the seven year period.

And now? He shook his head, he knew the answer. Now, the once high flying shares were destined to crash to earth. Now, this whole place was going to be worthless. Now, he was going to lose his job, every dollar he'd ever worked for and saved. Now, the company was going to go bankrupt. And now...now he was too old to start over. Alex continued to study the screens. Nothing changed. He couldn't save the company. He shut down his computer, pushed his chair back and tried to relax. It was impossible. He was going to spend his old age in a rent assisted apartment surrounded by deadbeats, divorcees, and welfare queens. He could see it coming.

He pushed back from the desk and headed for his door. Alex exited his office, turned left and headed for the elevator which would take him to the cafeteria. Maybe a piece of pie. His timing, though he didn't know it, was perfect.

Paula Pelitier was angry and frustrated. Her work was slow on a good day, lately she'd failed to make progress on anything. Her dreams of fame and glory, of being mentioned in the same breath as Pasture or Fleming had long ago faded. Now she just wanted the company to be modestly successful. It had been once, based on other people's work, wasn't now and that failure, more than anything ate away at her. Paula's pace was slow, almost labored as she approached the elevator which would take her to the small downstairs office she called home.

"Paula." Tolovek took her elbow. "We need to talk," he said.

"Not now Alex, I've got a lot of work and I've got to figure out what I'm doing," she squared her shoulders and faced the elevator doors.

"That's what I'm talking about Paula. What are we doing?" She glanced at him. "Paula, this company can't last like this, we need to take action."

She turned to the elevator doors. "We'll be okay Alex."

"Paula, I do the numbers. We're not okay, we need something now!" Alex could not understand how Paula and Sarah could not see the company was hemorrhaging cash.

Her cheeks flushed with anger, "What do you want from me Alex? I can't invent a miracle drug in a day." The elevator doors opened.

"I know what we can do Paula, we can get out of this." Paula stepped into the elevator, spun on one heel and studied him.

"Not now Alex."

He put his hand on the elevator door, "Paula, we're going broke, it's happening no matter how much she says it isn't."

"I've got work to do Alex," Paula spat. The doors began to close, he didn't stop them this time.

He had to do something. He'd thought about the next step for the past month. Sometimes the captain of a ship had to be replaced. He could do it, he could run this company. It was a betrayal of Sarah, but really, she had done the same thing, or nearly the same thing hadn't she? If life is a voyage then it's every man for himself isn't it? Well? What was different here? He had to throw Sarah overboard, take over this company and steer it to port. But he needed Paula, she had to stick with him, not Sarah.

Alex nearly ran back to his office, the pie long forgotten. He settled into his chair and turned on the computer. It took too long to boot. He thought about what he was doing. He'd heard the rumors, he knew there was a history there somewhere. But it was the only way, no one else would be able to help. Moments later and a few clicks of the mouse he had the phone number he needed. Alex took a deep breath, cast one last glance at the stock charts and dialed. A young woman answered the phone. "Metapalm Pharmaceuticals, how may I direct your call?" Alex pulled the cell phone from his ear and studied it. "Hello? How may I direct your call?"

"Thomas Langley please." Alex took the plunge.

Chapter 9

I

Twenty-two hours after applying her homemade leather softening cream to the saddlebag Bobbie Downing anxiously watched the clock. Viral BioTech paid her to work on drugs and viruses, but they didn't care what she did on her lunch hour and today she had no intention of spending that valuable hour in the cafeteria. Finally, the minute hand clicked to twelve and Bobbie felt free to return to her saddlebag.

Fighting the urge to grab a knife and cut her way into the bag's secret interior she carefully adhered to her plan for the bag. She would measure and note its dimensions, photograph the object, X-ray the bag and then, and only then would she begin the process of opening the saddlebag.

Twenty valuable minutes later, her measurements and photography complete, Bobbie carried the bag to the technician's room across the hall. A small X-ray machine dominated the little room, leaving just enough room to maneuver around the machine. She slid the object onto a flat radiographic table, then carefully aligned the extending tube arm. Satisfied the X-ray tube was properly positioned Bobbie retreated behind a lead lined wall to snap three images of the bag's interior.

Moments later she sat at the computer workstation and carefully studied the pictures. A large dark object with indeterminate shapes inside dominated the bag interior. At its bottom lay what appeared to be the nib of a pen. There didn't appear to be any flaws in the X-ray photographs themselves so she hit the print button. Then, just to be safe, she saved them to a flash drive.

A few minutes later Bobbie pulled the pictures from the

printer, pocketed the flash drive and returned to her office. Once again she made careful notes of the process and steps taken thus far. A quick glance at the clock and a smile, she had thirty minutes left in her lunch hour. At last, the moment had arrived.

Gripping a small ruler she carefully slid the plastic between the edge of the now softened cover and the body of the bag. Gently she worked the ruler back and forth until she had a gap large enough to insert a gloved finger. Then, she began to gently pry the cover upward from the underlying surface. Eventually she had the cover completely loosened from the front surface of the bag. Now, she rotated the entire bag to examine the buckles. They were attached to short anchor straps affixed to the cover flap. The anchor strap with its long row of holes wrapped from the bottom of the bag, up the side and into the buckle. The buckles and straps were still secured meaning that somehow she needed to unbuckle the rusted metal fixtures.

Removing a large magnifying glass she carefully examined the twin buckles. Several times she examined the X-rays. After considerable thought she decided the structural integrity of the square metal frame had not been compromised by their surprisingly light coating of rust. Two questions could not be answered. Would the leather strap separate as she pulled it tight to remove the prong and would the metal buckle prong itself withstand the stress it must endure while she worked it free of the strap? She referred to the X-rays once again. They didn't reveal any flaw in the buckle's metal prong, she would risk it.

Bobbie carefully worked a sheet of plastic between the straps and the bag itself. Then she began coating the buckles with penetrating oil. Gently she began working the leather straps back through the buckles until she had the tongues free. Then, while holding her breath she pulled the strap tight, lifted and was able to remove the metal buckle prong. Minutes later she had both buckles open.

Carefully she peeled back the bag's flap revealing the interior of the bag. She used a small pen light to examine the contents. The light revealed a neatly rolled bundle of oilcloth. Now she slipped her hands around the bundle and slowly pulled it free of the bag. At last it lay safely on the table. Suddenly the air was filled with cheers and applause. Bobbie had been so engrossed in her work that she hadn't noticed the laboratory staff silently gather around her. Cell phones snapped photographs, several people shouted questions, laughter filled the air and Bobbie couldn't help a shy smile. She felt like she'd climbed Mount Everest.

Viral BioTech's chief scientist, Dr. Paula Pelitier, raised her hands to quiet the room. "Okay, Downing, you've got us hooked. What is that?"

Bobbie did her best to look serious, but couldn't suppress a grin as she explained the state police contract and that she'd been sent into the field in a combination of her two specialties. "...so this is what I've got so far."

"So now what do you do?" someone called from the back of the room.

"I've got to see what's in this bundle, then we'll see where this fits in the historical record. I'm hoping to do some more exploration of the area."

"On your own time I hope!" Paula interjected.

"Absolutely boss!" Bobbie replied to the laughter of the room.

"Well, don't keep us in suspense, open that thing. Let's see what's inside," Paula pressed.

This surprised Bobbie, normally her boss was a stickler for following the rules, but this time even Dr. Pelitier couldn't control her curiosity. Slowly Bobbie unrolled the oilcloth. Gradually the fabric separated from a sheet of light brown leather hidden underneath.

"What's that?" someone whispered.

"Looks like deer skin," another answered.

Gently Bobbie began to unroll the leather. At last a bundle of documents and small packages were exposed. Reverently she began to remove the documents, laying them out on her table. Some were thick packages, most were secured with a wax seal and addressed to officials in Detroit. Others were addressed to cities and villages as far away as New York. Two were addressed to London, one to someplace in France.

She carefully laid the documents side by side on a long laboratory table. None of the letters were in envelopes, each had been folded to form a flap, each flap appeared to have been sealed with wax. She thought about that then smiled. Envelopes were not widely used when this bag had been assembled. Another clue to its age.

Some of the wax seals looked very official, others were simply an initial, still others were simply a lump of wax. Most of the seals had separated from their letters and Bobbie opened those letters, laying them flat.

"This is about as far as I can go," Bobbie said to her laboratory partners. "I've got to separate these, photograph them and let them adjust to the humidity. I can't open them for a couple of days."

Then, using one of the lab cameras she began taking pictures of each document. She was totally absorbed with her work when an alarm sounded on one of the many machines in the laboratory. Several pairs of eyes rotated to stare at the machine. Someone silenced the alarm. "Okay folks, let's get back to work and let Bobbie finish doing whatever it is she's doing," Pelitier announced.

After her coworkers had returned to their workstations Bobbie went to the lab storage cabinets and removed a pack of filter paper. Then, she carefully laid each page of each document on one of the absorbent papers. She didn't have time to read each letter now, but she was unable to resist the urge to scan each document. Soon she discovered a letter to the Michigan territorial governor, Lewis Cass which reported on the fur trade at Fort Mackinac, several letters to mercantile agents requesting goods be sent to the fort and even a few love letters. Bobbie smiled, then firmly told herself to remain detached and professional. It was impossible, her smile seemed to be carved into her face.

One letter caught her eye, it was addressed to Zephaniah Platt. This letter seemed out of place, Zephaniah Platt lived in the town of Plattsburgh. She knew the place well, it was now a city on the shores of Lake Champlain and she had been born on the base in the old Plattsburgh Air Force Base hospital. The opening line grabbed Bobbie's attention like none other.

My dearest friend, Zephaniah, I have the duty of describing to you a most unfortunate incident which I am thankful to note concluded in a most satisfactory fashion.

In moments she found herself sitting at the table deeply absorbed in the letter. The writer began to describe something which he could only attribute to *"a strange series of mystical, possibly demonic events."* She was now more intrigued than ever and continued to read.

A substantial period of robust winds from the northwest arrived. Birds not seen in the area were viewed as if fleeing a terrible fate. The hand of Death visited the natural world, the terrible wrath of God vented itself upon His own creations. At once, large numbers of waterfowl: gulls, terns, shorebirds, ducks, geese and swans and the like began to die. Flocks of domestic fowl, lively in the morning, were dead and burned by night.

Fear gripped our meager Fort. Pestilence as yet unknown to these parts, of a scope only seen in the corrupt societies of Europe, seemed to have been let loose upon this land. Soon, our worst fears were realized. Adventurers and trappers reported native villages decimated by disease as far west as the Sioux tribes and north into the Ottawa. A strange illness that had not been seen before gripped the natives. I hoped the disease would confine itself to the natives. I was disavowed of that hope when a pair of Canuck trappers lay down at my door.

Bobbie could envision the scene described by the writer. A terrifying, apocalyptic vision of death in the natural and human world. The author seemed especially shocked at the speed with which the illness killed. Fully grown, healthy young men were well in the morning and dead the next day. Bobbie shuttered. The doctor's helplessness was evident, he was forced to deal with a foe he could not identify nor hope to combat.

As she read she became more intrigued and fascinated by the similarity with illnesses she had studied. It seemed as if she were working on the same pathogens now.

"Dr. Pelitier, come take a look at this." Paula suppressed a grin, happy to get a closer look at Bobbie's special project. "This letter is from a doctor and describes an illness that sounds, well like a virus. Apparently it hit the natives first then moved into the French trappers. Sounds pretty serious."

Pelitier was now standing next to Bobbie, a sly smile creased her lips, "Sounds vaguely work related, what's the letter say? Pelitier had become intrigued.

As a physician I could do but little howsoever, as a man of God I was compelled to act. I sallied forth to the Ojibway encamped just outside the confines of the village of St. Ignace. A sad and terrible fate had befallen the poor heathens. Their young were stricken with fever, cough, and painful throats. Their very muscles tormented them. In some, their eyes oozed and discharged a torrent of fluid. Many could not breathe, as if an object of tremendous weight had been placed upon their chest."

I could not treat the pestilence. Sadly, scores of the heathens died. Some within twenty-four hours of being struck down with disease. I despaired of even alleviating their suffering until their time when suddenly I was touched by the hand of the Almighty Himself. Inspired to combine the worthless potions administered by the tribal healers with modern science I fashioned a broth, distilled it, then when fit to consume I bade my patients drink. Hallelujah but that it did not stop the progress of the disease! Gradually, ever so slowly I saw improvements. Within a fortnight my patients had recovered sufficiently to rise from their beds and by the next month they had recovered completely and were about their business.

In an effort to preserve this cure and to alleviate suffering I have written a detailed account of the manufacture of this broth and its distillation. I have endeavored to provide drawings fashioned by a skilled artist located here in the fort of each of the plants and herbs used in the hope that a physician's assistant with only a modicum of skill may collect *the necessary components without supervision.*

I have entrusted this letter and the accompanying journal to my close associate, Jeremiah Berstrom. I beg you will treat him with the hospitality you would visit upon myself.

I remain, Sir, your faithful and humble servant,
Dr. William Beaumont

Paula put her hand on Bobbie's elbow, "What's that first part there? Reread that please," she pointed to the opening paragraphs. "That's amazing. You know, I think you're correct, it sounds like he was dealing with a virus. A highly contagious virus at that."

"Whatever it was it moved fast," Bobbie mused. "And this part about their eyes oozing is pretty unusual."

"The dying birds are what caught my attention." Paula paused then stood erect, "You know, this sounds an awful lot like avian flu."

Bobbie slumped back in her chair. "It does, I agree with you." She thought about what she had just read, "Funny how they cured everything with herbs and broths back in those days." Bobbie picked up the letter then said, "I'm sorry doctor what-ever-your-name was, but a virus isn't cured by a hot broth."

"Don't be so sure Bobbie, only one percent of the plants in the Amazon rain forest have been tested and something like twenty-five percent of all drugs come from an ingredient or compound derived from those plants. Just last year the National Cancer Institute listed over 3000 plants that are active against cancer cells.

"You really believe he was on to something?"

"Bobbie, science happens in the strangest places. Who

knows? Maybe the common flu was cured in 1812 or whenever this happened and no one knew. The point, with apologies to Mr. Sherlock Holmes, is that whenever you have eliminated the impossible, whatever remains, however improbable, is possible."

"You can't be serious?" Bobbie asked, slightly taken aback.

"Who would have guessed mold growing on an old petri dish would end up being so important? I know I'd certainly like to see this journal," Paula said.

Bobbie thought about what Paula was saying, then made up her mind. "Well, the letter says the journal accompanied the letter." She gave a meaningful look to Paula, "I won't be in the lab for the next few days. I've got some work to do."

Paula's initial impulse was anger, the tests were expensive, time consuming, complicated and failing. But Bobbie was clearly determined to explore whatever it was that had produced this remarkable tale. Paula replayed their conversation, a doctor that may have cured bird flu? Impossible. But then hadn't she just said not to discount anything, that science sometimes just happens? The kid could be on to something. Making up her mind she said, "This better be worth it. See you on Monday."

II

Paula preferred to work at night with only her desk lamp. Tonight was no different. A large pile of folders sat on her left, a smaller pile on her right. Each folder contained the results of a different test or analysis of her anti-viral efforts. Slowly each was removed from the left, its reports, graphs, and analysis were read and evaluated. If she saw something amiss she made a note. Gradually the pile on the right grew. By nine o'clock Paula was no closer to figuring out why her tests were failing, what she did know was that another night had been wasted and there was no one home to care.

A faint sound wafted in from her office door. Paula sat up and listened. She couldn't place it. She peered through her office door, across the laboratory floor to the lab door. Nothing. She gave up and took the next folder.

"Paula!" The voice nearly exploded in the silence. Paula's feet ran in place and her head snapped up. A man in blue jeans and a sweat shirt stood just outside her office.

"Alex! You son of a bitch! You scared me half to death."

Tolovek stepped into her office. "Paula, I need to show you some charts. I need you to listen to me. We have got to work together on this."

She studied the accountant. "I don't have a lot of time Alex."

"You won't have anything else but time if you don't put those folders down and listen." He flipped on her office light, momentarily blinding Paula, and sat down across from her. "It's time someone else ran this company. We can't go on like we are."

She leaned back in her chair, "I'm not a trader Alex."

"Paula, it's not like we're selling secrets to the Chinese, we're talking about this company and the people who work here. We're talking about saving people's jobs, putting kids through college, keeping people in their homes." She didn't care for Alex Tolovek, but his insistence she review his data bothered her, maybe he was on to something. She shifted in her seat then steepled her fingers and rubbed the bridge of her nose. Finally she said, "Show me the charts."

Tolovek placed a binder on the desk. "I give this briefing to Sarah every Monday morning. It's not just the tests, it's the loss of patents. We're spending a lot of money and we're about to lose our biggest lines of revenue. It won't work."

Paula paged through the charts. "I knew it was bad, but...."

"It's going to get worse," Tolovek sat down in a chair next to Paula's desk. "Look at this," he flipped to the next chart. He couldn't say anything more, if she didn't see the truth now she never would. He nearly whispered, "We need to replace Sarah. There's no other solution."

The silence in Paula's office was thick. He'd played his trump, now he waited for Paula's decision. Paula thought about what Alex was saying. Finally she said, "How do we do that?"

Tolovek felt a rush of adrenalin. Maybe this would work after all. "We need to buy controlling shares of stock and then..."

Paula cut him off, "Alex, I don't have that kind of money!"

"Neither do I. But relax, I know someone who does. I made a phone call today."

Chapter 10

For years the world of viral research had been
dominated by the university system. Research was too
expensive for all but the biggest companies. Only the well
connected, well funded universities had access to the
government grants and large endowments necessary to pay for
the work. Millions of dollars of equipment and acres of
laboratory space was the price of admission. Decades were
needed to make even the smallest advances. Huge teams of
scientists reinforced with legions of laboratory assistants,
themselves aided by unpaid interns were required. And the
payoff was minimal, the secrets of the natural world refused to
give themselves up.

The system began to fragment with the completion of
the human genome project or HGP. The HGP was an
international effort made up of leading scientists in the United
States, Europe and Asia which mapped the basic building block
of human cells, deoxyribonucleic and ribonucleic acids.
Understanding of the DNA and RNA molecules was a large,
complex and long process. The molecules, made up of nucleic
acids, contain some three billion bits of data in small subunits
known as nucleotides. Mapping the structure and placement of
the individual nucleotides was the first step in any drug
development. The HGP's efforts to map the DNA and RNA
saved years of work and allowed hundreds of top notch
scientists to leap directly to the business of developing drugs.

Happily, one of those great accidents of history
occurred during the research. Virus nucleic acids were found
to have an eerie similarity to human nucleic acids. Learning
how to map human DNA and RNA allowed rapid mapping of
virus DNA and RNA. Now, research could be conducted by

much smaller teams. The university lock on research dollars faded. Legitimate and useful work by small companies could be done. A race for new medicines addressing everything from the common cold to athlete's foot was on. The winner of the race would reap the benefits, and the benefits were huge paydays.

It was one of the early winners in this race that Alex Tolovek had turned to, Metapalm Pharmaceuticals. Tolovek drove south on I-196. He was headed to Chicago for the day. This was not a pleasure trip and Alex did not want to make it. But, Langley had insisted they meet in person. Tolovek had thought of nothing else during the long two hour trip, now all he wanted was some quiet classical music and to not think of Langley, Sarah or his rapidly collapsing retirement savings account. He reached out to the radio and turned on the local public radio station, hoping for some new classical music. Instead two guys laughing about some poor woman's car noise filled the air. Annoyed he pushed play on the MP3 player and selected his habitual play list.

Alex had met Thomas Langley only once, at a small pharmaceutical conference he had attended while Sarah recovered from a burst appendix. Langley had made a play for Alex's services, even offering to increase his salary by five figures. Tolovek hadn't taken the bait. He was certain it was just to pry a wedge between himself and Sarah. That was then, this was now.

Tolovek gripped the wheel a bit harder and tried to concentrate. He was losing his nerve. What had been so clear was now cloudy. Maybe he had moved too quickly. Things were beginning to spin out of control. He needed help. More importantly he needed reassurance. Anyway he looked at the numbers he was going to be poor, very poor in a very short time. What Alex desperately needed was a crystal ball. He was trying to take over a company and using a competitor's money to do it. He knew it was crazy, but he couldn't see any other way to save his future and maybe save the company.

Thirty minutes later Alex had seen enough of the highway and exited. Soon he found himself on Lake Shore Drive, classic Chicago. The easy part of the trip soon ended and Alex turned off the four lane highway onto Michigan Avenue. Alex wasn't comfortable in the heart of the city. He quickly became fixated on the how of where he was going rather than the where. It was only at the last possible moment that he spotted the gray stone building's arched windows and gold lettered sign announcing his arrival. He braked hard, causing a loud blast of indignation from the cars behind. He quickly swung into the driveway of the Allerton hotel, stopped and climbed out of his Chevrolet Impala. A valet appeared and Alex handed over his keys. A few steps later he pushed open the bronze and glass doors of a 1920's jazz era hotel.

The lobby was grand, ostentatious and seemed to stretch to the horizon. A montage of reflections bombarded the new visitor. The gleaming floor was made of multiple colors of polished granite in a diamond motif. A tall ceiling, with raised copper ceiling tiles bounced and defused light. Echoes of Alex's shoes sounded as he crossed the lobby to the wooden engraved elevator doors. Wall mirrors and granite columns all reflected his image in hundreds of directions. A Chicago gangland feeling seemed to be in play. It wasn't hard for Alex to picture Bugs Moran sitting at one of the ornate tables, sipping bootleg bourbon and plotting his next move against Al Capone. The blood red flowers, arranged on tables which lined the lobby seemed to agree with him and waived as he passed.

Thomas Langley waited for him on the twenty-fourth floor, not quite the twenty-fifth, but close. Alex rode the elevator up and soon found the designated suite. He knocked gently, almost timidly on the door. Before his hand had returned to his side Thomas Langley filled the door.

"Thank you for coming to see me Alex," Langley said as he took Tolovek's hand. "I'm sorry I felt compelled to meet in person, but one must be careful in these things."

"Oh, yes...absolutely. No, it's not a problem." Alex's nerves were failing.

Langley hadn't released Alex's hand and gently pulled him into the room. "So, how was your drive?" He didn't wait, nor expect an answer. "Take a look over here," Langley directed Alex to the window. "Isn't that a magnificent view? What a sight. Makes me appreciate the people that built this great city." A moment later Alex had been steered to a large, deeply cushioned armchair. Langley poured a tumbler of scotch and pressed it into Alex's hand, then he continued with a brief history of the Chicago waterways. After several minutes Langley sat back in his chair and grew quiet. A moment later, in a voice that had suddenly become lower, steady and cold, Langley said, "But you didn't drive all the way here to listen to me did you?"

Alex, empty glass in hand, leaned forward. Was preserving something disloyal? Was saving your own future disloyal? Did he owe anything to Sarah?

"Mr. Langley, I've done the projections, I've calculated the effects on cash flow, long term debt, retained earnings and a host of other indicators. It all comes back to the same thing. Our share price will, inevitably collapse."

"That's a difficult thing Alex. You invested...how much again?"

"Everything, but it's not just the money. I sold my business, I mortgaged my house."

"Yes...well, sometimes people make bad investments." Langley studied the man. Clearly Tolovek was a man on the edge, the only real question was exactly how close.

"You said on the phone that you could save the Viral

BioTech. You were going to help me buy the company."

"Not exactly true. I said I'd be willing to save your retirement. I don't think I said save the company."

"But you said I could get back what I've invested. I wouldn't lose everything. How does that happen if you don't save the company?"

Langley leaned forward, "Alex, I intend to buy Viral BioTech. I intend to buy it for a very cheap price."

"That's not what we talked about!" Tolovek felt his blood pressure beginning to build.

"You were going to steal a failing drug formula and have me buy it? For enough money to fund the company? Then you were going to...what? Kick Sarah to the curb by some board vote? That doesn't make sense. The FCC will be all over that, you'll face lawyers and depositions. Sarah will have you all tied up in court so fast it'll make your head spin. The whole thing will take years to settle. No, I've got a better plan."

Alex could feel the nausea beginning to build. "What's your better plan?"

Langley smiled, "I'm going to buy Viral BioTech outright."

"You buying VB won't save the company. It won't save my retirement or my options."

"That's true, when I buy the company it of course will be liquidated. Your retirement will be gone and your stock options will be worthless. But, if you do something for me then obviously, I'll do something for you. I'll make your stock options good for Metapalm stock, you'll be a very wealthy man."

Tolovek was now into uncharted waters. He knew his call to Langley was disloyal to Sarah. He'd expected to sell some company secrets, get some cash, stop the money drain. But this was sounding like something much more. "I'm not sure I understand."

"Really Alex, it's not that hard. I intend to buy VB and I intend to buy it cheap. To do that I need information on what's going on inside those laboratories. I need to know details on how the tests are working out, which are going well, which are not. I need to know before the market knows. If I don't, well...the market will see what's happening to Sarah and someone else with deeper pockets will step in and begin buying up the shares. They'll buy before rock bottom. I don't want that to happen, I want to own the company. And, I want to own it cheap and outright. I'm going to be the one that personally gives Sarah her walking papers."

This was too complicated. Tolovek began to think he'd made a mistake. Langley could see the confusion, Tolovek was about to bolt, it was now or never. He had to close the deal. "Look Alex, the market won't know about your drug trials until next year. Your stock price won't fall very far until then. I want it to fall faster, I want it to be an onrushing train. One bit of bad news after the other. And this won't work unless I know what drugs the company is working on, how those tests are going and the formulas for those new drugs. I get that information and your future is secure, you're a wealthy man."

This was a sellout. There was no other term, he was being asked to betray Sarah and the rest of the company. The plan had been to take over the company, right the ship, save people from losing their jobs. Alex hesitated, then, "How can I get that?"

"Well Alex...c'mon now. You're a resourceful man. I'm sure something will come to mind."

"But, that's all protected. That information is locked up in Paula's laboratory each night. She protects those formulas like they're nuclear launch codes." Alex was becoming confused. "I don't get it. How does this help me?"

"Alex, if I know VB's drug is failing in test I can get that word out to the street. The stock price goes down. I pick up shares at a depressed price. If I know VB's drug is succeeding in test I announce Metapalm's testing in the same drug line is wildly successful and we'll be to market very soon. Again, VB's stock price goes down. Then, someone like you ensures the VB tests are not successful after that. And, presto, stock price goes down. Got it?"

Tolovek sat back in his chair and thought about Langley's plan. It was too much. He needed to get out of this room, just go back to Viral BioTech and forget the whole thing.

Langley pushed a bit more, "Alex, you're just accelerating what you know is going to happen."

"There aren't any new formulas, not really, we're just working..." He thought for a moment, "I won't be able to get the drug formulas."

Langley's patience was at an end, "ALEX!" he shouted. "You're not listening, I need those formulas. Any formulas. If you can't get them then I suggest you find someone that can. Otherwise, we don't have an arrangement and you'll end up shopping at the food bank!"

Tolovek flinched, his brother lived on Social Security, nine hundred fifty bucks a month. It wasn't the food bank, but it was close enough. Alex didn't want that, couldn't imagine ending up like that. He looked out the window, maybe he could open his accounting firm again. He glanced at Langley. No, it took years to build his little CPA firm, he didn't have that kind of time. Alex came to a decision, "Okay, alright, I'll get them...somehow. But..."

Langley smiled, "Don't worry. With you helping, and the legal issues VB is facing it won't be long before you're a wealthy man working for an entirely new company."

Chapter 11

Saturday morning Eve carried a large duffel bag to the back of their Jeep Grand Cherokee. With a grunt she lifted the bag and swung it into the cargo area behind the rear seat. "Anything else?" she called.

Jim carried a small, rolled up pup tent under one arm and sleeping bag under the other. "I think this is it." He thought a moment, "We didn't tell her what to bring. We should have told her what to bring. Ya think she'll at least bring a couple of changes of clothes and her toothbrush?"

"Jim, give the girl a little credit. She seemed to me like she was pretty comfortable in the woods. She'll figure out what to bring. Besides, just in case, I packed an extra toothbrush. She'll be fine," Eve replied.

"I'm just saying, she's a city girl and probably never camped before. I should have spent more time with her. At least tell her what to bring."

"Jim, c'mon, I'm sure she'll bring the basics. She's not stupid you know."

"I'm not saying she is, don't get me wrong here, babe. I just don't know if she's ever camped before. There's a learning curve, not a big thing, just having done it a time or two helps. That's all," Jim explained.

"Got it, and I'm saying I think she'll be fine," Eve answered then headed back to the house for Molly's bed and dog food.

Finished with the packing they loaded Molly the beagle into the back of the car. An hour later they were passing through the state capital and looking for the exit to US 127. Jim found their exit, turned north and set the cruise control. Eve settled into a novel and Molly snored. Another hour and they were turning into the parking lot at the Little Boots Diner one block from the Houghton Lake shoreline. Before Eve had finished walking Molly a yellow Jeep Wrangler parked next to their Cherokee.

"Hi Jim," Bobbie called while locking the Jeep's door. "Hope I didn't bring too much. I've got my camping gear and a bag of tools for the dig."

"Camping gear?" Eve asked while trying to hold back a beagle intent on a closer look at this new person.

"Yeah, you know, change of clothes, my tent, bedroll and pad, and of course my toothbrush!" she grinned.

Eve glanced at Jim and grinned, "Doesn't sound like too much at all."

After a quick lunch Jim and Eve led the way to the Mio Ranger's Station. They drove around the orange traffic cones and noted the signs marked "Ranger Station Closed". Bobbie parked her vehicle behind the building then stuffed a small black backpack which she used as a book bag and two bags of gear into the back of the Cherokee. The transfer complete Bobbie took her place next to Molly on the back seat.

Thirty minutes later they were bouncing along a dirt fire break road nearing the section of forest where Jim and Eve had set up camp the previous week. Soon Jim pulled the Jeep off the road and thirty feet into the forest. "Ladies and gentlemen welcome to Mio. Please be careful opening the overhead bins as items may have shifted in flight." Jim announced.

Eve glanced at Bobbie, "He thinks he's clever." Bobbie grinned and they got out of the Jeep. Eve took Molly for a short walk and Jim began removing gear. "There's a bit more than we normally bring, so we'll need to make two trips."

"Oh, I'm sorry, the dig tools took up a lot of room," Bobbie replied as she strapped on her backpack. "I kind of underestimated how much dig equipment I needed."

Jim pulled Bobbie's remaining bags from the back of the vehicle, then began piling the remaining camping gear next to them on the ground. Molly reappeared and eagerly began sniffing the new bags in the familiar pile. Seeing that Bobbie's backpack and sleeping gear looked well used Eve couldn't resist, "How come there's so many patches on your sleeping bag?"

"I was on a six week dig last October in Sault Ste. Marie. We had to get our bags up off the tent floor because it was already cold so I layered with pine needles then covered them with fern leaves. I screwed up and picked up a stick when I was grabbing the pine needles. The stupid stick tore the bag every time I rolled over and I didn't see it for a couple of days. Couldn't figure out why my feet kept getting cold!" she said with a laugh.

"Hummm...," Eve said and grinned at her husband.

"No one likes a smart alec," he whispered.

They pitched three tents, one for Jim and Eve, a pup tent for Bobbie and a second pup tent to hold fishing gear, spare clothes and Bobbie's tools. Jim gathered all the food stuff into a canvas bag and tied it off.

'Where are you going to put the food?" Eve asked.

"I guess the same place."

It took her a moment, but Bobbie quickly figured out what they were talking about. "Are there really that many bears around here?" she asked.

"They're moving south, used to be only in the top part of the state. Now they're south of Houghton Lake. Sort of a conservation success story I guess. But, I must admit, camping has become a little more interesting," Jim replied.

Molly ran after Jim as he headed off to tie the bag in a tree. Eve went the opposite way and began gathering firewood. Bobbie dug out several large rocks to increase the size of the old fire ring then began building a small pyramid of kindling wood. Eve assembled a metal tripod and placed it over the pile of kindling and branches, then she built a smaller formation of stone and placed a wire frame over that to hold their coffee pot. Jim returned just as the fire began to blaze. Ten minutes later they settled down to a hot lunch and Eve and Jim began to learn more about the dig site.

"What's so interesting about this particular site?" Eve asked.

"I'm convinced we've stumbled upon the location of an early 1800's courier or someone like that," Bobby explained. "How this person died obviously we don't know. If we find the rest of the body or more bodies we might be able to figure that out. Of course, the odds are that we won't."

"Why courier?" Jim asked.

"Well, when we were here last week I recovered half of a saddlebag. The saddlebag was remarkably well preserved. There was a bunch of letters, packages and official documents in there." Bobbie paused to take a bite of her stew.

"Official documents?" Jim asked.

"Yeah, several of the letters were addressed to government officials in Detroit. I haven't read those yet. I'm still drying them. There were letters to England and France. And, most interesting, at least to me as a scientist, was a letter to someone in New York. The writer talks about an outbreak of a disease. My friends at work and I all think it sounds a lot like avian flu."

"Avian flu? You mean bird flu?" Jim asked.

"The same," Bobbie replied.

"I thought that was a recent thing," Eve asked. "Didn't it come from Asia...Viet Nam or Cambodia, someplace like that?"

"Well, current thinking is that it may have. But, it's also possible that it could have been around for hundreds or thousands of years, just not as virulent or not recognized,"

Bobbie answered. "The letter seems to quote the symptoms pretty accurately. What's more interesting is that the letter talks about how the doctor treated and cured the victims. He documented his methods in a journal. I'd love to find that!"

"But still, it's just the flu right? People can just get a flu shot and that's that," Eve interjected.

"Almost," Bobbie answered. "The problem is the people who don't get the vaccine or that develop the disease even after getting the vaccine. Even the best flu vaccines aren't one hundred percent effective. And, for those who come down with the illness there is no cure, doctors can only treat the symptoms. With a bad flu like bird flu, sometimes that's not enough and people die."

"So you think the cure is in that journal?" Jim asked.

"Oh, I don't know. Probably not. Would be nice if it did. But, avian flu is a nasty virus." She took a sip of her coffee. "Modern science has a hard time with viruses. Look at AIDS or Ebola. Those are difficult to treat now. I can't imagine someone could treat for something like that way back then. But, you know, anything is possible. I'm just curious about the medical techniques used back then, that would be interesting to read."

They continued talking about the site and Bobbie's career for another ten minutes. Finally, Jim stood up and took the coffee pot, "Anyone want another cup?" Not receiving any takers he poured the coffee on the fire then went to the river to rinse out the pot.

Eve stood up and called after him, "Jim, we're headed down to the site. See if you can catch us some dinner. I've got more stew in case you don't," she grinned.

Eve and Bobbie began to fill two backpacks with archaeological gear, dry clothes and snacks. "Be careful with that red box Eve, that's my laser transit. Actually, the university's transit. I had to make a lot of phone calls last night to get that, I think I pledged my first born to the MSU hockey team to get it out of East Lansing."

"I'll treat it like a Murano treasure," Eve promised.

A short time later Eve found herself on one side of the dig site holding an orange and white pole with a round prism reflector on top. Bobbie stood behind a transit on the opposite side and was shooting laser beams at Eve. After each shot Bobbie would wave Eve left or right then re-shoot the beam. Eventually Bobbie would give a thumbs-up and Eve would pound a stake into the ground then label the stake with a dark felt pen. The process was followed by tying knots and more laser shots. After two hours of waving and pounding they had completed lacing white string around every stake. When the last knot had been tied Eve stood, arched her back then announced, "I think that's it. So now what?"

Bobbie smiled, "We get to be photographers." She removed a small digital camera from her backpack and began studying the site. "I think we'll start over here," Bobbie said. She handed Eve a white board, felt pen and small rag. "I'll tell you the caption, write it down and hold it so I can capture it in the picture." Bobbie slowly walked around the stakes telling Eve what to write and snapping pictures of the overall site, the surrounding area, the grid system and various protrusions in the ground. At last she finished.

Eve stood up from where she was kneeling and announced, "I don't know what we just did, but it's as beautiful a grid of string as I've ever seen in the woods. I'd want a picture too."

"We've established our Cartesian coordinates. That way, as we dig in different areas and down in depth we can accurately map where each artifact was located in the grid and how far below the surface of the grid, which I measure from the strings. Once a site has been disturbed you can't rebuild it. So, we map and locate everything. You'd be amazed at what people have discovered years after the dig was complete by looking at the maps. Sometimes entirely new conclusions."

"Okay, got that. So now what do we do?" Eve asked.

"Now, we establish depths." Bobbie answered. She produced a calibrated hand held GPS to determine the height of various areas of the grid. The elevation of each grid square was important, the site was embedded in the side of the river bank. Determining age of the find by sediment level was a long shot at best, but Bobbie felt compelled to document the levels of the dig regardless.

Bobbie and the state police had excavated a small portion of the site. This was now documented and photographed. The technicians from the crime lab had used a sieve to filter dirt in their search for clues. Neither Bobbie nor Eve approved of the location the technicians had selected. Together they selected a location closer to the river and began to assemble their own sieve.

At last the site was ready for the real work. Soon Bobbie was lifting an orange bucket full of dirt out of the site and passing it to Eve. Eve then dumped the bucket on the sieve and began shaking the box. Dirt and small bits of debris filtered through the mesh and formed a cone shaped pile beneath. Larger stones, sticks and other objects remained in the mesh box. Eve examined those objects and, if she found anything other than stones, sticks and dirt called Bobbie to take a closer look. Two hours later they had only found one button, which Bobbie noted on her site map.

Somewhere in the middle of the third hour Bobbie stood and yelled, "Eve come look at this."

Eve was busy shoveling the previously filtered dirt from beneath the sieve. Thankful for the rest she jammed her shovel into the ground and went to the side of the dig. She knelt down and watched as Bobbie began brushing dirt away from a slender strap which appeared to be attached to a bag. The bag looked to be about nine inches wide and six inches deep.

"What is it?" Eve asked.

"I'm not sure. Some sort of bag or pouch I think." She scrapped away a bit more dirt. "It's small."

Eve bent over her shoulder. "Doesn't look like a bag to me, looks sort of like a pile of brown leaves."

"It's all pressed together and dried up," Bobbie said. She put down her trowel and began digging by hand. Carefully she scraped away more dirt until she could lift the object. Bobby glanced at Eve, "This is cool isn't it?" she asked with a smile. Eve grinned and shook her head. Bobby turned the object over several times, examining it from several different angles. At last she said, "I'm thinking this might be what used to be called a possibles bag." Unlike the hardened but damaged leather half saddle bag she had worked on the previous week this bag was simply dried out and stiff. The cover would need to be softened to open, but this was a good find.

"A possibles bag? You made that up!" Eve laughed.

"No, really. A possibles bag was used to carry the items needed to fire a flintlock rifle. Stuff like extra flints, small tools, extra patches, maybe extra lead balls. Anything possible the frontiersman needed for the gun."

Bobbie pushed the bag to Eve, then stopped. "This looks odd," she pulled the bag back and turned it over. "I thought I saw an outline...," her voice trailed off. Bobbie examined the bag a moment then bent and scooped up one of her brushes. Quickly she brushed dirt from the underside of the bag then held it up to the sun. "Yup, look at this," she said, her voice just above a whisper. Slowly, carefully, her fingers traced a small square outline pressed into the leather from the inside. "There's something inside here. It's square, maybe six inches by eight," Bobby's voice was just above a whisper.

"Maybe a bible?" Eve asked, using the same hushed tone.

"We'll have to see I guess," Bobbie said. "It seems an unusual thing to put in a possibles bag, but maybe this isn't a possibles bag at all." Bobbie handed the bag back to Eve, noted its location and depth and turned back to her work. "Let's see if we can find something else."

Thirty minutes later Eve had finished another sieve full of dirt and found nothing. "I think that's going to have to do it for today Bobbie," she called. "We don't have a lot of daylight left and I don't want to be walking back to camp in the dark."

Bobbie looked up from the hole she was kneeling in. "Wow, it is getting late. I hadn't realized." She climbed out of the hole and brushed the dirt from her pants.

Eve handed her a bell hung from a clip. "Clip that to your belt or hat. It lets the bears know we're coming," Eve said then picked up one of their equipment boxes.

"Good idea, always want the bears to know dinner is being delivered," Bobbie joked.

They gathered up the remaining equipment and began the walk back to camp. A short while later they arrived to find Jim sitting next to a roaring campfire, dinner preparations laid out at his side. "I was starting to wonder if you two were going to dig all night!" he called as they approached.

Bobbie eyed the dinner preparations spread out next to the fire. "Looks like we're in for a feast tonight!" she exclaimed.

"You two get washed up and I'll do the cooking," Jim said.

Soon Bobbie and Eve returned from the river to find plates of fried trout, sweet corn, fried morel mushrooms and blackberries laid out on the camp table. "So, what did you find this afternoon?" Jim asked.

"We found this," Bobbie said, pulling the dried possibles bag from her backpack. She handed the bag to Jim. "We think there's some sort of book inside and we're hoping to open it once the leather is pliable enough."

Jim turned the bag over in his hands. "Seems pretty stiff..."

"I think with a little cleaning and my special homemade leather treatment I'll get this open," Bobbie said as she stood up and walked to her tent. Soon she returned with two bottles and a handful of rags. She sat one of the bottles on a stone next to the fire, then opened the other and poured the liquid on a rag. Jim watched her for several minutes then began the after dinner ritual of washing the dishes.

The evening passed slowly as Bobbie quietly worked on her find. An hour later Eve was fighting sleep when Bobbie announced she was ready to open the bag. Jim and Eve watched intently as she gently pulled the bag's cover back. Bobbie stopped and glanced at them, "This is kinda neat isn't it?" she asked, her face breaking into a smile.

"Don't stop now!" Eve cried, "What's inside?"

Bobbie's hand disappeared inside the small bag and she gently began removing the contents. Slowly a leather bound book, the size of a small notebook appeared. "Look at this," Bobbie exclaimed in a hushed voice. She put the book down then studied the inside of the bag. "That's it, nothing else," and she turned the bag upside down.

"What's the book?" Jim asked.

Bobbie picked up a dry paint brush and began dusting the surface of the manual. "I don't see a title," she whispered. Carefully she separated the cover from the first page, happily noting the remaining pages separated freely. "Oh, this is wonderful," she gasped, "Look at this!" The book appeared to be a diary, each page began with the date, temperature, rain fall and weather. Then brief comments on the events of the writer's life. Near the end the pattern changed. Suddenly the pages were filled with colored pictures of plants, insects, mushrooms and flowers.

Eve took the outstretched book, "Look at this

handwriting. That's some seriously ornate penmanship," she said.

Slowly Eve turned the pages, "And look at those pictures! Whoever did that was an artist." The colors were still rich and vibrant, the handwriting was precise and beautifully done. Each page listed the Latin name and common name of a plant or insect.

"What does it say at the bottom there?" Jim pointed at a small paragraph which seemed to be repeated on each page.

"It's hard to read." Eve tilted the page to the light. "I think it's a description." She turned a page. "Yes...it tells the best type of ground and lighting to find the plant on each page." She handed the book to Jim, "See here?" she pointed.

Jim read the paragraph then flipped several pages. "Look, this is different." Jim read for a moment then said, "It's like a cookbook. This part seems to be techniques for cooking the various plants, herbs and bugs." He studied the page, "Doesn't seem to be making a meal...what do you think this is?" he asked looking at Bobbie.

"I'm not certain," Bobbie replied, "The first part seems to be a journal, a diary of the day's events. But these pictures...maybe it is part of a cookbook?"

"A sauce book?" Eve offered.

Jim glanced at her clearly confused. "What's the difference?" "You know...desserts, sauces, soups...it's like a cookbook, but not for meats or pastries," Eve whispered.

"Oh," he murmured.

Bobbie continued to study the pages of colored drawings. "I don't think so. There's no soups mentioned, no meat or breads. There's only...herbs and mushrooms and..," her voice trailed off. Suddenly Bobbie stood, "I've got it! It's for a pharmacist! It's a pharmacist's notebook!"

Chapter 12

I

Sarah Cox had completed her bachelor's degree and her medical degree as a confirmed late night person. Beer, pizza and a background of the Late, Late Show had served her well from high school forward. Even her years as an intern and later a resident physician had been spent, mostly between the hours of midnight and 8 A.M.

Metapalm had changed all that. In what she considered an incredibly rude habit, her co-workers had insisted on morning meetings, afternoon lunches and leaving work for family at five. It was all very corporate, very routine. All very soul stealing. But, gradually, as the years had progressed, Sarah adapted and now, to her disgust, she too had become a corporate sellout and held morning meetings.

She checked her watch, swore under her breath and began gathering her materials for an early morning meeting with Alex and Paula. She knew she needed to kill the antiviral project. They couldn't do it. Maybe she had waited too long, maybe the hole they had dug was too deep. But she had felt the need to try, a success would have been history making. Only a few people are ever mentioned in the same sentence with a Nobel Prize, even fewer ever win one. This had been their chance. Now, she didn't see any choice, if VB was going to survive it was time to pull the plug. It depended on what Paula would say this morning. Just as she reached for her notebook the office door opened and Connie, the fat secretary with the dark hair on her upper lip leaned in, "Morning meeting in five minutes."

"I know!" Sarah snapped, a bit too quickly, then felt guilty about the abruptness. That was the problem with getting older she thought, she felt guilt more often now. Sarah turned this function of age over in her mind as she walked into the conference room. Every department head was there; Tolovek the company CFO, Paula Pelitier, her lead scientist, Personnel, Legal, Purchasing, Marketing and Production were all represented.

The meeting quickly progressed through production, marketing and HR issues. Paula Pelitier watched her colleagues closely. These were good people. She hated the idea of stabbing Sarah in the back, taking the company she loved from her. It was against everything she believed. She and Sarah were friends as well as colleagues. If she could solve the antiviral problem the company would be on top again. There would be no need to push Sarah out, everything would be okay. She needed more tests, more time, more data. If she could produce an antiviral with less toxicity and slower rate of decay the problem was solved. If she found the answer the whole idea of taking the company became a bad dream. She was close, she needed to run a few more rounds of tests. Just a little more time and she could save Sarah and the company.

Finally only the new developments and finance were left. Sarah had learned long ago these two issues were best discussed solely with their respective department heads. Minutes later only Paula Pelitier and Alex Tolovek were left in the room.

Alex began. As usual his presentation was all gloom and doom. Decreased sales, decreased revenue, decreased profit. Sarah had grown tired of Alex and his black cloud. Not that he wasn't correct, he was, Sarah knew that. "Alex, you're not telling me anything I don't already know," she finally blurted.

"Sarah, I've told you. I know that. But we've not done anything, we're bleeding cash and an artery is about to open."

Sarah bristled, "Nice analogy Alex, but I don't have any

stitches." She turned to Pelitier, "Paula we need something from you."

Paula inhaled deeply then began her presentation. She quickly ran through the over-the-counter drugs and elixirs her group was working on. The list included cough drops, antihistamines, and anti-nausea drugs. She stopped for a breath and Alex jumped in, "Those aren't going to generate the revenue we need, they're, well, they're just low return junk."

Paula grimaced, she knew Alex was right. Small improvements on common over-the-counter treatments really were, for all intents and purposes, just junk. These little projects were just to add revenue to cover overhead for the project she truly loved. But that project wasn't going well and she didn't want to hash it through again. She didn't want to talk about the antivirals. The discussion exposed her to the reality that she may not succeed. Maybe she was engaged in an unwinnable war against nature's perfect foe. She didn't know, she didn't believe it, but it was possible. The whole thing was becoming personal. Failure was not something that Paula had ever experienced and the concept was foreign. The trials were not going well. In fact, they were clearly failing. What was worse, Viral BioTech could only afford one more full round of trials. And, affording the trial and justifying the expense were two different things. Paula took a deep breath and plunged on. She reviewed the data, discussed strategies for moving forward and finally flipped to the cost projections charts. Her presentation had the smell of failure all over it.

As committed to finding a broad spectrum anti-viral drug as Paula was Sarah was more so. Sarah loved the research, loved the idea of defeating every virus from the common cold to Ebola. But the data didn't lie. She couldn't put it off any longer, "Paula, you don't have anything do you?" She didn't wait for an answer. "We're going to pull the plug. I'm killing the antivirals project."

Paula slumped. Failure of this project meant she had failed to save Sarah, failed to save the company. There was nothing to generate the revenue they needed, their only hope was the antivirals. "Sarah, one more test, it's all we really need. We'll have the data, we'll understand the toxicity issue."

"I'm sorry Paula, that's where we stand," Sarah said as she placed her tea cup carefully on its saucer. "If we were showing some successes, even a little progress, we might be able to fund one additional round, but right now, it just looks like good money after bad."

Paula had been through these types of issues before. She had been instrumental in the development of several statins and two antibiotics. She knew companies could not test forever. For the past several weeks she'd spent every thirty-five minute drive to work afraid today was the day the company pulled the plug on the best project she had worked on in years. And, every evening she made the drive home certain that tomorrow would be the last.

"Sarah, I've got one more idea. I think it needs a fair chance..." Sarah clearly wasn't pleased by this, but didn't say anything, instead she concentrated on her cup of tea, not wanting to listen to what Paula was about to say. Paula plunged ahead, "...there's already some evidence that we may be on to something."

Cox was surprised and snapped her head around to eye Paula so fast that her long hair lifted and swirled. "What? There's more and you haven't mentioned it? Paula, c'mon we've been doing this a long time now." Sarah's anger flashed, turning her gray eyes cold, her skin hard.

"I would have, I just didn't think of this until last night. I need a moment to explain." Paula was scrambling, a little put off by the flash of Sarah she'd never seen before. She knew that this better be good or she'd be looking at a body bruising takeover fight that she could lose. That was unthinkable, she could easily end up exiled from corporate funded labs. She might find herself as a high school chemistry teacher rather than a contender for a Nobel.

"Okay, let's hear it."

"Last week the new kid, Bobbie Downing, was sent out on a contract call we got from the State Police." "Yes, I know. She was looking at some sort of old body." Sarah snapped. "Yes, good you know. Anyway, the kid's pretty smart; has a Ph.D. in molecular biology and is about to defend a thesis in archaeology."

"I know, smart kid, confused. What's this got to do with our test failures?" Sarah asked.

"I'm coming to that. So Downing goes out to Mio and…"

"Where's Mio?" Alex asked.

"Up north, on the Au Sable River, beautiful place. C'mon Alex, who cares? The thing is, she does her job then proceeds to do a little archaeology on the side. Why she decided to start digging there I'm still not clear on, apparently something about the State Police find was odd. Anyway, lo and behold, she finds half a saddlebag. The bag she found contained a letter from some doctor in the 1800's."

"Half a saddlebag?" Alex asked, trying to sound as if he were following the conversation.

"Yeah, you know what a saddlebag is don't you?" Paula's disdain was physical.

"Sure, of course."

Sarah eyed Alex, he couldn't pull it off, she leaned forward, "Two bags connected by a wide strap. The strap goes over the horse's ass, one bag hangs down on each side." Returning her gaze to Paula she said, "So what about the saddlebag?"

Alex started to ask a question and Paula quickly cut him off, "Apparently the other half is out there somewhere," her frustration with Alex only modestly hidden. "Anyway, seems the saddlebag contained a letter about how some doctor treated the Indians for a virus, and did it successfully!" This last sentence had Alex's attention, but seemed to stir something more in Sarah.

"That doesn't even make sense. Someone was spouting a load of crap," Sarah barked.

Paula bristled, "I don't think so. I've only done a little bit of research, but this letter does coincide with a known flu outbreak in the northern Michigan territory at the time. The outbreak wasn't your run of the mill flu, it hit hard and fast. Victims were dead in a matter of days."

Sarah seemed to steady herself, "Spanish flu?" she asked, referring to the deadly pandemic of 1918.

"We can't really tell, this thing killed wild birds, flocks of domestic ducks and geese...the description seems to point to something more like avian flu. The point is, this doctor used some sort of combination of native ingredients to make a broth. He then distilled the broth like a beer or alcohol, we're not sure." Paula studied the faces of her colleague and boss. She had their interest, but she needed their support.

"This doctor says in his letter that he used a series of herbs and plants to treat the virus."

"Paula, c'mon, the science isn't there," Sarah had already dismissed this crazy idea.

"You're absolutely right, Sarah. There is no science that shows an herbal treatment attacks and destroys viral DNA. But, there is a growing opinion that herbal treatments help destroy viral DNA outside the cell, sort of in a supporting role to the white blood cells. And, more importantly the herbal treatments mark the virus before attachment to healthy cell proteins."

Sarah couldn't mask her skepticism, "Okay, suppose herbs do mark viral DNA, how are the herbs introduced to the body? Don't tell me it's a matter of making an herbal tea. I've never seen evidence that chicken soup cures a cold."

"It's not as simple as drinking herbal tea, but it could be as simple as drinking. Think about alcohol in the blood system. Grains, sugars, yeast, hops...put them together, distill them and alcohol is created. We know that alcohol accumulates in the blood. That same alcohol passed through the stomach, into the gut and was absorbed into the blood. That's what police are checking for when they administer a breathalyzer test. The machine measures the number of grams of alcohol per one hundred grams of a person's blood. And, we know that different chemical signatures of alcohol are created in different drinks. Except for the basic chemical structure the alcohol in beer is different than the alcohol in a whiskey. Very sensitive, very sophisticated tests can actually tell the different alcohols in a person's blood."

"It still sounds like science fiction. An herbal tea curing avian flu, I'm not buying it." Sarah was about to end the meeting. She began to gather the papers from the table in front of her in preparation for standing.

Paula refused to stop, "There's more Sarah. That's how he got what ever chemical the herbs released into the blood. He distilled the mixture and they drank it. The real magic occurs once the chemical is in the body. I believe that this chemical allows white blood cell identification of the virus before infection of the healthy cell. It marks the virus and it marks an infected cell."

Sarah stopped gathering her papers and focused on Paula. "Once the cells are marked the white blood cells eradicate the infected cell, even if the infected cell is a fellow white blood cell." Paula reached into her briefcase and withdrew a folder. "These three articles postulate the effect and have been reviewed. I'm telling you Sarah, it is possible." She handed a plain vanilla colored folder to Sarah.

Cox opened the folder and picked up the first article. Tolovek began to ask a question when Sarah cut him off. "Paula, look at this, this isn't any medical journal we've ever used. Who is this? Was the study truly peer reviewed?"

"Look at the next one. It's The Lancet for Christ's sake, what more can we ask for? I'm telling you Sarah, this guy developed a marker for the virus and didn't even know it. I think that's how his remedy worked."

Alex Tolovek raised both his hands in a stopping gesture, "Wait, wait, wait...he made a marker? What does that mean?"

"A virus is just a collection of DNA molecules. A marker is a unique DNA sequence in a known location within the chromosome," Paula answered.

"Okay, so there's a specific group of DNA on the string-thing, what's that called?" Alex asked.

"A double helix."

"Yeah. So, on the double helix there's a specific DNA?" Alex asked.

"Well, almost. The double helix is the shape of nucleic acids," Sarah murmured as she read more of the report.

"What's nucleic acids," Alex asked.

"Just think of nucleic acids as things like DNA and RNA."

"What's RNA?" Alex asked.

"C'mon Alex, you're not planning on becoming a molecular biologist today are you?" Sarah's agitation with Alex's questions grew. "We're not talking about RNA, we're talking about DNA." She shifted back to Pelitier, "Get to the point Paula."

"Just think of the DNA as the double helix. Got that?" Paula asked.

"And the double helix is...?"

"It's the structure of the DNA, get on with this Paula,"

Sarah barked, barely concealing her anger with Alex's basic questions.

"Okay, but I still don't know what a marker is," Alex whined.

"The marker is a specific sequence of parts of that double helix," Paula explained, doing her best to suppress her excitement. She turned to Sarah, "There are two types of markers, biochemical markers and molecular markers. I think this doctor developed an herbal broth that when metabolized by the body binds with a specific sequence in the DNA of the virus. In essence, puts a sign on the bad DNA saying 'Here I am'."

"So? Isn't the virus hard to kill?" Alex pressed on, ignoring Sarah and paying close attention.

"No, actually a virus is pretty easy to kill if the white blood cells can identify it. Most, in fact somewhere on the order of ninety-nine point nine percent of all viruses which enter the human body are destroyed immediately. The body's defenses, the white blood cells, simply identify the virus as a foreign body, surround and kill it. But sometimes, the virus is able to escape, then attach itself and hide in the surface proteins of one of the body's cells. It's those cells infected with a virus that need to be identified and killed."

Sarah stood up and poured herself another cup of tea. Tolovek seemed to be following what Paula was saying so she continued. "Once the virus is attached to the cell it makes its way inside the cell wall and begins to alter the host cell's DNA, forcing the host to reproduce the DNA of the virus, not the host."

"Okay, I'm with you, so what's the big deal about this 1800's doctor?" Tolovek asked.

"Right now the predominant treatment of viral infections is prevention. We immunize with dead or weakened viral cells. The body develops an ability to identify the virus

DNA before it binds with a cell and kills it. The problem is the viruses for which we don't have immunizations," Paula said.

"Or, the cases where someone is infected because they were too damned stupid to get the shot," Sarah added. "And, right now each separate virus requires its own, specifically developed vaccine. That's not at all as efficient as an antibiotic that treats a whole long list of bacteria."

Tolovek eyes hadn't completely glassed over so Paula continued. "Right now I'm..." She caught herself, "We're working on drugs that kill a broad spectrum of viruses within the body. Our problem has been the toxicity of our compounds. We're not only killing the virus, but we're also killing the host cells. We need the compounds to identify the viruses and the infected cells and kill only those." She turned to Sarah, "What if the compounds hunted the markers not the virus?

"It's possible I guess, assuming these are correct," she pointed at the folder Paula had given her.

"I think the Doctor's compound marked the virus and attacked the marker. Destroy the marker and you've destroyed the virus. He didn't inoculate, he identified the virus and the host body's own defenses killed the virus." Paula was tired. She'd put her heart and soul into this and she was sure she'd convinced her boss and company owner Sarah Cox to make one final push for success.

Sarah leaned back in her chair, she studied Paula then glanced at Alex. "I'm sorry Paula, that sounds good, but it's just not enough. I need a lot more than a nice story to get me to bet this kind of money."

Paula's shoulders sagged. Slowly she stood, she studied Sarah, then Alex. She'd lost. There was no changing Sarah's mind, she could see that. She took a moment to compose herself, she thought about quitting right now, but where would she go? There was still a chance the stock she'd been paid with for the past few years would be worth something. Finally she said, "Alright, I'll start taking the project down. We'll have everything cataloged, viruses destroyed and everything sanitized by say...Tuesday. I'll have the staff do their final reports and have them on your desk by Monday next." She turned and walked to the door. "It's a shame, I think Dr. Beaumont hit on something pretty profound."

Sarah straightened in her chair. "What? Paula, who did you say created this magic soup?"

"Dr. Beaumont. He was the doctor at Fort Mackinac on Mackinaw Island. Sort of a famous guy, studied digestion on some French trapper's stomach. But, he also did..."

Sarah's eyes glazed, she tilted her head to the right. Both Alex and Paula recognized the quirk and let her think. Slowly Sarah returned to them. "I know. He's...I remember... Paula, that story has been around for years. Look, we went over that in first year med school. There's no evidence, no one ever mentioned the village."

"Well, that's the thing. Apparently his entire cure is detailed in some journal. Bobbie is out there right now looking for it."

"So we need the journal?" Sarah asked.

"It would sure help, yes."

"Without it we'd be shooting in the dark wouldn't we?" Sarah's voice dropped into the depressed tone she'd been using moments before. "But, we could probably replicate his methods...given time," Paula began to get uncomfortable with how this conversation had just turned. She studied Sarah. "Maybe she'll find the doctor's journal," she offered. Sarah seemed to be lost in thought. "This is crazy," Sarah said, more to herself than Paula or Alex. "It's not possible...is it?" Sarah's voice trailed off, she was deep in thought.

"Sarah, maybe the history books are wrong, maybe he did save that village." Paula could see the vacillation. She needed to plant the worm, let it crawl around Sarah's brain and then, maybe, she would save her project. "Sarah, it happened. There's no other explanation. Dr. Beaumont did it, he found a way to target the virus. We can do the same thing! We're almost there. If Bobbie comes back with that journal we're golden." Paula could hear the pleading in her voice. She hated it, but couldn't keep it out. "Sarah, it could mean a Nobel."

Sarah studied Paula. "Maybe it is true," she whispered. "Maybe Beaumont did kill a virus." Paula gave one final, gentle push. "Sarah, we'll be famous."

Slowly Sarah grinned. "Okay, Paula, we'll do it just like he did."

II

Alex Tolovek's office was warm. A large heat duct ran behind the rear wall in his office, meeting with several takeoff ducts and flowing to other parts of the building. The oversized duct by virtue of radiant heat provided more than enough heat for the office, but Alex had insisted a register be installed. As a result his office was always above the building's average temperature, even in Michigan's brutal winters. By the same token, during the summer Alex's office would be cooler than the others. This was something Alex could not tolerate. Therefore he had the vent modified so that it could be easily and completely closed. And, he had an electric heater installed in the wall next to the vent. Alex Tolovek was a man who did not like to be cold.

This afternoon however, despite turning the thermostat to 80 degrees, he imagined the icy hands of death itself were gripping his heart. His plan, his arrangement, his future was suddenly in serious danger. He locked his door, then placed a black desktop MP3 player next to the door and pressed a button. Gloria Gaynor's voice suddenly filled the room proudly claiming she would survive. Satisfied that no one would hear his conversation he dialed his cell phone.

A light, almost happy voice answered, "Alex, how the hell are ya?"

Tolovek still didn't know if he should trust the show of camaraderie or if he should be afraid of it. But, in the interest of self preservation he had, from their first meeting, decided that fear was the more prudent action.

"I think there's a problem Mr. Langley," Alex said.

Langley punched the speaker button on his desk phone and flinched, "What the hell is that noise in the background?"

"Music, I didn't want anyone to hear me."

"That'll definitely drive 'em away from your door Alex. So, what's up? "Langley walked to his office bar and poured a small drink. His reward for dealing with this idiot.

"It's possible that we...she, can...she may have found a solution."

Langley whirled, punched the volume up on the phone and began to listen more closely. "Alright, Alex, slow down, take a breath. Now, tell me about it." Thomas' mind was running through at least a dozen scenarios while he listened. Barring a miracle drug he couldn't understand who or why anyone would invest in VB once they did a thorough scrub of the business. He thought about that, it wasn't quite true, after all, stranger things had happened. "She found a sugar daddy? Some sort of white knight?" he asked.

"Not a white knight, more of an outside chance that Sarah will be able to right the ship."

"And how can she do that? You told me her anti-viral drug testing is showing a colossal and expensive failure. That hasn't changed...has it?"

"There is one outside, almost impossible... I don't think it could happen, but....well, have you ever heard of Dr. William Beaumont?"

"The Beaumont story is a myth, it can't happen."

"That's what Sarah said, but Dr. Pelitier said that one of

our new employees found a letter or something that explained how it could. Apparently, Beaumont found how to address...no, mark, that was the word, mark. Beaumont found how to mark a virus in the body."

Langley felt a rush of adrenalin. Despite his current life as a CEO he had once been a top research biologist. Now his mind was racing. Genetically mark the virus? That was revolutionary. No one had been successful at that. If the body could simply find the virus on its own... With Herculean self control Langley brought his attention back to the conversation.

"Something about a helix with a part that is different after some sort of concoction is given to the patient. It's like a shot of whiskey. The white blood cells could then identify the infected cell and kill the virus. She said she thought it would work."

"What's the concoction?"

"That's just it. One of our new hires found a letter from that Dr. Beaumont telling about how he cured bird flu. The letter told all about the mixture, but not how to make it. Beaumont wrote a description and gave the details in his diary."

Langley refilled his glass. He walked to the window and surveyed the city. Chicago was short, not like New York or Hong Kong. This city oozed into the countryside. Alex had been right to call him. Could it be that his entire plan was threatened by some doctor from two hundred years ago? It was impossible, he couldn't let this happen. He had to stop her. He turned to the speakerphone, "Where's this diary?"

"That's what I'm trying to tell you. Now we're, well...one of our new kids is already looking for it. She said that if the letter is true and we get the formula then our production facilities, our entire testing process, our FDA licensing work and our current distribution network all fit the new drug. We'll be able to bring the entire thing to market in a few months."

Langley arched an eyebrow and thought about this. By good fortune Sarah was well down the path to drug approval. Having her protocols already established with the FDA put her two years ahead of anyone else. But if she didn't have this diary it meant nothing. He had to move fast. He leaned forward and whispered, "Alex, if you intend on retiring with a lot of cash in your piggy bank. If you don't want to spend the next ten years wearing a bright orange jump suit hoeing beans and having someone holding a shotgun watching your every move then you'll do exactly as I say."

Alex could feel the blood drain from his already pale skin. This was turning into much more than he'd originally imagined, "You just want me to get that journal right?"

"Exactly! Very good Alex."

"I'm not sure how to do that." Alex was becoming very aware of his shirt sticking to his back. "She's out there right now digging and looking for it."

"Then you'll need to take it from her won't you?" Langley was becoming irritated.

"But how...I just can't...I'm an accountant for Christ sake!"

"Then you'd better figure something out because we need that journal." Langley was nearly shouting. Alex was quiet for several seconds. Langley took a sip of his drink. "Okay, okay...I'll...I can do this." Tolovek cried.

"And Alex!" Alex flinched. "This is important... Are you listening Alex?" Alex hesitated, "Yes?"

"Good. This is key Alex, key, know what I mean? I need you to convince Paula."

"I know. I've talked to her, she's...she's hesitating."

"What does that mean Alex?" Langley demanded.

"We talked about it. I explained everything, I thought she was going to get on board...but she's...she's hesitating." Tolovek didn't want to admit that when he'd approached Paula she ultimately thrown him out of her office.

Langley fought down a burst of anger. He walked around the corner of his desk. He thought about what Alex had said, and didn't say. Several seconds passed, "How did you ask her?" The question confused Alex. "I just told her...what do you mean? I just asked her."

Langley leaned forward, his face hovering over the speakerphone. "Alex, she's not the kind of person who will..." Langley wanted to say "...who will betray her friend" but thought better of it. "Alex, she's not going to anger Sarah until it's absolutely necessary. We need to understand what motivates Paula. You've got to convince her she's making the right decision. Show her there's no choice." Thomas knew that Pelitier was as big a prize as the journal. He needed her. If Paula came with the journal he could have an anti-viral drug in months not years.

"I've tried, Mr. Langley. But she just doesn't think she needs to make a move," Alex whined.

"I don't think you understand what I'm saying. Maybe you need to be a little bit more forceful in your argument."

The phone went dead. Alex thought about what Langley had said. And, what he had not said. Alex needed some help, he began to punch in a phone number.

Chapter 13

I

Sunday dawned bright and clear. A furious squirrel barked at some perceived threat and rousted Eve from her sleeping bag. Quickly getting her bearings she dressed and noted that Jim was already on the river, hoping to catch the last of the bigger nocturnal feeding trout. A call to Bobbie and soon they had a breakfast fire, made coffee and had begun putting together a feast of pancakes with bacon and eggs.

Ten minutes later Jim returned from the river, calling, "That smells great!" as he approached the camp.

"Let's hope it doesn't smell too great," Eve replied. "I don't want any hungry bear wandering into our dining room."

"Yeah, about that...," Jim picked up his pack, studied the wind and walked into the woods. Once he'd gone some thirty yards he removed a spray can from his pack and began soaking a small brush with an artificial skunk smell. Then he moved to the other side of their camp and did the same thing.

"Oh, thanks, that smells wonderful," Eve chided when he returned.

"Yeah, well, bacon sent goes a long way. I guess I could have put that a bit closer?"

"No, I'm thinking that's plenty close enough," Eve grinned.

"You really think that helps disguise bacon scent?" Bobbie asked. Eve started to laugh, "Probably not, but who knows, it might help and I'm afraid of bears!"

Once they had finished their breakfast Bobbie began washing the dishes. Jim gathered the egg shells, left over bacon and pancakes into a paper bag. Then he picked up a camp shovel and marched off in the direction of the skunk scent.

II

The site was exactly as they had left it. Bobbie sat her backpack on the ground and began removing her gear. Once the tools were laid out she examined the web of string they had erected the previous evening. Satisfied that all was intact and Bobbie strapped on a pair of knee pads, settled into the dirt and began the painstaking task of scraping away the dirt and sediment from her target area.

Eve eyed the wooden frame and its wire mesh, which she now referred to as "her sieve" and decided the slag underneath had grown too high. She disassembled the sieve and moved it away from the pile. Then, using the shovel she began tossing the excess dirt away from the dig. Finished she reassembled the sieve and began working the first bucket of Bobbie's scrapings.

Gradually, Bobbie began widening her dig area. Each scoop of dirt went into the bucket, then the sieve. Eve shook the frame allowing dirt and small debris to fall through. Then she sorted the resulting find. If Eve discovered something interesting she summoned Bobbie to examine the piece. After three hours work they hadn't found anything of note.

Needing a rest Bobbie sat back on her knees and studied the side of the excavation. "I think I know why everything was so well preserved here," she said. "If you look at the ground around the site..." she pointed with her trowel, "...it's plain sand and a mixture of other soils. But, right up in here you can see it's all hard clay. I think this is some sort of unusual accumulation of clay. It kept air from getting to the artifacts. Because there was no oxygen, no decay."

Eve studied where Bobbie was pointing. "Pretty interesting, how did all the clay get here?"

Bobbie wiped her forehead with her sleeve, "I have no

idea. I'll have to get a pedologist in here and take a look."

"Oh, yeah... that would be a big help," Eve shook her head, wondering what a pedologist was.

Bobbie blushed, "I'm sorry Eve, no one knows what a pedologist is. At least no one who isn't an archaeological geek. It's someone who studies soils and their accumulation. A pedologist can tell us how this anomaly formed, maybe even when."

"Ah, got it. So someone may be able to date this just from looking at the dirt?" Eve wasn't convinced.

"Yup, that's it," Bobbie answered. "Normally the process only gets us within a few thousand years, but sometimes it can be very exact. I'm hoping this will be more the latter. In any case, knowing how this airtight clay pocket formed will be important."

Eve thought about that for a moment then said, "You know, that's all well and good. And I'm sure it's important, but I'm starting to think about lunch. You? Want to head back?"

"Eve! Holy cow! I don't believe this!" Bobbie suddenly began scraping dirt with a renewed purpose. A moment later she shifted to a dry paint brush and whisked away several layers of dirt. "Look, look! It's...it's...can it really be?" Bobby fell back to her knees and began carefully digging. Eve tried to see around her, but the view was blocked by Bobbie's shoulders. "Holy cow, I would have never bet on this." Slowly Bobbie stood. She was holding a dark brown, square object. "Look...at this! We've got the other half!"

III

Jim had just landed his third large brown trout of the day. He was attempting to remove the hook from the fish's jaw when a loud bang interrupted the silence of the forest. The blast was immediately followed by a second and Jim recognized the sounds as gun shots. The shots were in the direction of the dig and frighteningly close. Fear knotted his stomach and he began to hurry to the river's bank. His feet slipped in the rocky bottom. He reversed his fishing rod and began using the butt end as a walking staff. He felt as if he were running in quick sand. Finally reaching the shore he tossed the rod on the bank and, burdened by the chest waders, scrambled out of the fast flowing river. Struggling to climb the bank Jim cursed the waders. Finally reaching the top of the bank Jim began a laborious dash in the direction of the shots. The woods had grown silent again, only the steady "thump, thump" of his wading boots on the forest floor could be heard.

Then, in the distance he heard a motor start, sputter briefly then settle into a steady buzz. The branches tore at his legs as he ran, cursing the waders for the slow, plodding gait they imposed, but unwilling to take the time to stop and pull them off Jim pressed forward. He passed a small cluster of jack pines, none taller than fifteen feet. Just ahead he could hear branches snapping. Something or someone was coming fast, crashing through the woods toward him. He could hear the motor's volume increase. It was an ATV. If whoever was shooting came after him on that thing it was all over. The motor roared. The trees ahead moved; he tensed, but didn't slow. The branches parted and Eve burst through the gap between two stunted pine trees. "JIM! Someone is shooting. They shot Bobbie! We've got to help her!" she screamed as she crashed into his chest.

Chapter 14

I

Jim caught Eve without breaking stride, turned sharply left and kept running. He had to get her away from the river, away from the trail and away from whatever danger lurked up there and was coming after his Eve. Her feet dragged for a moment. She struggled to make her legs move in this new direction. Eve, supported by Jim's arm, finally caught her balance as her legs caught up with the momentum.

"What are you doing?" she shouted. "Bobbie is that way!"

"Keep running this way, off the path. Go! Go! Go!" Jim yelled back. Fear swept over him; he pictured bullets ripping into their backs. There was nothing to do now but run. Unarmed and facing a motorized foe willing to shoot them meant their only hope for survival was to get away and hide. They didn't break stride as they crashed through thick pine branches and up a small hill. Together they crested the hill and immediately tripped over a thick root running across the reverse slope. Eve fell first, Jim crashing down on top of her. They rolled twice and came to rest just short of a boggy, reed filled swamp. Jim scrambled to his knees, pushed Eve down in the leaves, whispered for quiet then crept back to the top. They were trapped between the swamp and whoever was out there.

They had only run some thirty yards off the path, but the woods were thick here. He studied the forest, peering intently between trees as far back to the path as possible. To his right the woods thinned and he could see the cluster of young jack pines he had passed just before crashing into Eve. The trees, the birds, the wind, everything was still as if waiting for some terrible event. Then, a small movement in the distance. Jim watched and wondered. What chance did they have here against armed men?

A man wearing khaki pants and a green sweater pushed through the tangled branches of the pines. He walked around the trees, peering into the cluster as if expecting to find a covey of partridge. Jim studied the stranger. He carried a pistol of some type. Jim couldn't get a good look, then reminded himself that it didn't really matter. Whatever it was it was deadly. The man's dark hat stood out against the green of the trees. His khaki pants were wet at the knees and cuffs. He stepped carefully, avoiding damp areas in the forest floor. His shoes were wrong, even at this distance Jim could tell they weren't boots. He was wearing loafers. The man studied the forest as he carefully walked toward Jim. He passed over the trail of upturned leaves and broken branches they had made in their mad dash to clear the area without looking down. Then, he continued across Jim's front for another ten yards. Finally he appeared to tire of the search. He stood fully erect, turned and carefully studied the forest. Slowly, he disappeared in the direction of the dig.

Jim slid back down the hill toward Eve. "He stopped looking."

"Jim, what the hell is that all about? What are we going to do? Who was that?" Eve's questions tumbled out in a low, terrified whisper. "What about Bobbie?"

Jim began running his hands over Eve's shoulders, back and torso. "Are you hurt?" he asked.

"No, and what the hell are you doing?"

"When people are shot they sometimes don't know it, shock hides the pain. I'm looking for blood."

The shock of the past several minutes began to set in and Eve began to shiver, "Jim, someone tried to shoot me." Jim was listening, but he kept glancing at Eve. She was soaking wet, bruised and bleeding from a cut behind her left ear.

"I know hon, but you're all right now." He wrapped his arm around her shoulder.

"Jim, what are we going to do?" her voice cracked.

"I have no idea, but we're not going to do anything for a while," Jim whispered.

"What? Jim, we've got to get the police! We've got to get an ambulance! They shot Bobbie!" She struggled to keep her voice quiet.

"No, we stay here. Those people are out there," Jim pointed in the direction of the trail. "That guy gave up too easy. He's watching the trail or our camp or he's watching this part of the woods right now. We don't need to move and we're not going to until we know it's safe."

Eve's face paled, "But Bobbie..." Jim shook his head. "You think she's..." Eve's face turned gray, "Okay, yeah...oh...you're probably right." She thought about what he had said, "Jim, he just appeared. He said something and Bobbie started to run and he just shot Bobbie then pointed his gun at me. I was standing next to the river so I just jumped in. I didn't help her Jim." Eve began to sob.

"There was nothing you could do," he whispered.

Eve caught herself, took a deep breath and asked, "Now what?"

"We survive," Jim answered then crawled to the top of their little hill to keep watch. Three hours later a stiff, cold and scared Jim and Eve Crenshaw climbed out of their hiding spot. "Let's see if they left anything at the site," Jim said as they approached the path leading to the site of their camp. A short distance later they came to the edge of the river and the dig site. Bobbie Downing lay next to the dig site, face down, the side of her shirt was blood soaked and the right side of her head was bloody.

"OH MY GOD!" Eve screamed and ran to her, Jim at her side. He quickly put his hand on Eve's shoulder. "We can't disturb a crime scene. Don't touch her."

Eve stood and buried her face in Jim's shoulder. "She's dead Jim, she's dead."

Jim looked past Eve's shoulder and studied the scene, Bobbie's body lay across the back of the excavation. Several other holes obviously dug without regard for archaeological technique had been dug around the site. Someone was clearly looking for something. At the top of the bank, behind the dig lay a black object. Jim pulled away from Eve and climbed up the small hill, "This looks like some sort of box. Does it look familiar?"

Eve turned to face Jim, took a deep breath and gathered herself, "I think that's what Bobbie found just before we were attacked."

Jim picked the box up, turned it over several times and opened the flap. "It's a saddlebag. Well, half of a saddlebag, empty." He threw the bag down then began walking back into the forest, "Looks like the killer went this way." Jim only went a few steps then returned, "We'd better go get the police."

Eve shook her head and the two began the long walk out of the woods.

II

Trooper Cheryl MacIntier passed the cream and sugar to Eve then watched as she doctored her coffee, her hands trembling slightly. Satisfied, Eve carefully sipped the mixture. She didn't look up, obviously still thinking about the day's events. Cheryl was becoming worried. She'd come to like Eve and Jim in the short time she'd known them and the day's experience would have been traumatic for anyone. Her friends had spent the last two hours giving statements to the state police detectives. She could see Eve was deep in thought and that couldn't be good.

"O'Brian's has great pie, the owners make it

themselves. True homemade stuff. I can honestly say that only because I think they live in this place during the summer." Cheryl smiled and watched Eve closely. Deciding her attempt at humor had fallen woefully short Cheryl said, "Eve, we'll find her killers. The detectives are good, we found where they hid their truck. We've identified the type of truck, we know it was pulling a trailer. We've got every cop in the state watching for it."

"I know Cheryl, I know."

"Who do you think would do this?" Jim asked. "Are attacks on strangers a common thing around here?"

"No, about the only crime around here is the occasional drunk tourist or a domestic. No, this is more than that. Some sort of sicko looking for kicks wouldn't have hung around digging holes after they shot somebody. They didn't run off after the deed was done, this is something more," Cheryl said in her most official voice.

"Why? That's what I want to know. Why her? Is she worth money? Was this an attempted kidnapping that went wrong? Is this payback for something she did? See? There's just too many questions." Eve gripped her coffee with both hands, more to keep from shaking than for warmth.

"All good questions Eve. You've just got to let us do our jobs." Cheryl examined her new friends. "Look, you two need to relax, our folks are on this. Let the detectives do what they're paid to do."

Jim grunted, "Relax is not what I want to be doing right now Cheryl."

"Jim, Eve, this sort of thing is pretty big. It stands out. I can't believe they haven't been seen by someone, somewhere. Or, that someone doesn't know what's going on. Don't worry, we'll find that someone who's seen the truck or the trailer or the ATVs. Or, we'll get wind of some idiot's bragging in a bar. Maybe someone will turn on them. It will come 'round. And don't forget, this is a shooting on federal land. We can get the FBI here if we need them. In fact, they should already have been briefed." She stood up. "Like I said, we've got this, okay?"

Picking her hat off the chair next to where she'd been sitting Cheryl grinned, "I've got to get back on the road, never know, someone might be speeding on I-75."

Jim smiled a half-hearted smile. Eve didn't even attempt a grin, "Alright, we'll leave it to you guys. Take care, be safe," he said as Cheryl spun on her heel and walked to the door then disappeared into the evening.

The door slowly closed and they were left sitting alone. Suddenly O'Brian's had become very large or they had become very small. Either way, they didn't like the feeling.

Chapter 15

Tonight the evening drive from the office to home was not fun; none of the mash the accelerator, press your back in the seat straightaways, no tight curves at high speed pressing her from one side to the other. Instead, the Laraway Lake Drive was lined with bright orange cones. Dump trucks growled at the passing traffic and forced the passing cars into one lane. Highway workers followed the iron beasts throwing steaming piles of black gravel into the road's annoying pot holes and cracks. Sarah crawled along, barely reaching twenty-five miles an hour. She desperately wanted to push the accelerator to the floor, feel the acceleration and let the adrenalin wash away, for however brief the moment, the crushing weight of a slowly fading business. She touched the radio. The melodic voice of an NPR host filled the air, then a blast of static ripped the Cadillac's interior. "When it rains it pours," Sarah muttered. The static turned into a ring as the car's Bluetooth system interrupted the radio.

"Yes?"

"Sarah, we've got some issues." Paula Pelitier's voice sounded over the car's speakers.

"Now what?" she couldn't suppress the irritation in her voice.

"We're still fighting toxicity and decay." They had decided to pursue their current theory for the antivirals while they waited and hoped that Bobbie Downing would return with some sort of never before seen recipe for a miracle cure. Sarah grimaced; if she was going to lose the company she'd go down firing all her guns.

Paula's voice blasted on, "It's the same as before. We're chasing shadows. The virus acts like it knows what we're

117

doing. I swear, some of strains seem to be mutating before we even introduce the compound. It's like they know we're coming for them."

Sarah asked a few questions, but already knew the answers. Paula sounded dejected. "Sarah, we can do this, but not in time."

"I know," Sarah could feel a bolt of panic gathering at the base of her skull. They had to find out how Beaumont had made his broth. "Any news on Beaumont's journal?"

"We're still researching. It's a near impossible task. I've talked to historians at both universities and they're clueless. We don't know what herbs he used, we don't know how much he made, and we don't know how he distilled the stuff. The letter is the only clue we have." Paula seemed to be on the verge of giving up.

"What about our little archaeologist? Where's she?"

"Not due in the office until Tuesday. I've called her cell but no answer. When she gets in I'll press her for more."

They agreed to meet the next morning and Sarah pushed a small button on her steering wheel. The call disconnected. Thirty long minutes and not many miles later she swung into the driveway of her large, tutor styled home. A dark gray Mercedes rested in the circular drive. Sarah parked in the garage and stepped through the rear door into the kitchen of her mini-mansion. She had two people on staff, a part-time gardener and a housekeeper. She told herself they were employed to clean and cook, but the reality was that she wanted someone else in the large house. The life of parties and frequent visitors she had envisioned when she bought the eight bedroom, twelve thousand square foot house hadn't materialized. She rarely had visitors and had begun to think of herself as a forty-something cougar without claws.

Dorothy James, her cook and housekeeper met her at the door. "Good evening Sarah, a Mister Langley is waiting for you on the patio. He said you were expecting him. I thought you were going to be home an hour ago so I asked him to wait."

Thomas Langley, CEO of Metapalm. She'd hoped she never see him again. Sarah's mind, like a computer doing a file search, automatically began accessing the memories of her time at Metapalm. She dug her thumbnail into her index finger and bit down hard on her lip, she would not think about that, not now, not ever again. It was no use, visions of a younger Thomas Langley, of Metapalm's research department, of her friends and tables of food and wine, birthday parties, weddings, co-workers all flooded back. Then she saw herself walking out the door with the secrets of an anti-herpes drug. Soon, she was running her own company and producing a wildly successful drug used by millions.

"That's fine Dotty, traffic was a bitch and I got out of the office late. Besides, I don't mind letting him wait." Sarah gave a reassuring smile. "I'll go see him now."

Langley sat on a deeply padded Adirondack chair overlooking a small but beautifully decorated garden in Sarah's backyard. He didn't see Sarah as she stepped through the large glass patio doors. She eyed him a moment. "What brings you to Michigan Tom?"

Langley stood. "Long day at a dying company Sarah?"

"I would have stayed longer if I'd known you were waiting for me," she shot back.

"You seem a bit...maybe a bit more tired than the last time we were together," he eyed her carefully. "Are you feeling alright? Work isn't too much for you I trust?"

"Your concern is much appreciated Tom." She sat down in an equally large and stuffed chair across from him. She knew Thomas Langley too well to know he hadn't flown his precious new airplane, he always had a new airplane, all the way to Grand Rapids to catch up on old times. "You want something, what is it?"

"Sarah, I was on my way to Toronto and realized you were just a small detour away. I thought I could spend some time with you, maybe you would take me out to dinner."

"Why on earth would I want to do that Tom?" Somewhere this snake oil salesman had laid a trap and she had no intention of blundering into it.

He glanced around the patio. "Those anti-herpes drugs seemed to have provided a nice home, your own little company, a good lifestyle. I think you owe me at least a dinner."

"I don't owe you a thing. In fact, I don't think you've sufficiently paid for what you did to me."

He locked eyes with her. She'd taken millions from him, she'd humiliated him, she'd nearly cost him the company. Metapalm's next generation of product had walked out the door with her. The company he had founded had barely survived. She owed him, she owed him much more than dinner.

"Ah, well, that was a difficult time I'll admit. But, Sarah, the past is the past and there's so much more to life in the future. Your money will be well spent, I have a proposition for you that, well...frankly, I don't think you can afford to turn down. So, dinner tomorrow night, I'll call you with the time and place." He stood and walked to the door, then turned. "And Sarah, I guarantee you don't want to miss this."

Chapter 16

I

The Holiday Inn served a full breakfast. Normally, Eve would have coffee, two pancakes with syrup, and a bowl of fruit. Today her tray was empty save for a cup of coffee. Neither had been willing to spend the night in a tent after Bobbie's assault so they had driven the thirty-five miles to Grayling, a small town straddling Michigan's aorta, otherwise known as I-75. The clerk at the Best Western had called a friend at the Holiday Inn and the miracle of an empty hotel room on a summer's night in northern Michigan was achieved. Now, Eve toyed with her coffee and studied the parking lot as if it held the key to understanding the universe.

Jim took a lazy bite from a bagel then idly folded his paper napkin into a small square. After several minutes of silence he said, "Eve, how long were you two at the site before the guy with the gun showed up?" It sounded like small talk and Eve was about to dismiss the question with a short quip when she realized Jim had leaned forward, arms on his knees. He was serious.

"I don't know, maybe...oh... I'd say four hours, maybe four and a half. I had just told Bobbie that we needed to think about going back for lunch. Why?"

"Did you hear anyone coming? An ATV motor?"

"No, we didn't hear anything. The river isn't even loud there, it just sort of gurgles along. I didn't hear or see him Jim," she caught a small sob, "He just appeared, like a ghost."

Jim thought about that for a moment. Then he said, "Why did he shoot?"

"I'm not sure Jim, it was all so fast. Bobbie turned and started to run. But she was just running over to me. I don't think she had heard him, she just was running to me."

Jim cataloged this, then said, "Eve, what happened just before he jumped out and fired his gun?"

"I was..." She stopped and thought this over, "I had just finished emptying the sieve. I thought I found something so I was rinsing it off in the river. Then Bobbie..." She paused and thought this over, "She yelled something, she was... Ummmm...she found something that got her all excited."

Eve sat back in her chair, frustration creasing her face. "Don't ask, I'm trying to remember, but I can't."

"C'mon hon, there's got to be more, what was it?"

"Jim don't yell at me....I don't think that. Wait a minute. Yelled. She got really excited, she yelled and pointed at something. I remember. She pointed at a...she pointed at the...." Disappointed, Eve looked up at Jim. "Jim, I have no idea what she was pointing at." Eve let her voice trail off.

"It must have been the saddlebag. Do you think what she found had anything to do with this guy coming out of the woods right then?"

"No, it couldn't, how could it? She barely had the thing out of the dirt. She was just holding it up and then the shots."

"Are you sure she didn't yell out something like, "I've found it" or "We're rich," nothing that would make this whole damn thing make sense." Jim found himself getting angry.

"No Jim, nothing obvious like that."

"C'mon Eve, think!"

"I am thinking! Do you think I'm blowing this off?" She glared at him.

He caught himself, "Sorry hon, I'm just a little frustrated." They both went back to playing with their coffee and studying the parking lot.

Jim couldn't shake the feeling that he was on to something. He tried again, "When you first arrived at the site in the morning did it look like it had been disturbed? Did it look the same as you left it the night before?" Jim's eyes locked hers, willing her to remember every detail.

"No, nothing that I could see..." Her voice trailed off. She began to picture the site and the minutes before the crazy jumped out from behind the trees.

"You know, it seems like you were being watched. Why appear right when she found the saddlebag or whatever it was that excited her?"

Eve shrugged, "Maybe he just walked up and saw us?"

"No, I don't think so. From what you've said that doesn't seem possible. You said you didn't hear anything. You didn't even hear walking in the woods."

"Okay, I guess that's true."

"Something happened. He was looking for something. I'm guessing he was watching you, when Bobbie pulled that saddlebag out of the ground he must have figured it held whatever it was that he's after." Jim's gaze returned to the parking lot. Eve stirred her now cold coffee, lost in thought. An overweight woman with a tribal tattoo around her upper arm, carrying a plate of bacon, eggs, sausage gravy and biscuits squeezed past. "I'm sorry, excuse me....excuse me," she said as she pushed behind Eve's chair.

"He must have been there waiting for her to find something," Jim whispered.

"Jim she didn't...she had just. Wait...I remember. Jim! She got all jazzed up, said something like "can it really be?" That's when the shots went off." Eve was becoming excited now. "I was trying to see what it was, but her back was to me. I couldn't see around her."

"I'm betting it was that bag. Bobbie found it and her killer saw that. That's why she's been killed. Then, the bag must not have had whatever he was looking for, otherwise why all the digging afterward?"

Eve pulled her cell phone from her jeans pocket. "Who

ya calling?" Jim asked, surprised.

"Cheryl, we need to tell her what really happened." A moment later Eve angrily punched her phone. "No power"

"Alright, then let's go back to the camp and get our gear packed up. We'll call her from the car and explain it to her. Then we'll take a look at the dig site. Who knows, maybe we'll find something there."

II

An hour later Jim and Eve's red Jeep Cherokee ghosted down the familiar logging road to their habitual parking spot. As they crested a small hill they saw they weren't the only ones using the two tracked road this morning. Jim parked the Jeep next to the familiar blue State Police car of Cheryl MacIntire.

"Wonder what she's doing here already?" Eve asked as they began walking in the direction of their abandoned camp site.

"Must have had site protection duty," Jim answered.

"Or maybe she's got something to tell us," Eve sounded excited.

"Let's not get our hopes up. She might just have more questions for us," Jim replied. "Bet she's at the camp."

"We should have told her we weren't coming back here last night." Eve stepped over a large log.

"We couldn't, we didn't decide that until after she left the restaurant. Think she's got a fire and coffee going?" Jim asked.

"Would be nice, don't count on it," Eve grinned, her first grin since running away from the site.

Jim ducked under a jack pine branch, straightened up then let out a loud "Aaahhhhhh....noo! Damn it!"

Their camp had been ransacked. Only one of the three tents stood. Bobbie's pup tent was now a sheet of fabric. It lay flat on the ground, having been sliced open. Eve and Jim's four person tent was collapsed and draped across the sleeping bags which lay on its floor. Only the small pup tent they used as a supply tent stood, fishing gear and cooler laying on the ground in front of the tent.

"What the hell!" Jim groaned.

"Bears?" asked Eve.

"Maybe, let's go take a look."

They walked the remaining ten yards to the camp and started assessing the damage. Gear bags had been emptied on the ground, sleeping bags were laying in the dirt and the tents were ripped. Jim began walking around the perimeter of their campsite. Stopping between the fire pit and the river he pointed. "Look at this." Boot marks were clearly identifiable in the soft earth.

"Not bears," Eve said, her voice hushed. "Why would anyone do this? What the heck is going on Jim?"

"I don't know...," Jim could feel the fear beginning to creep up the back of his neck.

They walked to the fire pit in the center of their former camp and surveyed the damage. "I'm glad we weren't here when whoever did this visited," Eve whispered and glanced at the surrounding woods.

Jim began searching the campsite more thoroughly. He circled the camp once again, half way through the second circuit he stopped at Bobbie's tent. Carefully he began pulling the fabric of Bobbie's tent back, revealing the patched up sleeping bag. Next to the sleeping bag one of Bobbie's gear bags had been emptied. Her toiletries, clothing and a novel were strewn about the shredded tent floor. "Looks to me like the tent was searched, then someone cut it up out of sheer meanness."

Eve went to the supply tent, knelt down and looked inside. The spare sleeping bag that Jim had brought lay in the rear corner. She reached in and pulled it out, revealing

Bobbie's small black backpack. "They didn't search very well, they missed this." Eve held out the backpack.

Jim took it and quickly rifled through the inside. "Nothing here that helps," frustrated Jim turned in a circle examining their former campsite. He extended the backpack's straps and slipped it over his shoulders then he walked to their own tent and began to pull on the fabric. Shifting his grip to the front of the tent he lifted it high and said, "Look inside, see if the poles are there. If they are, see if you can prop up one side so we can see what they took from in here."

Eve moved the door flap to the side, ducked, then squeezed inside. Suddenly she screamed. "Jim! Oh my God! Oh...Oh my God." Eve began to cry.

Jim held the tent in his right hand and reached inside with his left. He grabbed a handful of Eve's sweatshirt and pulled. Eve stumbled out of the tent, turned and gripped Jim as tightly as she'd ever held him before. "Cheryl. It's Cheryl. I think she's dead!"

Jim held Eve for an eternity. She sobbed twice, fought to regain her composure then stepped back. "We'd better call the police," she whispered.

Jim nodded then picked up the edge of the tent, revealing Trooper MacIntier's body. Carefully he studied the corpse. Jim could see a bloody wound centered in the back of her neck, there was no hope of reviving her. He tried to make sense of the horrifying scene. Cheryl's pistol was still in her holster, untouched. Her killer had clearly known how high her bullet proof vest extended. Her left hand held a wadded piece of paper, her right was clenched in a fist. A wave of nausea and profound sadness swept over him.

"She's holding something," Eve said in a hushed voice.

Jim reached forward and removed the paper from Cheryl's fingers. They moved easily, she hadn't been dead long. He turned it over and began smoothing it on his knee. The letters seemed to smudge. Jim studied the paper. "This is thermal paper, she must have a small printer in her car." Eve nodded, "What's it say?"

The paper was a form with blocks filled with names, addresses, dates. The form was entitled "Warrant For Arrest".

"It's an arrest warrant for...Eve, it's an arrest warrant for us!"

Chapter 17

I

"What? Why? Who would want us arrested?" Eve's eyes were wide, her voice bordering on panic.

"The police want us for the shooting and murder of Bobbie Downing," Jim read. Then he glanced at Eve, "Babe, we've got a serious problem."

"But we didn't do anything!" she cried.

"I know, I know...but someone wants us arrested. Here," he handed her the paper. Eve glanced at the smooth sheet and pushed it back at her husband.

"There's a time stamp on the bottom of this. Looks like it was printed about an hour ago."

Eve's voice cracked. "If we tell the police the truth we'll be okay, they'll believe us. We need to call the police and tell them about Cheryl."

A shiver of fear rippled Jim's back. "Right now let's get out of here. Whoever killed Cheryl could still be in the area. She was alive, in her car sixty minutes ago and she walked up here so that took some time. She's not now so that means she was killed just a short time ago. Her killer could be very close." Jim glanced around the campsite, then studied the woods. "I think we'd better get out of here now. C'mon, let's get moving."

"But..."

"No buts, this is the second time someone has been murdered in these woods and there's a good chance that Cheryl's killer is very close. We're in danger. Let's go and let's be quick about it." Jim grabbed Eve's hand and began running. A long five minutes later they were standing next to the two vehicles, breathing heavily.

"Now what?" Eve gasped.

Jim tried the door to Cheryl's police cruiser. It was open. He quickly slipped in and began looking for the ignition key. "Damn, if I'd been smart..." he muttered. Then he glanced at Eve, "I should have checked her for the keys."

"Jim, she's dead, we've got to do something," Eve was still choking back tears.

Jim grimaced then pulled down the sun visors. Nothing. Then he ran his hands between the seats, again no luck. A moment later he lifted the floor mat and held up the vehicle's keys. Neither bothered to smile.

"Eve, let's get away from here then we'll decide what to do about Cheryl. Now, get in the Jeep, follow me to the Ranger's station. I noticed Bobbie's keys clipped to a carabiner inside the back pack. We'll put our Jeep and Cheryl's car at the ranger station and take Bobbie's car. Hopefully no one will figure that out for a while."

"Why? Let's just call the cops!" Eve protested.

Jim turned to face her, "Hon, someone has framed us. There's an arrest warrant out for us. That was before they killed Cheryl. We're a target. Let's get this figured out then we'll call the cops."

She bit her lip, "Jim this isn't good is it?"

"No babe, we're into something scary here." He hugged her, "C'mon babe, we've got to get moving."

A short time later the police car and the Jeep were squeezing past the bright orange cones marking the entrance to the closed Mio Ranger's station. Jim parked in front of the building and motioned to Eve to park next to the police cruiser. They hurried around the corner of the building to Bobbie's yellow Wrangler. Jim quickly rifled through Bobbie's backpack and found the key ring. He tossed the backpack to Eve.

"We should call the police and explain that we didn't do this."

"Normally, I'd agree. But right now, I think we've been set up. And from what I can see it looks like whoever did it did a pretty good job. I'm thinking we need to figure this out before we turn ourselves in."

"I still think we need to tell the cops our side of the story."

"Eve, you know we can't do that."

"No, I mean...we could call them on the phone."

"A cell phone can be traced and located. We'd be in handcuffs an hour later, or some trigger happy rookie trooper would shoot us."

"Well then, we could leave a note," Eve insisted. Eve was in unexplored territory and she knew it. "We don't have the time do we?" Jim shook his head. "Jim, we can't go home can we? That's the first place they'll look." She leaned against him.

Jim put his arms around her. "I know babe, we're in a bit of trouble here, but we're going to figure this out. Don't worry, we'll be okay."

"Where are we going to go? Sherrie's?" Eve asked, referring to Jim's sister's cherry farm outside of Traverse City.

"No, that's the second place they'll look and then they would be in trouble too."

Eve took a step back. "Okay, so what do we do?" Tension turning her voice to a whisper.

"Look babe, we need to get some money, a change of clothes and we'll need a place to sleep." Jim opened the door of the Jeep, put one foot in and stopped. "Our bank has a branch in Grayling doesn't it?"

Eve got in the Jeep and slammed the door. "Yes, I think so, why?"

"Time to use our savings."

"But..." Eve had vacation plans for that money. "Why?"

"Checks, credit cards, debit cards can all be tracked. Cash is the only thing we're using until this is over," Jim explained. "You know, you've watched the same cop shows as I have."

"Damn! Okay, so we take out a bunch of cash, then what?"

"Want to go fishing?" Jim asked with no hint of a smile on his face.

II

Two hours later they had withdrawn several thousand dollars from their bank and were now creeping east on a two track path otherwise known as Glover Road. It took some searching, but eventually Jim found a break in the trees big enough to let the Jeep through and close enough to close in behind them. "Here we go, a life on the lamb," he said with bitter humor as he shifted the Jeep to four wheel drive and turned into the forest.

"Don't even joke like that," Eve whispered as their Jeep was swallowed by the Huron National Forest. Twenty yards off the road Jim stopped the car and they got out. An hour later they sat next to a small fire. Eve opened a package of hot dog buns, opened one and spread mustard and relish on the bread. Then she held the empty bun out to Jim. He picked up a stick which had been propped over their campfire and positioned a hot dog over the bun. Jim used the blade of his pocket knife to push the dog off the stick. After similarly fixing four hot dogs they sat down on the ground, leaning against a large pine tree. Birds chirped along the river to their right, otherwise the forest was silent.

Eve's mind searched for a return to normalcy. After several minutes she couldn't bear the silence. "Why do you always insist on Koegels hot dogs?" she asked.

"Just tradition, their plant is in Flint. They've been part of the culture around there since the early 1900s. And, their old advertisement, it always reminded me of home. "They plump when ya cook 'em," he quoted the advertisement and smiled.

The conversation died, they ate in silence for several minutes. Finally Eve picked up her paper plate and tossed it on the fire. "So now what do we do?"

Jim shrugged, "Our first priority is to stay out of jail."

"I'm all for that, but we've got to explain our side of this."

"Hon, here's what I think. I'm betting this is all about Bobbie, it has to be. Somehow this all relates to her and that dig. Whatever she found there, someone is after it."

"Alright, that makes sense. But I can't see what she found that was so important. I only saw a couple of buttons and that pipe thing."

"That's all she found?" Jim asked.

"Actually, I did the finding. She would scoop out the dirt, put it in a bucket and when the bucket was full would dump it in the box. I'd shake the box and anything bigger than a pebble would stay in the sieve. I saw everything and I'm telling ya, we only found a couple of buttons."

"You said the pipe thing, what pipe thing?" Jim asked.

"Remember? Last week when we first met Bobbie she found a pipe tobacco stopper thing. She was standing in that hole and showed it to us and Cheryl and Sergeant Meyer and the other troopers. You remember?"

Jim nodded his head. "Okay, so some buttons and a pipe. Anything else?"

"The possibles bag." Eve said.

"Yeah, okay but....I still don't see anything important about any of this. Nothing worth killing over." Jim idly pushed some small branches onto the fire.

"And why would someone kill Cheryl and frame us for it? What did we do?" Eve's voice was full of frustration.

"I'm not sure what we've done. I just don't get it either," Jim answered. They fell silent for several minutes then Jim said, "Look, I know you liked the kid but really we don't know a lot about her."

Eve looked at him, "What do you mean?"

"Well, was she a druggie? Was she involved with some bad people?"

"She wasn't a druggie and she wasn't some mafia don's daughter. C'mon Jim."

"All I'm saying is that we don't really know her. We need to know more."

She frowned, "This doesn't sound good."

"Eve, you know as well as I do, we don't know anything other than what she told us. Hell, she could be a con woman and her partners shot her for all we know."

"Jim!"

"I'm just saying..."

They fell silent for several minutes, both deep in thought. Finally Eve said, "So Sherlock, what do you suggest?"

"Watson, hand me yonder backpack." Jim pointed at Bobbie's black bag.

Eve couldn't help but grin. "Did you ever actually read Sherlock Holmes or did you just watch the movies? Holmes would have never said 'yonder' and that was an absolutely terrible British accent."

"I do whatever it takes to get you to smile." He put his hand on her arm. "We're going to figure this out and we'll be all right, don't worry."

"Yeah, that's easier said than done."

Jim turned the backpack upside down. A bright red fruit fell to the ground followed by what appeared to be a paper lunch bag, a small hardcover book, a small brightly colored pocket atlas, several energy bars, a toiletries bag, and a rain slicker folded neatly into a clear plastic pouch.

"Hey look, dessert!" He picked up the pomegranate and held it out to Eve.

"Let's stay on task. What else was in there?"

Jim unzipped the bag's pockets. A moment later he had stacked a note pad, a handful of pens and pencils and Bobbie's hair brush next to the other contents of the bag. Jim handed the toiletries bag and the book to Eve. He then opened the plastic pouch and pulled out the slicker. "There's one more," Eve said.

"One more? One more what?"

"One more zipper, there on the back of the backpack." She pointed at what appeared to be a seam running across the back of the bag. Jim unzipped the last pocket and removed a dried leather pouch. "That's the possibles bag we found yesterday," Eve whispered.

Jim could see Eve becoming upset, "Lets search this stuff hon, I know it's hard, but maybe we'll find something that will help us."

Eve nodded. Jim returned to the slicker. A quick once over and he was satisfied the pockets of the slicker were empty. He moved on to the paper bag. He unfolded the top and smiled. "Want a bagel?" he asked, removing one of the bread donuts. Eve declined and Jim moved on to the notepad.

Eve opened the toiletries bag and searched the inside, then she unzipped the outside pocket. Finding nothing but the usual items she picked up the book. "Here's a little lite reading for you," she said and read the title, "American Public Health in the Colonial Era."

Jim whistled, "Sounds like a page turner."

Eve fanned the book pages causing what appeared to be a folded piece of paper to fall to the ground. She examined the folded paper. "Jim, look at this."

Jim studied the document. "It's a copy of a letter...no, it's a photograph of a letter." He turned the paper in his hands. "Looks pretty old." He thought a moment then said, "Eve, this looks familiar! We've seen something like this before. It's the same handwriting as in that little book."

She took the sheet from him and tilted it toward the sun. After a moment she said, "I think you're right!" Then Eve began to study the document, "This is page two, or at least the last page of someone's letter. See, the first sentence starts in the middle and there's a valediction at the end. Wonder where the rest is?"

Jim nodded, "So what's it say?"

Eve had some difficulty with the elaborate penmanship but finally was able to make out the words. "It's just a formal goodbye. It says, '... *have entrusted this letter and the accompanying journal to my close associate, Jeremiah Berstrom. I beg you will treat him with the hospitality you would visit upon myself.*" It's signed by someone named Doctor William Beaumont.

"That's interesting..." Jim didn't finish the sentence.

"Yes it is, I'd like to know what the rest of the letter says, but I think we've got bigger issues. I don't see how it's going to help us."

"No, I'm not talking about that, I'm talking about this," he held out the atlas. "Check this out, Plattsburg is circled. And, so is Mackinac Island...and St. Ignace. Wonder why she circled those three places?"

"Do you think this letter is related to Mackinac Island or St. Ignace? Maybe that's where it was mailed," Eve said.

"Kinda makes you wonder what this girl was up to doesn't it?" Jim asked.

"So how do we find out?"

"I don't have a clue. I'll tell you what though. I think these towns are important. Otherwise why would she circle them? And, I don't think we know enough about Bobbie yet.

So, the only thing I can think to do is start finding out more about her. We might find something that puts two and two together," Jim was now studying Eve for her response.

"And how do you propose we do that?" she asked.

"Let's find where she works and then let's take a look at her house."

"Jim, if we go to where she works they'll report us to the police. We're wanted fugitives remember."

"Might be a risk we have to take. Maybe we could use a disguise or somehow talk to her boss without him knowing who we are?" Jim was guessing and he knew it.

"A disguise? Are you out of your mind?"

"Okay, not my best idea. But the point is we've got to get some information. I'll bet no one has even figured out where she worked yet anyway. So, let's just go talk to the guy, maybe we won't have a problem."

She studied him, "Suppose we do get away with that, what do we hope to find?"

He thought for a moment then said, "Well if I knew what we were going to find we wouldn't need to go talk to them would we?"

She put her fingers to her forehead and messaged her temples. "Oh, this is a terrible plan! And, what about her house. Are you really suggesting we break into her house?"

"Won't be breaking, I've got the key," Jim held up Bobbie's key ring. "It'll just be entering."

"Jim, this is one of your all time worst ideas. We're getting in way over our heads."

Jim shrugged, "What else can we do? We're looking at a murder charge or a murder charge with a dose of breaking and entering. Not much difference if you ask me."

Eve thought a moment then shook her head, "Ohhh...I hate this." She paused then said, "But, like you say, it's a plan, I don't know if it's a good one, but it's a plan."

Chapter 18

Just after 3 A.M. Jim slowly drove Bobbie's yellow Wrangler out of the forest's gloom. Coming to the edge of the drainage ditch his hand brushed a short black lever to ensure he was in four wheel drive and he gently pressed the accelerator. The Jeep didn't hesitate as it splashed through the three foot deep drainage ditch, climbed the side and eased onto the road surface. Jim glanced sideways at Eve, "Chez McDonald's for breakfast?"

"How long to Grand Rapids?" Eve asked in reply.

"I'm guessing, but I think it's about two and a half hours, maybe three if we stick to the back roads. Sunrise is a little before six. So, we're on schedule to get to her place in the dark."

"But it gets light right about then, who cares if we get there in the dark?"

Jim carefully checked for traffic then said, "My plan is to get there in the dark, get into her apartment and then have the morning sun up so that we don't need to turn any lights on once we're inside."

"That's actually a good idea," Eve said as she checked the map. Then she paused, "You didn't think of that on your own, you saw that in a movie! C'mon, which one?"

Jim grinned, "Actually, it was a spy novel, sounds like a pretty good idea though doesn't it?" Gradually he grew serious then said, "We're going to be alright you know."

"You keep telling me that," she answered.

They concentrated on staying off the main roads, not an easy task in that part of the state. Ninety minutes later they were passing through the small town of Harrison. Just short of the one village stop light they passed an overly large, neon lit sign which proudly identified the "Village Center Mall". The mall itself was nothing but a small, sad strip mall made up of a handful of stores, an insurance agency and a twenty four hour gym. Seeing the sign Jim had an idea and he swung the Jeep into the parking lot.

"What are we doing?" Eve asked.

"They'll be looking for Bobbie's Jeep soon. We need to switch plates."

The parking lot in front of Fitness Universe was full of early morning workout mavens. Jim half circled their lot, found a spot with a large pickup truck between themselves and the building and swung the yellow Jeep in. Then, as Eve stood look out on the passenger running board Jim knelt between the Jeep and a red Ford Focus. He struggled a bit, but soon had the rusted bolts free and the license plate in hand. Opening the Jeep's lightweight door he tossed the plate on the backseat, said "Okay, let's go," and climbed back in.

They found a local church and drove into the rear parking lot. There Jim switched the plate on the Jeep, pushing the old plate under the passenger seat. As Jim walked back around to the driver's side he noticed several stickers on the back of the Jeep. Not being accustomed to being on the run Jim didn't think about the stickers until he had turned the key in the ignition, then he muttered, "Damn!" and shut off the engine.

"What?" Eve asked, a flash of fear crossing her face.

"Forgot about the stickers, be right back." Jim returned to the back of the Jeep, took out his pocket knife and slowly peeled off the various markers. With that task completed Jim headed back to the driver's door. A moment later he slammed the door shut and started the Jeep, "We might succeed in staying away from the cops for a little while."

"Or get us in that much more trouble," Eve replied.

"There is that," Jim replied and pulled onto the main

road.

An hour later they were approaching the outskirts of Grand Rapids. "You find the address yet?" Jim asked.

"Yup, right here." Eve patted the plastic sandwich bag she'd found in the small glovebox. It contained Bobbie's insurance card and registration. "Let's get this over with." She opened a small map and began searching for the best route to Bobbie's apartment. "Wish I could just map this," she muttered after several minutes of searching.

"Keep looking, we can't use cell phones."

"I know, I know." Eve muttered, then she exclaimed, "Here we go, got it. Where are we now?" She began looking for a cross street. "Okay...yup, looks like..." She traced their route with her forefinger, "...four blocks then take a left."

Soon they had Bobbie's apartment building in sight. The structure was a two story, flat roofed building with gray wooden shingles for siding. Each second floor apartment had its own balcony making the building appear as if someone had glued a long row of gray shoe boxes to the side. Using Bobbie's keys they quickly entered the building, climbed the stairs to the second floor and found unit number 228. A glance in both directions and Jim unlocked her door.

"Not too bad for a single girl," Eve whispered as they explored Bobbie's home. A small kitchen looked over the living room and out onto a nice patio which itself overlooked a pool. A bricked wall formed one end of the living room. A short hallway ended at what appeared to be a coat closet. Two doors opened off the hallway. Jim opened the one on the left, peaked inside and found Bobbie's bedroom. A sliding glass door opened on to the patio and was covered with a lace curtain. Eve opened the opposite door and entered a second bedroom which had been converted to a home office. It was here they began their search.

"Jim, look at these diplomas," Eve pointed at four

framed diplomas behind the desk. This girl's got a Bachelors in biology and a Doctorate in molecular biology from U of M, a bachelors in history from State and last but not least graduated from Frankenmuth High School."

Jim was standing in front of the desk. "Would you look at how much paper this girl has on this thing!" Jim picked up a letter from the top of a pile. "Look at this." The letter had green Michigan State University letterhead. "She's scheduled to defend a thesis in archeology this August."

"She told me. Guess she likes..." Eve caught herself, "...liked both fields. She was a smart kid." Eve paused doing her best to put the pain of seeing Bobbie's dead body behind her.

"You okay?" Jim whispered.

"Yeah, I'm fine." She quickly scanned the rest of the office. "But I don't see anything to help us yet."

"Keep looking, there's gotta be something here," Jim answered.

"I'll check out her bedroom," Eve said. Time slowly crept by. Eve was alert to every sound. The neighbor's morning routine included a crying baby. "That baby wants to be picked up," she whispered, more to herself than anyone else. The baby kept crying. Several doors banged shut as the tenants left their apartments and made their way to work.

Fifteen minutes later Eve rejoined Jim in the office. "I found this," she handed Jim a book. "It was under the bed. She must have been reading in bed, put it on the floor and pushed it under."

Jim was looking through a small file cabinet. He stopped and took the book from her hand. It was a hard backed volume with no title on the cover, only on the spine. "Viral Diseases and their Diagnoses." Now, there's another page turner," Jim whispered.

Eve flipped the book open. "She was reading this on an

airplane."

"What?" Jim was still focused on the file cabinet.

"Look," Eve held up a boarding pass. "Looks like she flew to St Louis. And....." she studied the pass for a moment. "It was last week."

"Must have been a quick trip. She was with us on the weekend. Wonder why she went there?"

"Family?"

Jim thought for a moment, "I doubt it, no one goes to visit family for one day then flies home to go camping that weekend. Something else."

"Jim, remember the book she had in her backpack? That one was about diseases too."

Jim opened the book and fanned the pages. Chapter five appeared to be dog-eared. Flipping forward he came to a section entitled "Orthomyxoviridae", several paragraphs dealing with the diagnosis and treatment of disease were highlighted.

"Did you read this? It's about ortho-mox-vir-e-day," Jim struggled through the word. "It's the scientific name for avian flu."

"Jim, are we dealing with a bio terrorist?"

"I don't know babe, but let's see what else we find before we go calling Homeland Security."

Eve returned to the bedroom and Jim continued searching the office. A small bookshelf had been placed in the corner and Jim now turned his attention to this. The books were divided into three groups; biology, archaeology and science fiction. Jim smiled as he pulled the first of a series of outer space based novels from the top shelf. Jim was a fan of Isaac Asimov and it appeared Bobbie was too. Asimov's Foundation trilogy was prominently displayed. Jim quickly paged through each of the books. Nothing. He did the same for each book on the shelf. Again nothing.

Now Jim turned to the desk. One look told him it was too much. He ducked back to the hallway closet and removed a small green sports bag. Then he returned to the office and scooped up the papers on the desk, dumping them into the bag. A large hardcover novel lay underneath the pile and Jim noted the title with approval. "The Andromeda Strain" by Michael Crichton.

Suddenly Eve hurried into the office. Jim held up the bag, "I've got all that paper in...."

"Shhhh....listen!" Eve grabbed Jim's arm. Unconsciously they both tilted their heads in the direction of the front room. A slight thump, then a click. Finally a low voice said, "Got it."

"Someone just opened the front door!" Jim whispered. Eve's eyes opened wide, "We've got to hide!"

"C'mon," Jim pushed Eve into the bedroom and silently closed the door. Then he went to the patio door and slowly slid the heavy glass door open. They both stepped onto the patio. Jim began closing the patio door behind them but stopped. A voice filtered in from the hallway, "...then the bedroom. She must have taken it out of the...." A motorcycle roared in the parking lot below claiming the rest of the man's sentence.

Jim gently pushed the door closed and joined Eve at the near end of the balcony. "Now what?" her voice was tight with fear.

Jim did a quick look around and over the side. Jumping to the ground was impossible. "Next patio, we're going to have to jump for it."

The voice sounded again, this time from inside the bedroom, "You start on the office, I'll look in here. I just can't believe it's here, when did she have the time?"

"Jump? Are you out of your mind? I can't make that," Eve's fear was palpable.

"It's five feet, you can do that babe, now we have to

move."

Jim steadied her as she scrambled to the edge of the patio wall. She took one look down, quickly counted to three and jumped. Her right foot landed on the neighbor's patio wall, her left foot hit the patio's sidewall catapulting her forward. Eve landed with a sharp cry of pain on her outstretched hands and one knee. Jim threw the bag over the side, a muffled "Ouff" came from over the wall. He quickly stood on the patio wall and jumped, landed on the far wall and fell to the patio floor. Eve lay where she landed.

"Quick, slide your back to the wall, fold your feet in and keep your head down," Jim instructed.

"You hit me with that bag!"

"Shhhh....." The sound of Bobbie's apartment being searched kept them huddled behind the patio wall for the next twenty minutes. Twice they heard someone on the patio they had just escaped. After thirty minutes only silence came from Bobbie's apartment.

"Think they're gone?" Jim whispered.

"Let's wait," Eve whispered back.

Five minutes later they still hadn't heard anything from Bobbie's apartment. "Let's go," Jim whispered.

The living room door opening onto this new patio was locked but the bedroom door wasn't. They gently opened the apartment door and peered down the hallway. "Let's get out of here," Jim whispered and they quickly ran out of the building.

Chapter 19

Thomas Langley enjoyed the view from the twenty-seventh floor of the Grand Plaza Hotel. Lake Michigan stretched away to the west and north and maybe those lights to the south were Chicago. The city of Grand Rapids was laid out at his feet as it was supposed to be. His 'date' was late, but then he wasn't surprised. She didn't really want to be here did she?

She had worked for him. They had done wonderful things at Metapalm. He thought she was happy, he'd expected her to stay with him for the rest of her life. But, an affair with some Brit in the Congo had ruined his happy life. Then, suddenly, without warning she resigned, and weeks later it became evident that she'd stolen a fist full of trade secrets. Of course he would even the score, she had to know that. She just didn't know when. Could she really believe that now, after eight years he had forgotten. She would be on her guard, he knew that. "But it's what makes the game fun isn't it," he thought.

Sarah Cox stepped off the elevator wearing a tight fitting, spaghetti strap black dress which extended to just two inches above her knees. Flesh toned silk stockings with flowered garter straps, matching high heels and a push-up bra completed the ensemble. She calmly walked to the maître d's stand and announced she was here to meet Mr. Thomas Langley. The man's eyes quickly swept over her, as did the eyes of several of the men sitting in the dining room behind.

"Your party is already here. Right this way," the man turned on his heel and led the way between tables to a wall of windows. Thomas stood, Sarah could see his eyes expand; watched him fight the urge to look her up and down, lose the battle and then greedily take in the scene. "Good," she thought, "Don't go hunting for bear with a BB gun."

"Thomas, I would thank you for the beautiful view, but since I'm buying I'll withhold that." She smiled.

"Sarah, you look lovely tonight. Thank you so much for agreeing to see me. We have a lot of catching up to do."

"I'm not so sure I'm interested in catching up. I'm here simply for the view, the food and to see what kind of fool you intend to make of yourself."

"Sarah, I'm hurt. I'm cut to the bone. Tell you what. Let's enjoy a civil dinner and I'll not mention business until dessert. Let me catch you up on your friends...your colleagues back in the lab and you tell me what you've been doing. We'll have a nice evening."

She studied him closely. A delaying action, he was planning to delay, then distract and confuse her. Then he would attempt to overwhelm her with charm or cash or a combination of both. Finally, she was sure, if he still hadn't achieved his objective his last attack would be on the legal front.

She smiled, she was ready for all three. She'd spent the day prepping. All morning she had reviewed Metapalm financials with her accounting team and practiced countering potential takeover bids with the help of her attorneys. She had spent the better part of that afternoon preparing for "The Presentation". Then two hours on the hair, makeup and dress. She fully intended to look like a model, to make this man remember her as the sexiest woman he'd ever seen. This was going to be a fun evening and Thomas Langley was going to go back to an empty bed a frustrated man and frustrated business owner. Sarah smiled, "Alright Thomas, you have a deal. Tell me how the ol' gang is faring."

Sarah played the game. Thomas faithfully reported the news, whose families had expanded, which of her former circle had divorced, where so-and-so worked. His conversation was friendly, warm, inviting. Almost too easy. Sarah was starting to wonder what his game really was. He continued to eye her like a hungry wolf, but didn't make any suggestions about after dinner. That seemed odd, not the Thomas of old.

At last their waiter brought two servings of a white chocolate cheesecake drizzled with a dark chocolate brandy sauce. Thomas slowly, thoughtfully cut a bite. He slid his fork into the cheesecake, brought it to his mouth and said, "Sarah, I've lived up to my side of the bargain. But now, we have dessert, time to talk a little business." He slid the cheesecake into his mouth and waited.

She eyed him, "Thomas, I really don't intend to do business with you. I'm perfectly happy. My company is doing well, what more could I ask for?"

He swallowed, then dabbed the corners of his mouth with the cloth napkin. "Well? I would have thought you'd use a different adjective to describe VB. Maybe something like 'struggling'."

"Struggling?" she smiled. "No, Viral BioTech is doing fine, our revenue exceeds expectations and our new product line is strong. I'm perfectly happy." This was what she'd expected. Now he would threaten her with another lawsuit. She was certain he was still angry about the anti-herpes drugs.

"I hear that you're going to lose the Praximtine case. That could be pretty expensive."

"We maintain a healthy legal reserve fund just in case we lose a case like that." She took her own bite of the sweet dessert. A bit too fast, she thought.

"Yes, I'm sure you do. The real question of course is do you have enough?"

"I think we do Thomas, I'm not worried. And, who knows, a year from now the judge may decide differently."

"Good, glad to hear that. But, why a year?" He cut another bite.

Sarah didn't change her expression, "That case won't be decided for at least a year Thomas, you know that." Her fork hovered over her plate.

"Oh. I see...well, I'm sorry Sarah, but my sources tell me it will be decided next month." The cheesecake once again slid into his mouth.

"No Thomas, that's not possible. The second round of briefs were filed just last week," she studied her opponent. "It will take at least three months for the judge to even read that mound of paper."

"Maybe Sarah, maybe." He slowly chewed, his eyes never moving from hers. The hairs on Sarah's neck began to stand, he seemed very sure of himself. She watched his Adam's apple bob up and down as he swallowed. He couldn't suppress a smile, "Except a motion for summary judgment was filed on Friday and my sources tell me it's going to be granted." It came out in a half whisper, quiet enough that only she heard the words, loud enough to penetrate deep into her heart. Sarah's smile faded. He followed up with a sniper shot to her wallet, "And, well, I hate to bring bad tidings, but it seems you haven't heard. The judge is looking at twenty, maybe twenty-five million in damages. Not five."

She struggled to find a snappy reply, found nothing and defaulted to denial, "Your sources are wrong on that Thomas. He couldn't possibly decide this case in less than twelve months. And, while we may lose the case the liability is significantly lower."

"Oh, that's good. Reassuring in fact. It's just not what Judge Rappapore told me last Saturday night," he put on his best "I'm concerned" face and locked Sarah's eyes with his own.

Sarah studied her opponent, cheesecake now forgotten. Her stomach churned, the acid boiling up her esophagus, but she didn't say a word. Seconds ticked by. Finally Thomas' eyes turned to his glass, "Hummm, interesting, I guess we're hearing from different sources."

She couldn't decide. Maybe she had it all wrong, maybe he really was bluffing. "Your sources are wrong and you know it. What's going on here Thomas?" She desperately hoped he was.

"Going on? Nothing, just a conversation," his eyes had returned to hers. "I did want to ask you about Zanatoval and Matatoval. How's that patent case coming? My lawyers tell me a decision is coming soon on that as well."

"You mean you think you've paid the judge enough? How much does a federal district judge cost anyway?"

The shot missed, "I understand you're not able to extend those patents? That's a shame...you know it really is a shame. After all the money you spent on those...oh, wait, sorry. After all the money I spent on those products. But, you did a fine job of bringing them to market."

"It always comes back to that doesn't it Thomas?" she was playing defense now and not well. "What are you doing Thomas? Where is this going?"

"You've got a cash flow problem coming Sarah. Once those drugs turn into generics your cash flow drops by, what...?" He took a sip of his wine. "I'm guessing somewhere in the neighborhood of...fifty percent?" Sarah's heart skipped a beat. He knew too much, had information her team had developed only recently. She was now staring intensely at the western horizon. She concentrated on a picture of the Lake Michigan shoreline and the gentle waves rolling up the fine yellow sand beaches. "Picture harmony, peace, calm yourself," her voice was smooth in her mind, doing her best to slow her heart rate.

After a moment he leaned forward, "Sarah, what new drugs to you have ready for market?"

She studied him for a moment, "Thomas, you know I

won't discuss that."

"I'm sure you won't. There's good reason not to. You can't, you don't have anything ready for market Sarah. You have nothing in the pipeline," his voice had turned from soothing, syrupy to mocking and hard. "One more thing. Don't count on your antivirals. As I hear it, the T2 and T3 tests on the anti-flu drugs have all failed."

At the mention of the failed T2 and T3 tests Sarah's stomach clenched. She could feel the color drain from her face. "Face it Sarah, you're a couple of years, if ever, from bringing anything in that line to market." Her heart began to accelerate. How did he know the tests had failed? How did he know the tests even existed?

"With any new drug there's going to be some test failures. You know that." She was firing blindly, just spraying, hoping to hit something, knowing her shots were missing badly.

"Yes, true. It's the nature of the business isn't it? But when you have a toxicity issue," he took a sip of his coffee. "Wow, to be this far in the process and still dealing with toxicity on that scale. That's a problem."

He knew about toxicity issues? How did he know that? That was a closely guarded company secret. How did he know all this? And, he'd known about it before she did. He must have. He had invited her to dinner before the tests were complete. What was going on here?

Thomas leaned forward. He could sense victory. Now was the time to be aggressive, his opponent was stunned. This was when he could deliver the maximum amount of pain. "There are seven members on your board. There are ten million, two hundred fifty thousand shares of stock outstanding. Your board and more importantly your shareholders authorized another five million shares be sold only when your stock price exceeds thirty dollars a share."

"Yes, that's all public knowledge. The thing is Thomas, I own the controlling vote."

"Well...that's not the end of the story is it? You own three million shares. That's oh...about sixty million dollars...if you could sell them. But you can't, not for another year. Your underwriters didn't want you leaving the company did they? Odd that you structured your IPO that way, but some people can get greedy and I'm sure they didn't want to see that happen. But, I digress," his smirk had returned. "I'll grant you that no one else owns anything near three million shares. You clearly have the controlling vote, but not the majority of shares."

"Get to it Thomas," she demanded.

"Once news of your company's failures is made public your share price will collapse. It will sink to somewhere near book value. Which I calculate at somewhere under two dollars a share. That's a long drop from the twenties isn't it? I'll buy every share I can get. And, I can buy them on the open market." He studied her, "You can't do that. You'll have to deal with SEC filings, insider trading rules and regulations...it gets messy. More importantly, it's a slow process. I'll buy shares faster than you will. It won't take long, I'll own three million then all of a sudden it will be five million, one hundred twenty-five thousand and one share. I'll own the company." Her glare was as hard and cold as she could make it. It didn't stop him. "And when I own the controlling interest, well, you will be out. Publicly, loudly, and all over the cover of every business journal, newspaper and television show I can think of. Then I'll ask the board to file civil charges against you. I'll claim that I offered you a substantially higher share price at this dinner and you turned me down. Shareholders will sue you for failure to protect their financial interests. A ton of your money will go to the lawyers, the rest will go to the victims of your mismanagement. You'll be lucky to keep your car let alone your house."

Even in the dimed light he could see her face flushing red, her eyes beginning to glaze. Tears were too much to hope for but maybe...

"Go to hell Thomas," she stood, knocking over her chair in the process. Several heads turned in their direction.

Langley smiled, "Sarah, if you lose the company either by me buying it or the board throwing you out, I don't care."

Sarah's face burned. She could feel her throat tighten. She pivoted on her heel and stormed out of the room.

Chapter 20

They left Bobbie's apartment building and drove a short way east. Jim was accelerating slightly as they rounded a bend in the road when Eve gave a surprised cry. A police cruiser lay hidden under a large oak tree, its occupant pointing a pistol like device at the traffic. The officer had one eye on the traffic and the other on the speed readout of the laser detector. Jim concentrated on maintaining a steady speed, then as he came abreast of the cruiser he gently switched lanes, putting a large family van between himself and the officer. A quick glance in the rear view mirrors assured them they hadn't been noticed. "Who would have ever guessed driving past a cop would make me so nervous?" Jim whispered.

"You're doing fine," Eve said. Jim was about to say thanks when she added, "...just don't screw up." A mile later Jim turned into the drive of a small one story motel near the airport.

A young woman with dirty blonde hair, a tongue ring and several other piercings sat behind a large counter separating her from the nonexistent lobby. She handed Jim a key hung from a large slab of plastic and he passed two twenty dollar bills under the bullet proof glass which had been bolted to the face of the counter and an imposing iron bracket at the ceiling. Jim didn't care, the motel's rear parking lot backed up to a strip mall dotted with four businesses which were open twenty-four hours. He could hide the Jeep among the other cars in that lot. Eve took the room key and set off for their room while Jim moved the Jeep to the middle of a grocery store parking lot.

Their room seemed to spring from a 1970's TV detective show. Linoleum floors, bed with a hole in the middle and large T.V. on a cheap dresser. Eve checked the bed, pronounced it bedbug free then washed the room's coffee pot and cups using the small jar of shampoo on the counter. In a minute a small two cup coffee maker had done its job. She handed Jim a cup and asked, "Now what? We didn't learn anything by searching Bobbie's house and we nearly got killed. All in all, one of our more successful adventures."

"Did I ever tell you that you clinch your teeth when you're being sarcastic?" Jim grinned.

She tried to glare, failed, then said, "JIM, what's the plan? We've got to come up with something."

"We're not done, we've got these papers to go through. Let's get that done, see what we come up with and that should help us figure out our next step." She glanced at the green bag Jim had set on the bed and nodded. Jim moved the bag to the table. Then reaching in with both hands he scooped out a large armful of papers. "This will get us started," he dropped a stack of papers in front of Eve then emptied the bag opposite himself.

"What are we looking for?" Eve asked.

Jim looked up, he wasn't ready for that question, "I'm not really sure, something that doesn't fit, or maybe something that does fit with what we already know. Like I said, I'm not really sure."

They began sorting through Bobbie's life. For ten minutes the only sound in the room was papers being shuffled. A small pile began to build on the floor between them. Finally, Jim said, "She's late on the cable bill."

Eve didn't reply, didn't even look up. Several minutes later she stretched out a long three inch wide piece of paper and sighed, "Why do people keep grocery store receipts?"

"Ummm-kno," Jim grunted without looking up.

Another twenty minutes and Eve stood, stretched her arms out in front of her and flexed her stiff back. "She doesn't buy Tide with bleach. She buys the regular Tide. That means she has to add bleach later." Eve tossed the receipt onto the floor. "Who does that?"

Jim sat a bit straighter, "Hey, here we go, look at this." He smoothed a sheet of stiff photo paper on his knee. "Look at this. It's a picture. It's not a...this looks familiar, I've seen this before." Jim held the photo paper out to Eve.

"You're right, we have seen this...look at the handwriting. It's the first part of the letter we found in Bobbie's backpack!"

Eve hurried to the other side of the room, picked up Bobbie's backpack and began rifling through the contents. A moment later she found what she was looking for and held up the small book Bobbie had removed from the possibles bag. She quickly fanned the pages, stopping when she came to a sheet of paper which had been folded in half and placed inside. "Yup, here it is." Eve pulled a letter sized sheet from between the pages of the volume. The paper was stuck to the binding of the book. Its removal loosened the ancient glue and the pages of the book poured to the floor like water from a pitcher.

"Damn! Oh, look at this." Eve turned to Jim but he had already begun picking up the scattered pages.

"Aside from destroying a priceless early American diary, what exactly were you doing?" Jim asked.

Eve dropped to one knee and began gathering the remaining pages. "No one likes a critic," she shot back through an embarrassed grin. A moment later Eve stopped, lifted the document she had originally removed from the book and handed it to Jim. "See, check this out. Same handwriting. So, what's the story with this letter?"

They both studied the now complete document. After the third time through Eve placed her finger on the letter pointing to a specific sentence and said, "Seems like he cured some disease."

"Must have been a pretty bad disease too. Here, look

here," Jim pointed at the description of dying natives.

"He cured the disease though," Eve said.

"No, can't be. They didn't have antibiotics then. Whatever it was just ran its course, this guy's timing was good though."

Eve suddenly grasped Jim's arm. "Look at the handwriting on the letter." She held up the ancient book, "It's the same handwriting as in this little book. I'll bet this little book is the journal the letter is talking about!"

"But I don't remember..." Jim pointed at the letter. "Look right here, the writer says he provided, 'drawings fashioned by a skilled artist located here in the fort of each of the plants and herbs used.' And, that's in the journal the letter describes."

"They're there, in the back. The cookbook part, remember? What else could this be? This has got to be the journal the doctor was talking about," Eve protested.

She began stacking the pages they had picked up from the floor in their proper sequence. "Look at this page," she handed Jim a surprisingly detailed water color painting of a mushroom. Jim studied the picture for a moment. Then a car door slammed in the parking lot and caught his attention.

"Think the police have found us?" Eve whispered. Jim went to the window and studied the outdoor staircase. "No, but I'm starting to worry about more than just the police," he whispered as he closed the right side of the curtain and went to the left.

While Jim studied the exterior of the hotel Eve returned to her page sorting. Finished she said, "Jim, remember the paperback book she was reading? The one about viruses?"

"Not what I'd picture as a light read."

"Exactly. Why was she reading two books about viruses? She had one in her bedroom and one in her backpack."

Jim turned from the curtain, "Yeah, you're right. She was. She was reading one of them on an airplane. Remember the boarding pass?" Jim said.

"I do. And both were about viruses. Chapter five, on the flu, was highlighted. And this letter was stuck in the old book. That letter talks about a cure to some disease." She pointed at the photocopies.

"So?" Jim asked.

"So? So, she was working on a cure for the flu." Eve said.

"A cure to the flu? No, that's already been done," Jim dismissed the idea.

"No it hasn't."

"What? Of course it has, we get a flu shot every year."

"Flu isn't cured," Eve's voice had a slight insistence to it, "...we get a vaccine, but some people get the flu anyway and there's no cure once they get it. Every year we see stories of some kid in high school or a baby or someone who we wouldn't think would get that sick from a simple case of the flu that dies from it. It's not curable once you get it. That's it, you've got it. They can only treat the symptoms and hope."

"Really? So you think soup made out of forest plants really worked to cure some disease not just prevent it?" Jim asked.

"Well, I don't know. But, if it does then a lot of people would want that recipe wouldn't they? I would think it had to be worth a bunch of money."

"I wonder if that's what this whole thing is about?" Jim studied the little book.

"Well, something is going on. We were just camping by the river, we didn't do anything."

"So if it wasn't our fault it was her fault..." Jim's voice trailed off as he thought about what Eve was saying.

Eve grimaced, "I don't know if I'd use the word fault,

but yeah, if we didn't do something then Bobbie did. Why she was shot we don't know, but she did something that started this whether she knew it or not. It looks like a good chance that this letter was fairly important to her."

"If that's true then we've got a big problem." Jim was pacing now. "We must know something we're not supposed to know, otherwise why set us up by killing Cheryl?"

"We've told the police everything we know."

Jim paced in silence while Eve studied the letter. Finally he said, "We're looking at this wrong. We must be."

Eve put the letter down. "Do we go to the police?" she asked hopefully.

"Eve, no, we can't go to the police, they'll lock us up for months before this gets straightened out. We're suspected of murder and not just one!" They were silent for a long minute, each trying to assemble a puzzle they couldn't see. Finally Jim stopped his pacing and said, "I think we need to find out if this is at all possible. I say we go visit where Bobbie works."

"Ohhhh...that isn't a good idea," Eve shook her head.

"Got a better plan?" Jim insisted.

"No, but I don't have to have a better plan to not like the one we've got!" she said and put her head in her hands.

Chapter 21

I

"Our meeting is at one, you'd better hurry." Eve hated to be late, even when being on time seemed like a shortcut to prison. Jim didn't reply. "So how are we going to get anyone to talk to us?" she asked. The address on the Jeep's parking sticker continued to slide closer as she studied her gas station map.

Jim shrugged, "Bluff, that's our only choice. It's possible no one has contacted Bobbie's boss yet. She was shot on a weekend, today is Monday. Maybe the cops didn't get here yet. We'll be the first here so we'll act like we're coming to tell them, then we'll ask our questions."

"That's never going to work," she paused. "What happens if the cops are there when we get there?"

"Got any better ideas?"

"No."

They rode in silence for several blocks. "What happens if the police have been there? Or, if someone called her boss? Or, worse if they show up while we're there?" Eve asked.

Her questions struck home, the thought of her in jail terrified him. Jim glanced across the Jeep at his wife. "It won't be good." He took a deep breath, "Look, hon, I'm going to drop you off at the library. You go in, grab the phone book and find us a good criminal lawyer. I'll talk to these folks."

Eve turned in her seat, "And what good does that do? I'll tell you what good it does. Nothing. I'm staying right here. We're in this together, we'll figure it out together."

"Eve, now c'mon."

"No, forget it, I'm staying."

Jim studied her for a moment. "Pay attention to your

driving," Eve said and crossed her arms.

Moments later they arrived at a long, low, two story building with dark windows. Five separate company logos were scattered along the roof line facing a large, grass island dotted parking lot. A red and blue glowing sign, significantly larger than the remaining signs was affixed to the second floor roof line and clearly proclaimed Viral BioTech as the major tenant. Each company had their own entrance doors. They found the one marked with a VB logo and parked as close to the entrance as possible.

"We may have to make a run for it if someone recognizes us," Jim said as they walked to the building.

"Good plan," Eve shot back and rolled her eyes.

Ten yards farther they approached the large glass front doors of the company. Jim reached out and held Eve's arm, "Let's not put all of our cards on the table."

"What's that mean?" Eve asked.

"You know, let's not tell them everything."

"Like what? What do you not want to tell them?"

"Well, seems like we shouldn't let on that we have a copy of that old letter and the journal," Jim answered.

"Jim, she worked here. Who cares if they know we know about those? It doesn't make any difference. Let's just ask them about the cure and get outta here," Eve countered.

"Okay, we'll do it your way." He put his hand on the door handle but didn't open the door. What are you mad about?" Jim asked.

"I'm not mad."

"You sound mad."

"I'm a little nervous okay, so let's just get this over with and see where we are in an hour."

"Okay...long as you're not mad." Jim said as they entered the building. A short distance inside the building they were greeted by an imposing granite receptionist desk with a young woman in her early twenties hidden behind. Jim leaned over the counter and asked to speak to the company president. The receptionist had begun a well practiced deflection of this stranger when Eve leaned over the counter and began telling the young woman that a dear friend of theirs and a company employee had been injured. Minutes later they were being escorted into a small conference room. They took their seats and, before they could finish glassing the room, a well dressed woman followed by a balding man and a middle aged woman marched in.

"Good morning, I'm Sarah Cox, president of Viral BioTech and this is our leadership team," she waved her arm to indicate her two partners.

"Good morning, I'm Alex Tolovek," the man said extending his hand.

"And I'm Paula Pelitier," the older woman said.

Jim and Eve introduced themselves while Sarah directed them to seats. A secretary placed a tray with water and glasses in the center of the table and quickly retreated. An awkward silence followed. After a moment Jim decided everyone was waiting for him. He sat forward in his chair and began to explain their relationship with Bobbie Downing, ending with a brief description of the events surrounding her murder. Sarah paled and gripped the table edge with both hands.

"Are there any suspects?" she asked, her voice tight and coming from a long way off.

"Not that we've heard so far," Jim answered.

Eve waited several seconds while Sarah and the others digested the news. Then she asked, "Have the police been here?"

"No, we've not been contacted," Sarah replied, still struggling to maintain control of her emotions. "Thank you for bringing us the news." Eve casually leaned back in her chair and did her best to hide a wave of relief.

"Why would anyone do this?" Tolovek asked.

"We really have no idea, we were just her friends on a camping trip," Jim answered. "We just wanted to ensure you folks knew what was going on. I understand she doesn't have any family in the state and figured someone ought to tell her employer."

"Thank you, we appreciate that," Sarah answered, obviously still shaken.

Jim glanced at Eve then decided to push ahead with their plan. "Bobbie was an interesting camping companion." Eve watched Sarah nod. "We spent several hours just watching the campfire and talking. She knew an awful lot about medical history, there's some pretty interesting stories there."

Jim glanced around the room to see how his narrative was playing. Sarah seemed to be paying attention but looked melancholy. Paula Pelitier was studying the window and occasionally glancing at the accountant. Jim couldn't remember his name, but he was oddly focused on Jim's every word.

Jim took a sip of water and continued, "She mentioned that what she was working on might help her at work. She had a document that you folks may be interested in." Jim pulled a copy of both pages of the letter from his pocket and slid it across the table to Sarah. "It's very old, apparently some doctor cured a terrible disease in an Indian village."

Sarah picked up the letter and began reading, her face impassive. Eve filled in the silence, "I know this is a bit off topic, but Bobbie was reading a book about viruses and the flu."

"We do research on the flu here," Paula Pelitier spoke for the first time since Jim had begun the meeting. "It's an important and expanding threat. Bobbie was a big part of our efforts."

"Expanding? What does that mean?" Eve asked.

"New viruses are being discovered every year. We're seeing viruses now that were not known fifty years ago. Even familiar viruses are dangerous. Last year over three hundred fifty people died from influenza in California alone."

"From the flu?" Jim asked, slightly surprised.

"It's a deadly virus," Sarah whispered as she read.

"Can it be cured?" Eve asked hoping to learn something they didn't already know.

"It can be prevented, but technically there is no cure for the virus. At least not yet," Paula answered with a slight smile.

"Bobbie mentioned that letter and a journal that may hold a key to finding a cure," Jim said. "She said that a mixture of herbs and other items might be the key. Is that possible?"

Tolovek leaned forward, about to say something. His timing was off, Sarah finished with the letter, laid it on the table and said, "Well, certainly it's possible. Many, many medicines are derived from plants. But for a disease to be cured by a mixture...a hot herbal tea, no matter what the herbs are...well, that's a bit of a stretch."

"A journal?" Alex asked, "Did she have the journal?"

Jim turned to Alex, was about to answer then caught himself. Eve filled in the sudden silence, "She didn't. She said she was looking for it while we were camping."

"Did she find it?" Alex asked, his question a bit rushed.

Eve ignored Alex and asked a question of her own, "I imagine that journal and its magical herbal broth would be important?"

"Absolutely," Sarah answered. "I've heard of this," she pointed at the sheets of paper laying in front of her. "I've always thought it was a legend. From the text it would seem this journal could hold a valuable bit of information."

Alex Tolovek could feel the excitement building in the pit of his stomach, this was the journal he needed. He shot a quick glance at Paula. She ignored him.

"You think this could really work?" Jim asked still watching Alex.

"We've been working on finding a method of attacking the flu virus for a long time. If we can treat that virus on a generic, non-specific level...well, that opens up an entire new field of drugs." Paula seemed relieved to have added to the conversation.

"You've actually touched on one of the big debates in virology. It's a complex discussion, but there's evidence to suggest herbs have a role in the battle against these diseases," Sarah interjected. "So, if you happen to find that journal please bring it to us. I'd like to take a look and see what that magic tea is made of."

"After we leave here we're heading home. I wouldn't have a clue where that journal is," Jim replied.

"So, you don't have the journal?" Alex asked again. "Do you know where it is?"

"No, we have no idea," Jim answered. "She didn't find it as far as we know."

Alex studied Jim. "Yes, hummm, that's a shame." Jim met his gaze. No one said anything and Eve quickly moved to fill the unnatural pause in the conversation. "Thank you for meeting with us. We just wanted to make sure you folks knew about Bobbie. And, we're sorry for the loss of your friend." She stood to leave.

"Thank you for bringing us the news," Sarah replied as everyone stood. They walked to the conference room door. Jim stepped aside to let Paula pass, causing Eve to stop for the small traffic jam.

Eve took advantage of the pause, turned to Sarah and asked, "How much would that magic tea be worth?"

"Oh, millions I'm sure," Sarah answered, "A broad spectrum antiviral drug is the holy grail of drug research."

"Really? That's amazing." It was Eve's turn to exit the room, she extended her hand to Sarah and smiled, "Good luck with what you're doing here. Hopefully we'll never need your products!"

II

Alex Tolovek watched Jim and Eve leave the conference room. There was a journal, he was now certain. Instinct told him these two had it. There had been something odd about the meeting with the Crenshaws. He couldn't put his finger on it but there was no such thing as coincidence. They had appeared now? It was...impossible? Odd? Whatever it was, it wasn't natural. Plus, there had been a strain in their faces, he fancied himself a poker player and he could tell those things. Alex spoke a few pleasantries to the secretaries in the outer office then walked down the hall to his own office and closed the door. He sat down behind his computer screens, his thoughts focused on that damned journal. This was important, that couple was involved. Things were moving, events were spinning. Not out of control yet, but spinning. He picked up the phone and began to dial Thomas Langley's cell phone, then stopped. He needed Paula firmly on board first. It was now or never.

Paula Pelitier's office door was closed. He didn't knock. Paula was concentrating on her computer screen. "Don't you knock, you little worm?" She glared at Tolovek. Her response was unexpected, what was she so high and mighty about?

"Paula, we need to talk."

"About what?" she didn't really like him, he knew that.

"Paula, I've been presented with a deal, a special deal."

Paula didn't say anything. Alex continued, "This company is headed for the door. We're a takeover target if we're lucky, bankruptcy if we're not. That means all those stock options Sarah has been handing out; all the bonus shares that we can't sell for another year, all that collapses." He studied Paula, her eyes, her hands. She was good, no tells except one. Her fingers, just her fingers began to shake. "The stock price is going to take a nose dive. We can't sell before that happens, we're barred from selling by the original underwriters and that's enforced by the SEC. In another year we'll be lucky if there's a building with a sign on it."

Her forehead seemed to have a bit of a glow to it, not exactly sweat rolling into her eyes but just a glow. "But, we can come out of this..." he paused, searching for the right words. "We can come out of this just fine."

Paula studied him, she did know, she didn't understand all the numbers, but she could read the tea leaves as much as anyone. He took her silence as permission to continue, "I just need to deliver that journal to a friend." Tolovek crossed the room and stood looking down on the parking lot. "Those two have it."

Paula watched Tolovek walk around her desk. He was aggressive, almost angry. She knew the finances, but what was he talking about? She didn't understand what was going on here and decided to stall. "What makes you think that?"

"There's something about those two. They know about the journal and they were with Bobbie." Paula still didn't respond. Alex turned and asked, "Did you hear her ask Sarah how much the journal would be worth. It's always about money."

It was those two, he was focused on them. Paula began to relax, "Think they're gold diggers? Bobbie was a smart girl. Maybe she found it and they took it from her. Do you think....maybe they killed her?"

He toyed with his tie for a moment. "Maybe they did. I don't know. Why come here in the first place? And, why give Sarah a copy of the letter if they were trying to keep everything for themselves? But, they've got the journal, I'm sure of that. Paula, I need you to commit to getting me that journal. Once we have it we're out of VB, with a bonus that makes up everything we're losing and a salary that doubles what we're making now."

Paula's eyes widened. Maybe she could get out of this. Still not committing she stood and followed his gaze out the window. "Everybody has a game, what's theirs?" He glanced sideways at her. "Paula, we need to get it. If we have to go through them then fine, but we need to get that journal."

She had been with Sarah too long, she couldn't just stab her in the back. The journal would save VB, keep them working, keep her in the lab. She made up her mind, "Let's let it go Alex. It's not that big a deal."

Alex Tolovek, the mild mannered, bookish little man suddenly squared on Paula. He reached out and grabbed her upper arm. His face hardened, his eyes narrowed and somehow he transformed into what she could only describe as a thug, "Shut up Paula," he hissed. "It is a big deal. I've got more invested in this than you'll ever know. I sold my business, mortgaged my house, cashed out my 401s. I lose everything. Don't think I'm not in this up to my aching ass!"

"Alex, you're hurting me, let go," she whispered.

"You listen to me, you little worthless…" His face contorted, Paula's arm now screamed, he seemed to take a breath. "When this company goes under you lose a few bucks, you'll live on Social Security and alimony for the rest of your life. But I'm screwed, I've got nothing. So don't ever tell me to let it go. His fingers cut deeply into her arm. "Don't ever tell me that it isn't a big deal."

She couldn't scream, she tried but the sound, the air, her vocal cords, nothing worked. Finally she squeaked out, "Okay Alex, I get it."

His grip lessened a fraction. It was only for a moment,

"Don't ever go back on me, do we understand each other?" his grip returned, even harder this time, hot pokers sliced through her arm. The feeling in her hand and fingers was slipping away.

"I'm sorry Alex, I know you're trying your best," her eyes watered, a bit of desperation creeping into her voice.

He relaxed his grip. "We're partners now Paula, partners. Do you understand that?" She nodded. "Good. Now, tell me, did you get their phone number, address, anything?"

"Should be on the sign in log." She rubbed her arm, certain that purple bruises would decorate her arm for weeks.

He turned to the office window. He could see Jim and Eve approaching the Jeep and climbing in. Above them, Paula rubbed her arm as the yellow Jeep below came to life then slowly drifted across the parking lot and stopped, waiting for traffic to clear.

"They're driving her Jeep." Paula said.

He didn't reply. Then, "We're both in this up to our necks Paula. We need that journal, we need this to work. It's the only way." He watched the Jeep disappear in the traffic.

Paula wasn't stupid. She knew there was another company out there, lurking in the shadows, just waiting for a sign of weakness from Viral BioTech. Once spotted the phantom would move heaven and earth, or at least Wall Street and Broadway to gobble it up. A career would be gone, she'd be wiped out. But, maybe if she had the journal. "Then we have to get it, don't we?" she didn't take her eyes off the Jeep.

"One way or the other," he whispered.

Paula looked at him and wondered what he was capable of. "I've got a meeting in the lab," she said by way of an excuse to get away from this man.

"Then I guess you'd better go," Alex replied, his attention still focused outside of the picture window. Silently Paula crossed the office and slipped out. Alex turned. He pictured a dog and wondered. Did the dog wag the tail or did the tail wag the dog?

Chapter 22

Jim turned east on the Paul Henry freeway and accelerated. He wasn't certain what they had learned by their visit to BioTech, but he was certain they had hit a nerve. Glancing at Eve he said, "That woman, Sarah, seemed like she was genuinely surprised by the news about Bobbie."

"Yeah, I guess," Eve answered, her thoughts clearly not focused on Sarah Cox. "What did you think of the other two?"

"The woman seemed alright. A bit of a hard hearted old bat, but otherwise all right," Jim grinned.

"Very descriptive, I wouldn't have used those exact words..." Eve laughed, "...and I'm not sure I agree with you. There's something about her, I don't know what, but there's something." She thought a moment, "What about the man?"

"I didn't get a good feeling. Seemed like a geek and a self-centered SOB. Didn't care one way or the other about Bobbie."

Eve thought that over. "I picked up on that too. He cared, I just don't think he cared much about her. He looked at the older woman when we said that Bobbie was murdered. Normally a person would look down or off in the distance, they don't normally look directly at someone else. And, he cared more about the journal than about her. Did you notice how many times he asked about it?" Eve had turned in her seat to face Jim. "I didn't like him."

"You're right, he did seem a bit too interested in that journal. But, really, they all sort of were," Jim answered. They exited the freeway and turned into the grocery store parking lot behind their hotel.

"But he had a more than casual interest," Eve insisted. Jim parked the Jeep, they got out and walked to the store. After several steps Jim said, "Okay, yeah, I guess he did. You know, now that I think about it, he asked us if we knew where the journal was even after we said that Bobbie hadn't found the damn thing."

Just after walking under the building's overhang they turned right and walked to the far corner of the store. Two employees, their butcher aprons spotted with blood were taking a cigarette break. As Jim and Eve approached one waved a cigarette in the direction of the parking lot, "Wonder what the cops are doing?" he asked his friend.

Jim glanced in the direction the man pointed and spotted a Grand Rapids police cruiser slowly rolling to a stop behind the yellow Jeep. The officer got out of his car and carefully circled the Jeep. Then he reached to his shoulder and spoke into a microphone clipped there. All the while he scanned the grocery store front.

Jim instinctively grabbed Eve's arm, stopping her. A shadow of fear crossed her face then she regained her composure. "Hey buddy, got a spare?" Jim asked. He then maneuvered so that both their backs were facing the parking lot. The man gave Jim an odd look. Jim said, "I'm trying to quit but need one right now." The man hesitated.

Sensing trouble Eve said, "I won't let him buy the things. It's a nasty habit." The shorter man shook a blue pack at Jim. He took the cigarette, moistened the filter and leaned over to the lighter now being offered by the man's friend. Jim inhaled, coughed once, glanced at Eve. The two meat shop employees laughed, "Man, I feel ya. I quit maybe six times, never sticks."

"This is my fourth," Jim answered.

The two men finished their last puffs and tossed the butts into a plastic container. "Gotta get back in, the bus from the old folks home will be here any minute. Later dudes." The two store employees slowly ambled back inside.

Jim turned slightly and studied the police officer. The man seemed to be watching the front door, maybe Jim's attempt to blend in with the smokers had worked. The cop seemed to be ignoring them. Sirens wailed in the distance, grew closer and then two police cars turned into the grocery store parking lot. The first officer turned his back to the store and waved at his two partners. Jim saw their chance and quickly grabbed Eve's arm. They ducked around the corner of the building before the man turned around. "Let's go!" Jim hissed and began a quick jog never letting go of Eve's arm.

"Where?" Eve half shouted back.

"Away from here!" Jim now picked up his pace. They rounded the back of the store, then sprinted across an open area and reached the back of their motel. Pausing at the bottom of the outside staircase they caught their breath and studied the back of the grocery store, no one had followed them. Satisfied they hurried up the stairs and to their room. Jim turned the key in the lock and pushed the door open, "Grab the journal and anything else we absolutely need. We've got to get out of here fast."

Eve was in the bathroom stuffing their toothbrushes into a small bag when a loud knock sounded from the front door. Frantically she scanned the room, looking for an escape. A window, a door, a vent, some way to flee. There was none. Slowly she put the bag down and walked into the center of the room. Jim reached out for her. She hugged him tightly, "Guess this is it," she whispered.

"Yeah," was all Jim could say. A new round of pounding erupted.

"You'd better get the door," Eve said.

Jim opened the door to find himself face to face with a big man wearing a full white beard. The man's fist was poised to crash down on the door one more time. Jim's surprise left him speechless. Eve was the first to recover. "Dan?" she cried.

Ranger Dan Hubble walked into the room. "Hello Eve."

"What are you doing here?" Eve's confusion was evident.

Hubble nodded toward Jim. "You two have something I need." Hubble didn't look directly at either of them, instead he quickly studied the room. Then he turned to Jim. "I'm sorry it's got to be like this," he said, then Hubble pulled a pistol from under his jacket and shot Jim in the chest.

Chapter 23

Alex Tolovek's shoes clicked on the tile floor of the main hallway in the laboratory wing of the Viral BioTech building. Paula glanced up from her lab table and watched him through the large glass windows separating the hall from the laboratory area. There was something about him, she wasn't sure what it was, but he was changing. She noticed he walked with a bit of a swagger. That was something new, what happened to the man-in-green-eye-shades? The man with only a bit part in the company? Now that she thought about it, Alex had been acting differently the past several days. The incident in her office had scared Paula, unconsciously she rubbed her arm. The bruises where his fingers had pressed hard into her flesh were bright painful purple. The lab door opened.

"Paula, I've got some good news." Tolovek closed the door then pulled a stool up to the table across from her. "We're not going to be here much longer, we're moving to a different company."

Surprise then a flash of panic swept over Paula. "What? What do you mean? Where...why would we leave?" Paula did her best to sound nonplussed but felt she failed badly.

"Paula, we've been fighting to save this company for months. You know and I know that it's a lost cause. This place is going belly up and there's nothing we can do about it."

She could feel her eyes widen. "Paula, we've got to leave," he didn't leave room for argument.

"Where would I go Alex?" She didn't wait for his answer, "Look, we agreed that we'd get the journal. Once we had that I'd make the drug. We'll take over the company, we'll make a ton of money here. All we have to do is find that journal."

He began to smile. "I've changed the plan Paula. We're not saving this company, we're not taking it over. We're selling it now."

"What? Why? Why would we do that?" Paula now knew how a lab rat felt waiting for its turn on the experiment table.

"Why? Paula, I gave up everything to help her. She treats me like the hired help. She sits in that royal office of hers and acts like I don't matter." His right fist rhythmically pounded his left palm. "I do matter and I'm not going to be the little man anymore. We're going to Metapalm. They'll pay us. Don't worry about our little pile of shit for nothing stock options and our little 401(k) here. In six months they'll be worthless. Metapalm will pay for the journal, for Beaumont's journal."

"I don't want to work for Metapalm." Paula nearly screamed, then thought better of it. "I'm happy here. I'm so close, I've done so much work. With the journal I can...Alex, I'm on the brink of something important here. I can't replicate all the viral work I've done here."

"You'll have more. You'll have more laboratory workers, more research money. You'll have everything at Metapalm. You won't be able to do all that here, even if we do get rid of Sarah. If I deliver the journal they'll make us rich, we won't be saddled with this crappy little company and we'll still be rid of Sarah."

"Alex, it's not that easy. The journal is key, yes, but there's a great deal of work, months, maybe even years of work before we see any new drugs from it." She studied Tolovek, he wasn't listening, he seemed to be looking into the distance while he talked to her. "Alex, do you hear me? Do you understand what I'm saying? We've got to stay here, we can't just pick up and leave."

"Paula, this company isn't going to be around long

enough for you to finish making the drug. Don't you get that? We leave or we're screwed. We lose everything!" Alex gripped her arm.

"I can't...it's just that. I never wanted to leave Alex."

"You've changed your mind haven't you?" It was more an allegation than question, "You've decided to stick with Sarah. After all she's done to you. After every insult you've endured you're staying here?"

"No, no...it's just that it's so hard to start over. You've got to understand how lab work goes."

His face seemed harder, different somehow. "Paula you need to decide. Are you with us or not?"

"Us? Who's 'us' Alex?"

"You don't need to know the details..."

"The hell I don't!" Paula's voice bounced off the laboratory walls. "What's going on here Alex?"

He slumped back on the stool. "Paula, Metapalm will buy us out. Think about it, we can live in California or Florida or someplace in South America. No more winter! We'll spend weekends at the ocean or in the hills. It's beautiful there Paula. I've already made the deal. My brother got us the journal. We can do this."

"I don't want to go to another company, I don't want to move to California. What 'we'? Why would I spend the weekends with you? How did your brother get the journal? Did...? What did you do Alex?"

"Paula, you and me. I've made sacrifices. She had it, Dan has risked everything. He's going to..."

"Dan?" she nearly screamed. "Who's Dan? What risk? Tell me Alex! What did you do?" Paula's confusion was now complete.

"My brother Dan. He's a ranger. He knew all about Beaumont. He does reenactments and knew the story of Beaumont saving the village. He got us the journal. I was there," Alex seemed to think this explained everything.

"What did Dan risk? All he did was tell you about the journal."

"It's more than that Paula. He's...he's been very important."

Paula's throat seemed to be closing, her voice cracked. "You, he...that's how the kid was killed. You...you killed her didn't you!" Paula was now backing away from the lab table.

"No! I didn't Paula. It was Dan, but it was an accident. He didn't mean to shoot her. We were just trying to scare her into running."

"WE? You were there? So you killed her..."

"Paula, are you with us?" Alex stepped around the laboratory table and began walking toward her.

"This is more than I can..." her voice trailed off. "You killed her," she whispered. Fear began edging up her spine.

"It doesn't matter Paula. We needed that journal, she had it." He could see it. She wasn't going to come with him, she was going to back out, abandon him. She was going to betray him like Sarah had betrayed him. Alex's hand slid along the black granite lab table. His fingers bumped into a laboratory support stand. Slowly he wrapped his hand around the steel rod protruding from the iron base.

"She was a sweet kid Alex," Paula whispered.

"Yes she was. But it was an accident Paula. Nothing but an accident."

Paula was backing up now. Tolovek followed her around the table. Paula could see what was about to happen. His fingers were already curled around the lab stand. This man had become a killer. He'd killed before, he was willing to kill again. She thought she knew him, but now he was different. Now he was someone else entirely.

"All right, all right Alex. I'll go with you. I'll go to Metapalm.

He stopped. Maybe she did see. Alex's stare seemed to hurt. She couldn't bear the gaze and finally turned away. "Paula, you have to be sure. It's important Paula. There's no going back on this."

"I won't change my mind. I won't Alex." Paula fought down the temptation to cry. "You're right, Sarah has treated me like a slave."

"Good, I knew you'd eventually get it Paula. I knew you'd come around." Alex's hand slid off of the lab stand and along the table. He approached her, she didn't move. He put his hands on her shoulders. He could feel her shutter. "It's going to be fine, no worries." Slowly his hands moved in, pausing at her neck. Panic swept over her. He moved his hands a bit higher, holding her head. He forced her to look at him. "We're going to leave and never look back. We're going to be rich." Alex turned and walked out of the lab.

Chapter 24

Warily Eve studied Dan Hubble as he methodically searched the hotel room. Her hands and feet were tied to one of the room's two table chairs. The electric cords Hubble had torn from the table lamps cut into her ankles and wrists. She could feel a bit of the sticky, half-dried blood on her ankles. She watched Hubble tearing the mattress apart, stabbing a big hunting knife into the material and ripping from one end to the other. He didn't appear to have any plan, didn't seem to know what he was doing. She knew if he asked her she would tell him where the journal was, especially after seeing the size of that knife. He had, but only once and she'd lied. It seemed only right to at least try to resist a little bit. She told him she didn't know anything about it. He'd ignored her answer, in truth, it seemed as if he'd not even heard it. He had just started tearing the hotel room apart. She almost smiled, Hubble would be a joke if he weren't so dangerous.

Eve glanced at her husband. Jim sat slumped in the other table chair. His hands and feet were tied with a thin green rope she had heard him call para-cord. Jim's head rested on his chest, drool covered his chin, his breathing seemed steady. A tranquilizer dart still hung from the center of his chest. Hubble's state issued animal tranquilizer gun lay on the floor where he'd thrown it. Satisfied Jim was alive she turned her attention to the electric cord around her wrists, she desperately wanted to move her hands, stretch the cord, maybe find some slack and free herself. A glance at the hunting knife quickly convinced her that now was not the time to attempt her escape.

Hubble gave up on the bed mattress and went into the bathroom. It didn't take long. He pulled the neatly folded towels from the rack, bouncing them off the closed toilet and spreading them across the floor. The leather possibles bag flew across the room, hit the wall and slid to the floor. A minute later he emerged from the bathroom. "Were you going somewhere with this?" He held up the journal, seeming to wait for an answer. An angry silence filled the air. She desperately wanted to make something up, some answer that would fool Dan into believing she didn't know what he held. She couldn't, she could feel her lips begin to form a word but had no idea what word to form. Her mind was a blank. Finally, he announced, "Eve, we need this."

"What do you need an old book for?" She studied the man, his mask seemed to crack for a moment. She could see him searching for an answer. He paused, seemly to think the answer to her question over. She didn't wait, Eve fired another arrow, "Dan, do you really know how to turn that into a drug? Someone is using you. You know that and I know that." Eve's eyes were fastened on his. Maybe she could plant enough doubt to convince him that his plan, whatever it was, wouldn't work.

Hubble's head began to swivel, carefully he examined the hotel room and the clutter and mess that he had made. It seemed he was looking at it for the first time. Then, without warning Hubble's fat hand slapped the small desktop. "I know what you're thinking. Believe me, I do. But, what do they say? In for a penny, in for a pound. Well, that's it now isn't it? I'm in too deep."

"It's never too late to do the right thing Dan."

"No, I made my choice. I've got to deliver this book. We'll get our money and then get to someplace that doesn't have an extradition treaty with the United States." He stopped, gazed into the distance a moment then said, "And has beaches and warm weather."

Eve tried to keep her voice calm, "That's what I mean."

"What? What do you mean?" Dan was confused by the statement.

"Do you think your partner is going to let you keep all the money? It never happens. One partner always betrays the other."

Dan seemed to be thinking finally he said, "Not Alex, maybe someone else but not Alex."

"What makes him so special Dan? Ever heard the saying there's no honor among thieves? They don't say that for nothing."

He stared at her. "My brother would never betray me."

Alex was his brother? It hit Eve like a bucket of cold water. She struggled for a retort, wanted to keep the conversation going. She had been doing her best to humanize herself, but this announcement left her without a response. Alex was his brother, Alex was the balding man at the company. No wonder he looked so nervous. She turned this new information over in her mind. It made no sense, what could a ranger and an accountant do with the journal? Eve studied Dan for several seconds but couldn't answer her own question. The silence grew uncomfortable. Finally she said, "Look Dan, we met with the people Bobbie worked for. We were there today. They can do some good with that book. They can use it to stop disease, to help people." He didn't move. "Dan, you just need to turn that book over to the authorities and this will all be forgotten."

"Nothing will be forgotten. C'mon, you know that. They'll put it all together." Hubble walked to the window, stood to one side and studied the parking lot.

"Put what together? How you got the...." Suddenly Eve knew what had happened. "It was you! You killed Bobbie and you killed Cheryl!" Eve's voice was tight. "You did didn't you!" Forgetting the cords binding her to the chair Eve attempted to stand up, nearly causing the chair to fall to the side. "Why

Dan? Why did you kill them?"

He stared hard at her, then his eyes grew tired and old. "I didn't mean to kill the girl. I was just trying to scare her, but she started to run. It just happened. I tried to shoot next to her, I was just trying to...but..." his voice trailed off. "It was an accident."

"You killed Cheryl! Was that an accident too?" Eve demanded.

"She figured it out. I don't know how, she came back to the park. I was out at the camp ground, she just walked up to me and expected I'd go with her. She just told me she'd figured it out and that I should turn around and let her put the handcuffs on me. She didn't even unholster her gun." He seemed to be apologizing, then his voice fell to a near whisper. "We were friends you know. But...well, I couldn't, I'm too old to go to prison."

"Are you going to kill us Dan?" Eve wasn't afraid. She'd lost her fear when she saw her husband collapse on the floor.

"There's been enough killing. I didn't mean to Eve, you have to understand that. I didn't...she just got in the way." Hubble was growing uneasy. "All I need is a little time. Who's going to even look for me? You're the murderer here."

"What? I'm not, we're not murderers! We didn't do anything...we were just..." He held up his hand silencing her. "The truth doesn't matter. I'll have the cops here fifteen minutes after I walk out that door. You'll be arrested for killing a state cop and maybe for killing the girl. I won't have to worry about you for a long time."

"We didn't kill anyone, no one will believe you!" Eve cried.

"They don't have to believe me," his laugh was now tired. "They just have to burn a couple of months on you. By the time they figure out you were just a set up we'll be long gone."

She was mad now, her fear forgotten. Rage and disgust consumed her thoughts. This man had killed two people she knew, whom she liked. "I'll tell them, I'll tell them everything," she spat.

He smiled, "You'll be in jail. Maybe for a few days, maybe a few months. It doesn't matter, I'll be gone. No one will believe you. At least they won't for awhile." He tucked the journal under his arm and walked to the door. He stopped but didn't turn around. "I could kill you. You and Jim. I could. Maybe I should. But there's been enough. I didn't mean for it to go this far Eve. Really, I didn't." Then, he was gone.

Immediately, Eve began pulling against the cord surrounding her wrists. It was slow, painful work. Soon she could feel blood oozing down the back of her hands. Several painful moments later the blood provided the lubricant she needed. Wrists screaming she squeezed her right hand from the looped cord. In an instant the other hand was free. Quickly she untied her feet and ran to Jim. His head lay against one shoulder and slowly lolled from side to side. She pushed two fingers into the side of his neck, searching for a pulse. Finally, she found it, not strong, but not weak either. Satisfied, Eve lifted his chin and pulled his right eyelid up. The motionless black pupil nearly filled Jim's normally blue iris.

"Jim, c'mon back to me baby," she slapped Jim's face and checked his eye again. This time she detected a slight movement. Eve was fighting an overpowering urge to collapse; to just sit and sob. "Jim, listen to me Jim. Do you hear me? Jim! Jim!" she slapped him again. Jim gave a small grunt. "We've got to get out of here." Eve was afraid of being in jail for months trying to explain that Dan Hubble, Michigan State Ranger was framing them for a pair of murders that he had committed. She began to untie Jim's hands and feet. "Jim, c'mon Jim, we don't have much time."

Then, like a bolt of lightning she had an idea. "Oh,

you're not going to like this," she thought. She did a quick scan of the room and spotted what she wanted. A waste basket sat under the small table next to the bed. Eve picked up the basket then ran out of the room to the stairwell. As expected an ice machine stood in the corner. She quickly filled the basket with ice and ran back to the room. She ran past Jim into the bathroom and topped off the bucket with water, then returned to Jim.

"Jim!" his head rolled to the side, he tried to open his eyes. "Jim, we've got to get out of here." He tried to lift his head but only succeeded in a slight nod. "Okay, we'll try this," she said. Eve pulled his shirt collar outward and poured the icy water in.

A loud moan erupted from Jim's throat. His eyes opened and he stared at her. She had her face right in front of his. "We've got to get out of here Jim, now. C'mon, move!" The urgency in her voice cut through the fog filling Jim's brain. Suddenly his right hand grabbed her arm and he tried to stand. "Hold on, hold on," she whispered. Eve lifted his arm over her shoulder and said, "Stand up babe."

Slowly Jim got to his feet, his weight pressed down on Eve's shoulder. "Okay, now we've got to get to the door. C'mon, move." Eve said with a grunt. She began to push and carry Jim in the direction of the door.

"I'mmmm kkkoooooooooolldd," Jim said.

"Yeah, sorry about that. Now let's move a little faster hon," Eve gasped. She was bent under his weight.

Jim's muscle control was gradually returning. Slowly they made it to the door of the motel room, then outside and to the stairs. Carefully Eve maneuvered Jim down the steps. At the bottom she could hear a siren in the distance. Eve fought down another wave of panic. If those police cars arrived before they were gone it meant months of jail, maybe years of prison.

They rounded a corner of the building and now faced a

central stairway, a maid's cart blocked their way. Eve leaned Jim against the wall then quickly grabbed the clipboard on top of the cart, pocketed the master key card clipped on the front and scanned the list of rooms. Room 210 had a red line drawn through it with the words "COMMODE ORDERED" written in a terrible scrawl. Jim's legs were steadier now. The siren grew closer. She quickly scanned the hallway, found the room and maneuvered Jim in that direction.

An eternity later she reached the door. Using the master key she opened the lock, pushed open the door and shoved Jim in the direction of the bed. Then Eve turned and ran back to the maid's cart. She quickly slipped the master key back in its place and returned to their new room to find Jim snoring softly on the floor.

Chapter 25

Thomas Langley swung his Mercedes E550 off Chicago's north Lakeview Drive into the entrance to the underground parking garage of his apartment building. An elevator ride and several minutes later he entered the two story apartment, snapped on the lights and made his way to his home office. There he settled into a large leather desk chair. A touch of a button and two computer monitors blinked, rendered an annoying little sound and the desktop icons appeared. A moment later he had four screens open and overlapping.

On top was the day's market chart for Viral BioTech. The stock was holding its own, hovering between eighteen and nineteen dollars a share, off five dollars from its yearly high. A click of the mouse and he arranged an overlay of the daily volume chart. The volume of stock sales was shown by small vertical bars, spaced to reflect fifteen minute increments throughout the trading day. Increments where the price was higher than the previous increment were colored green, those with a lower price were shown in red. The daily charts were beginning to show a distinct trend, more red than green. The market smelled something. Thomas smiled, he suspected it was the lack of news on new products. They were right, there were no new products. In this case no news was bad news and that alone would succeed in driving the price down another twenty percent. Then again, it could be his little misinformation campaign was working. In any case, things were looking good, but he needed to get on with his own antiviral drug, that would crush Sarah's little company.

He removed a cell phone from the center desk drawer. He studied the face of the phone for a moment, more seeing the man he was about to call than the phone itself. It took a moment, the man irked him, then he was ready, game face on. He keyed in the number from memory.

Alex Tolovek answered on the second ring, "Alex, my man! How's things there?" Alex's reaction was bumbling confusion, the friendly greeting was out of place, Langley was not a lighthearted man. "They're fine, why?" Thomas smiled, the unsettled voice was exactly what he had intended to elicit. "Alex, what's going on with that journal?"

"Downing gave it to her two friends..."

Thomas cut him off, "Alex, that's not what I wanted to hear."

"It's okay, it's okay. I've...," he quickly corrected himself, "We've got it. It took a little time, but I've got it now, no worries. I, we had to..."

"Don't bore me with details Alex. I'm just glad you have it. Now I want you and Paula to...."

"Paula may be a weak link."

Langley sat upright. "Why? She's still coming to Metapalm isn't she?"

"I talked to her about it this morning. She's fine, she's happy coming to work for you." Alex did his best to cover this little lie.

"I need her in this deal Alex." Paula's defection could seriously delay bringing any product to market. Her history with the project, with this method of viral treatments, her past experience with virus treatments and more importantly with the Feds and the protocols already established made her a very valuable and important acquisition. Without her his team would be nine, maybe twelve months behind. He couldn't afford the delay.

"She's a weak link. We need to be careful of her is all," Alex's protest was sounding hollow even to himself.

"I'm not sure I follow, what does that mean? Weak link. You said she would come over to Metapalm. What's going on

Alex?"

Tolovek's frustration was growing. If he could just reach through the phone, shake this fool with his 'holier than thou' attitude, make him see what kind of risks he had been taking for him. "Look, if she decides to bail on me, if she decides she's going to the police...Langley, I'm hanging out here. I can't afford to have her telling everyone about what's been going on."

"That's your issue Alex. But I need her. You need to make sure she comes to Metapalm."

"If she decides to go to the police..."

"She won't."

"I may have to take some steps." That sounded ominous, Thomas was now standing beside his desk. "What does 'take steps' mean Alex?" The line was silent, finally Thomas said, "Look, I don't want to know. I need her, this project needs her. Whatever you do, don't you hurt her Alex. We can't afford anything like that, we can't be involved with that," Langley insisted.

Tolovek listened but didn't say anything. Silently he cursed Langley and wished he'd approached one of the European drug makers, maybe the Chinese. Finally he said, "I may have to."

The phone exploded, "Dammit! Alex, we need her. Don't you understand? She's important. She gets us the antivirals."

Langley's attempt at intimidation didn't work. "Look, I got you the journal, I've told you about the experiments, I got you the formulas. I've done what you told me to do!" Tolovek's anger was growing. This high and mighty social climber didn't see the big picture, didn't know how things were really done. Did this fool think he could just give an order and things would magically happen? "That should be enough! You'll have more data, more money to experiment with than Paula ever did.

Why can't you make whatever it is that everyone keeps talking about? Sarah said all they need is the journal, we got it, what's the damn problem?" Alex was beyond reasoning with now.

Langley picked up a small granite bowl filled with paperclips and hurled it across the room. The bowl smashed into his paneled door with a loud bang, leaving a deep gouge. "All right. You're right, we can do that, no problem. But the thing is we need her expertise to move this along quickly. We don't want to reinvent everything she's done. You get that don't you Alex?" Thomas was doing his best to fight off panic, frustration, the overwhelming urge to rip this little shit's throat out. He needed to be very careful in these next three minutes. Langley was pacing now. "Look, I want you to deliver the journal to me tomorrow, I'll be at Gerald R. Ford airport, the general aviation terminal at one o'clock."

"Alright. We'll be there. But check her attitude, she's a weak link I'm telling ya." Tolovek pulled the phone from his ear and pressed the disconnect button.

Rage, anger, contempt, it all filled Thomas Langley. Alex Tolovek was a self serving idiot. He would have to rid himself of the man as soon as possible. He needed Paula, she could contribute, Tolovek was simply a useful tool. Langley stood to his full height, muttered "damn" then let his body go rigid, disconnecting conscious thought from his surroundings, clearing his head and allowing himself to become rational once again. Finally, Langley sat down at his desk and punched a new number into his phone. The company airplane, his airplane, would be fueled and ready to go in less than an hour. Satisfied, he walked to the kitchen and made two sandwiches. He ate one and wrapped the other in wax paper, a habit he'd picked up from his mother. Thomas then hurried to the bedroom and changed to jeans, hiking boots, pullover and sweatshirt. Ten minutes later the doorman called to inform him a car waited to take him to the airport.

Chapter 26

Early evenings in Sarah Cox's home were the worst. Tonight was especially bad as both her housekeeper, Dotty and the gardener, Mister Wilcox, had gone home early. Sarah curled her legs underneath her and sat on the couch, trying to lose herself in the latest mystery set in Italy and Paris. It wasn't working and she moved to the media room to watch a rerun of her favorite show, "House of Cards". Ten minutes later, at 8:30 P.M. she found herself heading upstairs to put on pajamas and go to bed.

She stopped in front of a large gilded mirror which faced the landing from the building's main staircase. The image in the mirror was of some stranger complete with crow's feet at the corners of her eyes and traces of worry lines on her forehead. She studied the stranger's hair, several strands of gray hid under the darker colors around her temple. The coloring the salon used seemed to fade quicker with each use. "I am forty-three years old and unmarried...," she stopped in mid-sentence, the face in the mirror didn't move, "...hell, not even divorced. And, I live alone." The stranger just gazed back at her. She finished her climb to the top of the stairs. Pausing, she looked over the rail. "Nice house Sarah. Who did you buy this for?" She leaned over the rail and studied the floor. In a voice that echoed off the stone floor she said, "With my luck if I jumped all that would happen is I'd break my leg." She shook her head and went into the bedroom.

Ten minutes later she decided a glass of wine would be appropriate. She kept several bottles of Peninsula Cellar's 2011 Cabernet Franc, a nice dry red wine that she had grown fond of while sponsoring the Michigan wine competition, in the wine cooler build-in to the butler's pantry just off the dining room.

She padded down the stairs and through the dining room to fetch the wine. She was just about to peel the foil from the bottle top when she heard the sound of glass breaking in the kitchen. Thinking quickly Sarah ran to her study and pulled a Smith and Wesson snub-nosed .38 pistol from the desk drawer. It was then that Sarah realized she had left her cell phone in its charging cradle next to her bed. Carefully Sarah slipped out of the study, turned and crossed the dining room. She had nearly reached the staircase when a sudden, surprised scream erupted from the doorway behind her. Sarah whirled and leveled her pistol.

"Wait-Wait-Wait!" a nervous voice shouted and Sarah found herself facing a middle aged man and woman.

"Don't shoot! Don't shoot! We just need some answers," the woman shouted, her hands stretched over her head.

"Ms. Cox, do you recognize us? It's Jim and Eve Crenshaw from the other day in your office," the man said.

Sarah studied the two intruders, "What are you doing in my house?" she asked, not lowering her pistol. At precisely the moment she asked the question the woman introduced as Eve wheeled on the man, "I told you this was a stupid idea! We could have been shot!"

The man dropped his hands and faced the woman, "Well what choice did we have?"

"We need to get to the police Jim!" she shot back.

"We can't, you know that. She'll..."

"Hey! I asked you two a question!" Sarah shouted.

The pair seemed to have forgotten her. "Yes, yes, you did. Look, we need..."

The woman didn't let him finish, "We thought you were a killer..."

"But, of course you're not," the man interjected.

"...but then we were attacked by a mad man we thought

190

we knew and..." Eve took a breath, "We needed to tell you about how Bobbie Downing died."

"We've been framed, the police think we did it and we didn't. We need your help."

Sarah kept her gun focused on Jim's chest, "What do you know about Bobbie?" she asked.

"Like we said, we were friends." Jim's eyes focused on the pistol. "Ummm...This is going to be a bit of a long story, maybe you could point that pistol someplace else?"

"We're really just here to talk, and we'll replace your window," Eve added.

The tension in Sarah's face began to drain away, "Well, it's pretty clear you two aren't professional burglars." She seemed to make up her mind, "Why don't you two take a seat and tell me what's going on." She lowered the gun and pointed to a large, beautifully decorated living room.

Together Jim and Eve detailed what they knew of Bobbie, then they began explaining about the work she had been doing while camping. Eve fought back tears as they told of her death. Finally, they explained about Cheryl McIntire and how they had discovered her body.

"So you believe this Dan-guy set it up so you two would look like the killers and give him time to get out of the country. Okay, I get all that, but I'm not clear what roll I play in all this?" Sarah said.

"We think this all revolves around a small book that Bobbie found," Eve said.

"It appears that she placed that book in her backpack. Her killer didn't find all the pockets on her backpack and missed it, we found it," Jim explained.

"And we think that little book is the journal mentioned in the old letter," Eve added.

Sarah stood, "Let's go into the study." Sarah led the way from the living room into a brightly painted room.

Shelving lined two walls from the floor to the ceiling. Many shelves were decorated solely with flowers or vases, others were heavy with medical texts. Jim noticed several rows of romance novels. The room had a light, homey feel even in the artificial light of the lamps. A fireplace stood centered in a third wall with a bank of cabinets on each side. The fourth wall was a row of four French doors opening to the landscaped backyard.

"I've got something to show you," Sarah lifted a flower vase and removed a small key from beneath. "I collect antique medical books." She opened one of the cabinets and removed a small box. "Antique books are kept laying down, not on shelves standing up. It helps preserve the bindings," she said as she handed the box to Eve. "I believe I've read the letter you're talking about."

Eve glanced at Jim, then said, "So you knew all about this when we were at your office?"

"Absolutely. I didn't know you had found Beaumont's pharmacy book, but I suspected Bobbie had."

"Beaumont. That was the name on the letter, right?" Eve asked.

"Yes it was. Dr. William Beaumont. He was an eighteenth century medical doctor. Now open that box please."

Eve lifted the cover off the box and removed a small eight inch by ten inch leather book. "It's a doctor's pharmacy book," Sarah said in response to the unasked question. "In the early days of medicine pharmacies did not exist. Each doctor made their own medicines following recipes which were published in medical journals or handed down by tradition. Often the doctors consolidated those recipes in a single journal along with instructions of where to find the different ingredients. You're holding one such volume now. They've become collector's items. I have five."

"It looked very much like that," Jim said as Eve gently turned the pages. "Only the beginning was more like a diary."

"But it was full of pictures and recipes. Each picture was of a different plant or mushroom," Eve passed the book to Jim.

Jim examined the book then looked at Sarah, "In the book Bobbie found there were several pages of text. Then several pictures, each picture was annotated with how and where to collect the plant. Those were followed by what we believed to be recipes for different concoctions. I...we, assumed each one was a different medicine."

"I think you better get comfortable, now it's my turn to tell a story." Sarah turned back to her library cabinets. She paused, spotted what she wanted then removed a leather bound book from the drawer. "This is an original copy of his book, 'Experiments and Observations on the Gastric Juice and the Physiology of Digestion'. He published it in 1833."

"Beaumont?" Eve asked.

Sarah nodded.

"I'm guessing that didn't make the New York Times best seller list," Jim quipped.

"Probably not," Sarah deadpanned. "I've been a fan of his since med school. He was the post physician at Fort Mackinac. But he also tended to patients in the village outside the fort and in the surrounding areas. In fact, his famous patient, Alexis St. Martin, wasn't a soldier, he worked for Astor's American Fur Company."

"Wait, John Jacob Astor? The richest man in America?" Jim asked.

"The same," Sarah replied. She opened the book to the title page. "This is a sketch of Dr. Beaumont. Aside from what we know about Beaumont, there are rumors, many admittedly, unsupported like the one I'm about to tell you."

Twenty minutes later Jim and Eve were spellbound. "So

this Indian village was saved because of the plants in the book? Amazing!" Jim shook his head.

"And you really can make a cure for the flu from this?" Eve asked.

"We really don't know until we try it. But, this could be very big. If Beaumont did develop some sort of marking system, well, that's very powerful. If it really works, then it allows the body to defeat a marked virus, not just the flu. If we're right, viruses of all types will be marked and the body's own defensive systems will defeat them. This means the cure to a great number of viral infections. AIDS, Ebola, the common cold. It's as important as penicillin was in the 1940s."

"Okay, I can see why this is such a big deal." Jim leaned forward, resting his elbows on his knees. "But, there's no way a Michigan State forest ranger knew all that. Someone else is driving the train, Dan Hubble can't turn Dr. Beaumont's soup into the next super drug."

Eve shook her head, "You need to think Ms. Cox, who else knew about the book? Who would benefit from getting this?"

"Apart from a few on our staff, no one. If this were a recognized, viable means of developing an antiviral drug then any of the pharmaceutical companies would love to get their hands on this. The big companies would pay millions." Sarah stopped, thought a moment then added, "But all the current anti-viral research is DNA related. Nearly every virus researcher is attempting to alter the DNA of the virus or the DNA of infected cells. I can't think of anyone attempting to mark the DNA and letting the body's own white blood cells do the work. We're pursuing this because, well basically we're doing this on a hunch. No one else would go after this unless they were desperate, like we are, or a great deal of science had been done which convinced them of its merit."

"You said some people on your staff. Who were you

thinking of?" Jim asked.

"Really, the only people who even know we're looking at this are...let's see...our lead scientist, Paula Pelitier." She paused, her eyes flicked up and to her left as she concentrated, "Bobbie." She thought for another moment. "Oh, Alex was in a meeting where we talked about it. Alex is our CFO. I guess that's about it then."

"I didn't like that guy," Eve said.

Sarah shook her head, "He wouldn't know what to do with the journal."

Eve glanced at Jim. "It doesn't make sense then. Someone outside your company places a great deal of value in that book. They killed two people and, except for a crisis of conscience, would have killed Jim and me."

Jim straightened in his chair and turned to Eve, "We're looking at this all wrong. Maybe it's not about someone trying to steal the journal from her company; maybe it's about keeping her company from getting the journal?"

Eve turned to Sarah, "Who benefits from you not getting it?"

"No one, all of our employees lose their jobs. Our investors lose their money, I go broke. It's a disaster." Cox looked around the room. "I lose all this."

The three sat in silence for several moments. Suddenly, Sarah looked up, "I know. I should have thought of this before. There is one person who benefits from us not getting the journal. One company, one man." Her eyes grew distant, "Thomas Langley." She whispered the name.

Jim looked at Eve then back at Sarah. It was clear there was a long back story here, "Who's that?" he asked.

"A former boyfriend. I left him."

"Former lovers can be vindictive, but would he kill because you dumped him?" Eve asked.

"I did a terrible thing, more than one in fact. I...we had

been engaged. I kept dragging it out. I wanted to start my own company. I lied, I left him, I just," her voice trailed off. Sarah closed her eyes, seemed to gather herself then said, "Now he's making me pay." Sarah's face was filled with an obvious sorrow. "I took something from him."

"Must have been a rough breakup to kill over, or cause someone to attempt to destroy a company," Jim observed, obviously skeptical of Sarah's explanation.

Sarah seemed to shrink into herself. "You don't understand, I did something horrible. I was young, hungry, and anxious to start my own company. I was working for Thomas. He was...is a brilliant scientist. Absolutely a genius. We graduated from medical school together. But, he liked biochemistry more than medicine. A few years after we graduated he started Metapalm and..."

"The drug company?" Eve asked obviously impressed.

"Yes. I went to work for him a year or two after the company started. We became...involved, a short time later."

"And?" Jim prodded.

"Look, I'm not proud of it, but I left him. Just left him while we were planning a wedding. That isn't bad enough; I stole things."

"What things?" Eve asked.

Sarah was in another place, another time. Finally, she said, "I took the formulas for his anti-herpes drugs. I used those formulas to start Viral BioTech. They were worth millions." Sarah's voice was low, barely above a whisper. "It was unforgivable."

"That was some time ago, why do you suspect him now?" Jim asked.

"He visited me a few days ago. He'd changed. He's angry..." She thought about that. "No, he's beyond angry. He threatened me, told me he was going to drive my company into the ground and then buy it just so he could fire me." Sarah put elbows on her knees and hung her head.

No one said a word, thirty seconds passed, then a minute. Finally, Eve glanced at Jim. Her distaste for Sarah Cox was obvious. "In order for us to prove we're innocent we need to prove this Langley guy had Dan kill Bobbie and Cheryl."

Jim didn't move, he was studying Sarah. She had grown smaller, somehow taking up less space than before. Her shoulders shook gently as she quietly sobbed. He stood, "Yeah, I know. And to do that...Sarah, we need your help."

She shook her head, not looking up. "I'm sooo sorry. This is my fault. I killed her, I killed them both." Sarah buried her face in her hands and continued to weep.

Several moments passed. Jim glanced at Eve. She shrugged her shoulders then said, "Sarah, we need your help. You've got to pull yourself together." Sarah didn't move. "Sarah," Eve's tone was a bit sharper. "Sarah, there will be time for that, right now we've got other problems. Will you help us?" Sarah nodded her head.

Jim's voice softened, "Good. Sarah, the first thing we need is for you to loan us that recipe book." He pointed at the small boxed volume Sarah had shown them. "Then we need a couple of smart phones. And right now, we're going to need to know everything there is to know about Thomas Langley."

Chapter 27

Sarah Cox sat on the edge of her black leather desk chair, a thin white towel wrapped around her hand. Slowly she dried her feet. Gray skies and a cold spring rain had left large puddles in the parking lot and water covered the sidewalks surrounding the Viral BioTech building. The water had made a mess of her new shoes.

Her secretary leaned in the office door and reminded her of the finance meeting in five minutes. She nodded, examined her shoes once more, frowned and tossed them under the desk. With bare feet she padded across the room to a long mahogany credenza. Its surface was covered with a row of three ring binders and a small bouquet of flowers. She opened one of the sliding doors and removed a pair of Stuart Weitzman pumps just as Alex Tolovek, Paula Pelitier and Dave Conners from marketing entered the office.

"Take a seat, I'll be there in a minute," she said as she squeezed her damp feet into the dry shoes. She took a step, winced and said, "Okay, so where are we this week?" Sarah didn't waste time with pleasantries. Alex immediately gave a general outline of the week's revenues. On cue Dave Conners began a review of the various product lines, expected sales, marketing efforts ongoing and planned. Several minutes of questions followed and Dave was excused from the remainder of the meeting.

Sarah waited until the office door was shut then said, "Let's take a look at new products Paula." Paula began running through the various tests being done in the labs. Several products looked good, testing was going well. But Sarah knew their market was limited.

Other tests, specifically the antivirals were failing. And

the cost associated with continued work on this line was growing. The conversation quickly stalled on the high end products. After several minutes of this Sarah tired of the debate and ended the discussion. "Alright, what's next?"

"Sarah, we're going to have to raise more capital," Alex slid his binder across the table toward her. She eyed him suspiciously, "And how do you propose we do that Alex?"

"That's up to you. We could release more shares, but with the SEC filings and disclosures I don't think we'd sell many. In fact our share price would take a hit."

"Then that's not a plan is it." She glared at him.

"We could borrow, issue bonds, go to the bank, and take out a loan." Tolovek didn't seem to have an answer. Paula eyed Tolovek and wondered what game he was playing at. She knew he didn't give a damn anymore about this company or about Sarah. What was he doing?

"Alex, I need a recommendation, not just suggestions. Which one? How do we raise additional capital?" Sarah was trying to pin Alex down, make him commit to a recommendation. "Sarah, there's a number of ways. We'll have to do some more research." He wasn't going to commit himself. Paula let her mind drift, Metapalm didn't have this problem. In the distance she heard Sarah say, "Or I could just sell the company. How would that set with you Paula?"

Caught not paying attention Paula could feel her face flush. "I...well, that's a pretty severe, I mean, are you sure that's what you want to do?"

Sarah eyed Paula for a moment then closed her binder and note pad. "No, Paula, but sometimes we do what we have to do." Sarah stood, signaling the end of the meeting. Tolovek and Pelitier stood and glanced at each other, an uncomfortable silence filled the room. After a slight hesitation they went to the door. "Paula, one last thing," Sarah called before the pair exited her office. "Could you check Bobbie's cube and her locker for her personal effects? We'll have to send those to her family."

Paula turned to face Sarah and gave a weak smile. "Certainly. But, shouldn't personnel do that? I mean, isn't there a legal reason or something?" She clearly did not want to be associated with this task.

"Yeah, probably, but you were her supervisor and knew her best. If there's anything embarrassing or personal then it's best that you do it." Sarah watched Paula shift on her feet. "Oh, well, yes, I guess that's right." Paula was caught and there was no way out of this uncomfortable request. Sarah nodded and watched the pair exit the outer office.

Tolovek waited until they were well down the hallway then wheeled on Paula, "See, I told you! She sells the company and walks away with a ton of cash, but where does that leave you and me? Screwed, that's where. Nothing but a thanks and a kick in the ass!"

Paula didn't even glance at the terrier beside her. "Forget it Alex, just forget it," she finally said. They entered the laboratory and crossed to the row of cubicles on the far wall. "Grab a box out of the storeroom there," she pointed. "I'll get Bobbie's stuff together."

Tolovek did as he was told and Paula began searching the desk, gradually building a small pile of nic-nacs, pictures and other personal items. Finally, her feet tired, Paula sat down and attempted to slide her knees under the desk. It didn't work, they collided with a soft object. Bending to look under the desk Paula discovered a large zip-lock baggie taped to the underside of the desk drawer. Without getting out of the chair she reached under the desk, slid her hand over the bag, identified two strips of duck tape and peeled them away from the hard underside of the desk drawer. The baggie fell to the floor.

She picked the baggie up and set it on the desk top.

"Alex, take a look at this," Paula whispered. Inside the baggie was a cell phone and a small dark brown book. "Is that the..." Alex was talking to himself and didn't finish the sentence. Instead, he opened the bag and placed the items on the desk.

"I don't know. But, why keep a cell phone with it?" Paula asked.

Alex ignored the question. His mind raced. Dan had called, had told him he had the journal. But Bobbie had hidden the journal under her desk. From some far off place Paula's voice broke in, "What do you think the cell phone is for?" she asked.

"No idea, but it must be important, otherwise why keep it hidden with the book?" His reply was curt. He turned the small book over in his hands. Were there two volumes to the journal?

"Be careful with that," Paula said reaching out to take the book.

Alex ignored her and simply fanned through the book. "It's handwritten," he held the book open and studied a few pages. "Old fashioned script, ornate."

"Let me see that," Paula took the book.

"Give me..."

"Shut up," Paula cut him off. "Let me see if this is what we're looking for." She began to study the first few pages. "It starts with a list of herbs and quantities. Look, here's drawings of an herb, fever few. Humm...don't know that one. Here's southern wood, calendula, tansy, jasmine, mint, it's all here." She continued to page forward. "Here's a recipe for a purgative, here's tincture of laudanum, vinegar of roses..." Despite her misgivings Paula smiled, "This is it, we've got it."

Tolovek forgot his misgivings and pumped his fist as if they'd scored a touchdown in the Super Bowl, "Paula, we've found it! It's all been worth it, we can leave with this!"

Paula glanced from Tolovek to the small, leather bound

volume. It was decision time and she knew it. She hesitated, she tried to come up with some way out of this massive mistake. Roles had reversed, she could no longer bully Alex, he now did the bullying. Alex's voice cut through her fog. "Paula, you'll cure viruses. You'll be famous."

She began to protest, was going to back out when suddenly Alex grabbed her arm and squeezed. "Ouch, stop that!" The hard face had returned. This was not the man she knew. "Paula, that journal has Beaumont's secret in it. Bobbie died because of that. We killed a cop because of that. You're in this up to your neck. Now, give me the journal and let's get this to Thomas."

She always thought she could back out before she was in too deep. Alex had been off the reservation. He'd gone too far, but he'd done it all on his own. Now, there was no more hiding, no more kidding herself. She was going to follow Alex to Metapalm. She was about to betray years of friendship and work with Sarah. It also meant keeping her mouth closed about the murder of Bobbie Downing; being an accomplice to murder.

There was a choice, she could take the journal to Sarah, tell the police about Alex and Bobbie; turn her back on the money, the truly big money. Her eyes flitted from the small, dark brown book to Alex. She glanced at the sad little pile of, now meaningless, junk on Bobbie's former desk. Alex squeezed again, "Paula?"

It wasn't a choice she was willing to make. She made up her mind. "Now what?"

Alex smiled and tapped the journal, "That's all he needs."

Paula put the phone and the journal back in the bag. "What about Sarah?"

"What about her? To hell with her, she doesn't care about us," he spat.

"Just like that?"

"Yeah, just like that. Look, this is it, we've got it."
Tolovek let go of her arm, "Now we just take it to the airport.
We go see Thomas."

Paula looked at Alex and rubbed her arm. She was in
this now, there was no backing out, "Okay, we're going to
Metapalm."

Chapter 28

I

Jim flicked a switch and the windshield wipers began a steady "ba-whish, ba-whish" as they swept the rain from the windshield of the dark blue, four door Land Rover. The SUV belonged to Sarah and they hoped no one, and by no one they really meant Alex Tolovek or Paula Pelitier, would recognize Sarah's "play car". They sat at the far end of the Viral Biotech parking lot, partially hidden by the night time cleaning crew's vehicles and a small elm tree struggling for air from a small, oblong patch of dirt. Apparently this island of dirt was meant to differentiate between the parking areas and the transit areas of the large lot. Ten minutes after their arrival Sarah's Cadillac had appeared and parked in its accustomed space. Now, time slowly ticked by.

"How long has it been?" Jim murmured.

"About an hour."

"Not enough." Jim drummed his fingers. Finally, in a low, quiet voice he said, "I guess we just wait then."

"Waiting, my favorite thing." Eve whispered back. She took a sip from her Styrofoam coffee cup then turned in her seat. "Jim, I hate waiting. Why are we not just, I don't know, CALLING THE POLICE?"

"Shhhhhhhhh!!!" Jim flinched, "Are you crazy?"

"Jim, we don't have any business going after someone who kills people. We're not the cops, we're just...we're just us. What if you get hurt?"

"Me? Why would I get hurt?"

"You're always getting hurt, have you counted your scars? Why should this be any different?"

"Look, we agreed, we wait until Sarah gives us the signal and then we'll have them. We'll be off the hook, just be patient."

Eve settled back into her seat. "This better work. That's all I'm going to say, this better work."

"Promise?"

"Promise what?"

Jim grinned, "That's all you're going to say?"

Despite herself Eve smiled. "Look, we need someone saying they're responsible for Cheryl's death, otherwise we're still the number one suspects. This will work Eve. It has to," Jim put his hand on her arm. "We'll be okay, don't worry."

II

Inside Viral Biotech, Sarah Cox was stunned. She disconnected her cell phone and took a deep breath. Sarah couldn't believe what she had just heard. Paula was selling her out. They had been together for years, had attended birthdays, shared diets, gone to yoga, Pilates, and pure barre together. Now, she was going to give the journal to Thomas. Sarah couldn't understand, couldn't believe the betrayal. Slowly she came to a decision. This wasn't about Jim and Eve. This was about her, her life, her company, and Paula's betrayal of her. She left her office and hurried to the laboratory.

Sarah's shoes clicked on the linoleum as she approached the open laboratory door and her confrontation with Paula. It was that noise, or more probably blind luck that caused Alex to step into the hallway just as she approached. His face first registered surprise, but he quickly recovered. "Sarah, I was just going over some numbers with Paula," he said.

"Save it Alex, I heard everything. You found the journal, you're going to Metapalm. Both of you betrayed me." She pounded her index finger into his chest. Alex flinched, fell back against the wall and stared, wide-eyed at her. "How did you...," he didn't finish the sentence.

Sarah held up her cell phone, anger boiling up inside. "You little fool, a cell phone doesn't have to light up to be on and they don't all have little red lights either. I heard, I heard everything. And you're going to jail."

Sarah pushed past him, shoved her forearm against the now closed door and flung it back against the hinges. "Paula, how could you!" she demanded as she stepped into the cold white room.

Paula was standing behind the rear laboratory bench, placing the last of Bobbie's items in a box. She felt she owed Bobbie's parents that much and had refused Alex's demands to leave immediately. Now she put a small glass figure down on the black marble bench top and turned to face the mad woman rushing across the laboratory in her direction. Confusion, shock and surprise all washed through Paula, then what Sarah had said registered. She knew, she knew exactly what Paula intended to do. No, had done. Now Paula was embarrassed, maybe she could explain. "Sarah, I didn't want to..."

She didn't finish her sentence. Suddenly Sarah's head disappeared in a cloud of noise and white vapor. Paula heard Sarah cry out in equal parts surprise and pain. Then, a loud thunk sounded in the room and Alex appeared from the now dissipating cloud of smoke holding a large, bright red fire extinguisher. He smiled at Paula then began running along the two rows of laboratory stations opening the butane gas stopcocks as he went. "C'mon Paula, we've got to go," he yelled.

"What did you just do?" Paula screamed. "What did you do to Sarah?"

"Forget her, we've got to go," Alex yelled back. He had now reached the far wall of the lab and was examining the cluster of exposed piping there. Spotting a green valve labeled

"Oxygen" he twisted it open. Then he ran back to the unconscious Sarah Cox, picked up the fire extinguisher and began swinging it at the chrome oxygen valves located at each workstation.

"C'mon Paula or you can blow up with her!" He swung again and a valve was knocked to the floor, a hiss of pure oxygen formed a white fog above Alex's head.

"Are you crazy? What are you doing?" screamed Paula.

"She heard everything, she knows what we're doing. She knows what we did. Now she's going to be gone and so is this company and it will be months before anyone figures out how. Are you coming or not?" Alex swung the tank again and a jet of propane gas erupted from the counter.

Paula ran to the wall and began twisting the valves shut. "You can't, there's people in this building. You'll kill them all."

"What are you doing? Stop that," Alex yelled and ran back to the bank of valves. "It's got to be this way don't you see," he shouted. Alex began beating the valves with the extinguisher.

"Stop Alex, just stop!" she shouted.

He couldn't take it anymore. He swung the fire extinguisher. Paula saw it coming, got her arms up but wasn't able to ward off the blow. The tank crashed into the side of her head. She collapsed in a heap.

Chapter 29

Eve sat straighter in her seat, "Jim, something isn't right." She pointed at the building. Several people were walking out of the building. They didn't seem to pause they just kept walking, almost casually toward the very spot where Jim and Eve had parked Sarah's Land Rover. Slowly a long, thin line of office and laboratory workers formed as more and more people exited the building. Then a long pause with no one exiting the building. Suddenly a cluster of five or six people ran out of the building, yelled something and sprinted across the parking lot. Behind them Jim watched a man run out of the building, stop and survey the parking lot, then race to the building's corner and around. Jim glanced at the building evacuees. The line was breaking into three distinct groups. Each group began hurrying to a specific point in the parking lot where a man or woman held a red, green or white flag over their head.

"Looks like a fire drill," Eve said.

"Not a drill Eve, look at the ones coming out now. Ever see anyone run out of a building during a drill?"

Eve studied the door and the few remaining people now exiting the building were coming at a dead run. "You're right. Not a drill." She searched the crowd. Finally, in desperation she asked, "Did you see Sarah?"

"No. But I did see something odd. Someone came out of the building and instead of joining the crowd sprinted around back."

"Jim, what's happening here?" A touch of fear had crept into Eve's voice.

"I don't know, but we'd better find out." Jim started the Land Rover, drove around the gaggle of people surrounding the elm tree and raced to the building's front door. The SUV's wheels skidded and Jim's door was open before the vehicle had come to a stop. He hit the ground running. Eve scrambled to catch Jim who was now running toward the building.

The lobby was empty, a red light flashed behind the receptionist's desk. A klaxon blared from the end of the hall. In the distance Jim could hear the Grand Rapid's fire department sirens. He needed to find Sarah. More importantly he needed to find out if she'd gotten the recording he and Eve so desperately needed. "Check the front office, I'll check here," Jim shouted and they both ran in different directions. Thirty seconds later Jim had finished with the conference room and was running toward Sarah's office when Eve cleared the outer office door.

"Nothing," she shouted, trying to be heard over the sound of the klaxons and the sirens.

"Downstairs, maybe the labs," Jim shouted back. They met at the stairway door and sprinted down the steps.

"Oh my God!" Eve exclaimed as they opened the door to the laboratory level. A high pitched squeal hit their ears, grating on their nerves like fingernails on a chalkboard. "What is that noise?"

Jim's nose identified the noise first, "The pipes are squealing, it's gas!" he shouted. "This whole place could blow up as soon as that gas hits a hot water heater or an electrical switch is thrown." Jim coughed, his eyes were stinging. "Don't turn on any lights!"

"Look in here," Eve was pointing at a hallway window. Behind the window glass two rows of laboratory counters, each over fifteen feet long, were arrayed ten feet apart. The counters each had plumbing assemblies equally spaced about three feet apart. Each of the assemblies was easily identified by the fountain of yellow gas attempting to touch the ceiling. "What is that?" Eve shouted, trying to be heard over the noise of the high pressure geysers.

"Gas, they must color the gas so they can see leaks," Jim struggled to be heard.

"So now what?" Eve's face clearly showed the pain the squeal was inflicting on her ears.

"Find Sarah, I'll see what I can do about the ....." Eve didn't hear the rest. Jim attempted to open the door of the laboratory. His attempt quickly failed as the steel door was locked. He leaned back and was about drive his shoulder into the door when Eve yelled, "Here try this!" She pointed at a fire extinguisher cabinet. Jim opened the cabinet, yanked the red cylinder from its stand and in one unbroken motion hurled it at the door window. The glass shattered, immediately filling the hallway with a horrid stench. Jim unconsciously put his hand over his nose, reached in and unlocked the door.

"You go that way!" Jim pointed to his right. He ran to his left and began searching for a main shut off valve. Reaching the end of the aisle Jim turned sharply right and immediately spotted Paula Pelitier laying on the floor. Over her were the main line gas valves controlling the distribution of gases to the lab. Forgetting Paula for the moment he began shutting the values. It was no use, they were jammed open.

Jim's head was spinning. The poisons in the gas were replacing the oxygen molecules in his blood. He knew what was happening, but there was nothing he could do to stop it. At the far end of the lab he could see Eve. She was leaning against a counter, she seemed to be swaying from side to side. Helplessly he watched as she slowly sank to the floor. Fear was wrapping itself around Jim's gut. He couldn't believe he was going to die here, in a laboratory devoted to finding cures to the most gruesome sorts of disease. Desperately Jim searched for an escape. He couldn't shut off the gas, he couldn't get Eve out of the lab, his stomach rolled and he fought down the vomit. Then, like a bolt of lightning he had it. He struggled back to the door, picked up the fire extinguisher and made his way to the outside wall. His leg muscles seemed to twitch, he could barely stand. He knew he had only one chance, with his last bit of strength he smashed the eyebrow window to the outside. A blast of cold fresh air fell in the window.

The cool air seemed to stop the confusion. Saliva filled his mouth as his body prepared to vomit. He struggled to the next window. He smashed a second window, then a third. Cool, fresh air fell in on him, he sucked in one breath, a second. Now he felt a bit of strength. He tried to hurry to the hallway but hurry was a relative term now. At last he made it. Things were a bit easier now, he began smashing windows, allowing the remaining gas to escape into the wider downstairs. At last there were no more windows to break. He went to Eve and found her sitting up, back to the wall. Before Jim could say a word she said, "Wow, that stuff is horrible!"

"We've got to get out of here," Jim whispered.

"Sarah is lying back there," Eve pointed.

"Paula Pelitier is over by the wall," Jim answered.

"Is she all right?" Eve asked.

"Haven't had a chance to check. I'll be right back." Jim stood and went to Sarah. Her breathing was weak and a large gash bled from her head. Jim put his fingers on her neck to check her pulse. Sarah groaned and lifted her hand to her head, she would be alright. He hurried to Paula. Her head was bloody, her breathing irregular and shallow. He got to his knees and checked her pulse. It was weak but steady. A wave of nausea and weakness swept over him. He needed to rest. He put his hands out and lowered his head, trying to stop the spinning.

"JIM!" Eve's call brought him back to earth.

"Yeah, okay, I'll be right there." He struggled to his feet and returned to Eve's side. "Can you get up?" he asked.

"Give me another minute. Can't you get that gas shut

off? The noise is killing me."

"Forget that, let's get Sarah and get out of here. The fire department is probably already here." Feeling slightly better now Jim helped Eve to her feet. Together they lifted the now conscious Sarah to her feet and moved her to the hallway.

Just as they cleared the lab and turned right in the hallway Sarah groaned, "Guys, guys...I'm going to..." She leaned over and vomited. "Ohhhhh..." she panted. Wiping her sleeve across her mouth she gasped, "Get Alex, get him. He's going to the airport. He's meeting Thomas there."

"Which airline?" Eve asked.

"Not an airline," Sarah panted. "Thomas has his own airplane. A big one I'm sure, he's a pilot." Sarah struggled to be heard over the hiss. "It worked, I'm sure it worked. I used the app. The phone didn't show any lights, and recorded everything. I heard everything. We got the confession." Her diaphragm convulsed again and she doubled over, this time there was nothing in her stomach and she simply groaned. "Oh...oh...I set the cell phone," she moaned again. "I set the cell phone to record everything, but he took it. He took the journal and the cell phone."

They could hear noises in the stairwell. "Jim, c'mon, we've got to go!" Eve pulled at Jim's arm. "Sarah, you'll be alright, the firemen are here. You'll be okay."

Jim leaned over Sarah, "Paula is alive, over by the wall, she's hurt but alive." With that Eve grabbed Jim's arm and they ran to the back of the building and out the back door.

Chapter 30

I

Jim and Eve walked around the building to the front. The automatic sprinkler system had come on, wetting down the sidewalk and the edge of the parking lot. One fireman was yelling at another one, telling him to shut off the sprinklers. Distorted red shapes reflected off the wet concrete. A crowd of people stood at the far end of the parking lot. Sarah's Range Rover was right where they had left it, only now it was surrounded by firemen wearing breathing apparatus and carrying fire axes.

"Act like we belong here," Jim whispered. They walked directly toward the crowded front entrance to the building. "Who's in charge?" Jim shouted, "I'm blocked in."

"Hey buddy, that your Range Rover?" The fire marshal's anger was clearly evident by the spittle flying from his mouth as he yelled.

"Yeah, we were making a delivery," Jim shot back.

"You're in a damned fire lane! Can't you read a sign?"

"Hey look, it's in and out, only going to be in there a minute." The fireman was about to erupt. Jim followed up with, "Man, I'm just doing my job."

The man thought for a moment, "Delivery? What kind of delivery? That's not a UPS truck."

"Medical. We do it all the time. Lots of medical items move by unmarked, private carrier."

The man's radio crackled to life, "Command post, we've got two victims. One is non-responsive"

"Pal, move that or I'll have it towed. You're lucky the trucks didn't just run it over. Now get that damned thing out of my way." The fire marshal then put his radio to his lips and began barking orders.

Jim and Eve quickly got in the Range Rover and drove out of the parking lot.

"The airport. Sarah said that Alex is going to the airport." Eve glanced at Jim, "And what about his big brother? Is Dan going to be there too?"

Jim glanced at Eve, "Let's hope not, but somehow I think he will be."

II

The big SUV careened from side to side as Jim pushed through traffic on the normally placid Patterson Avenue. Reaching Oostema Boulevard he swung the wheel hard left and began looking for the general aviation terminal. A pair of Air Force A-10 ground attack jets visiting from Selfridge Air National Guard base lifted off the runway as he found the driveway to the large private aircraft terminal. Their distinctive whine somehow calming and focusing Jim on their mission.

"Jim, we should just call the cops now," Eve said.

"Eve, we need that cell phone. Otherwise we're looking at months or even years in jail while some lawyer we don't know who doesn't really care one wit about us tries to clear our name. It becomes our word, maybe Sarah's word, against theirs. But the evidence is on their side. Which means we're screwed. Who knows what could happen? Without that recording there's no evidence to clear our name."

"So what's the plan?" an obviously unhappy Eve Crenshaw asked.

"I don't have one. Just stop them from leaving I guess. Then get the cell phone."

Eve tried to find a better answer, failed and said, "Alright..." she gripped the door handle, "Okay, let's go find their airplane."

The two cautiously approached the door to the general aviation building. A wooden door attached to a small, five foot by eight foot weather entrance with windows on both sides protected the main door. The little room was meant to keep snow and rain from blowing into the building through the main, metal door. On the left of the metal door was a small intercom and sign which read, "Press one for Dutch Aviation, two for Davidson Aircraft Engine." They glanced at each other. "Okay, here we go," Jim said as he pushed an intercom button.

His efforts were rewarded with a cheery voice, "Dutch Aviation, can I help you?" A young woman's voice danced from the speaker.

"Two for the Metapalm aircraft," he said and glanced at the dark orb suspended over their heads and a few feet to their left. The voice didn't answer. Instead a buzz indicated they should pull the door open. They entered a short hallway leading into a foyer. A wall of glass on their left allowed light into the area. Two doors were embedded on the opposite wall. The door on the left was painted green and the words "Dutch Aviation, LLC" were stenciled in gold across the door. The door on the right hadn't been painted and was still covered with only a pale blue primer. A small, black sign was mounted next to the door and read, "Davidson Aircraft Engine".

Jim and Eve opened the green door and found themselves in a bright lobby. An old fashioned popcorn cart sat next to a coffee bar with refrigerator and snack machine on the wall to their left. To their right a young, red haired, woman wearing a blue golf shirt with the words "Dutch Aviation" embroidered over her heart was pulling luggage from a storage closet behind a long glass fronted counter. The counter displayed various supplies, charts and gadgets for pilots. At the other end of the lobby was a pair of glass doors centered in the middle of a wall of glass.

The young woman had just removed a bright green and white golf bag from the closet and placed it on top of a stack of suitcases. The bag immediately tilted to the opposite side causing several of the clubs to slide from the bag to the floor. The girl muttered under her breath, pulled the bag off the pile, sat it on end and replaced the clubs. The weather channel played on the muted flat screen television behind her. A lobby of faux leather chairs and couches were arranged so that their occupants had a clear view of the floor to ceiling glass panels making up the airport side of the building. Directly in front of the building two Cessnas and a Piper were tied to metal rings embedded in the concrete. Jim checked the concrete aircraft parking area known as the "ramp" in both directions, but there were no business sized aircraft to be seen. By now the woman had removed a black wireless phone from its charger which sat at the end of the gray granite topped counter.

Eve approached the counter and, before the girl could dial, said, "Excuse me miss, we're looking for some friends of ours."

The girl put the phone back in the charger and said, "Oh, hi! I'm sorry I thought you went into the hanger. I'm Bonnie, welcome to Dutch Aviation."

"Yes, hi. Bonnie we're looking for some friends of ours. They're flying a business airplane, but we don't know where they are."

"Oh, sure. Must be the guys with the King Air. They just came through here. I think they're doing their preflight. They're in the hanger."

"Is it too late to catch them? We've got some items they left at the office," Eve deftly invented a cover story.

"No, shouldn't be a problem. Just go down that hallway, flip the deadbolt and let yourself in. I think theirs is the only airplane in there." Bonnie pointed to a short hallway ending in a metal door with a large wire screened window filling the upper half. "Oh, would you tell them I'm calling the fuel truck now and then I'll get the tug and have them out of the hanger in a few minutes please."

"Sure will, thanks," Eve muttered and took several quick steps to catch up with Jim who was already on his way to the hallway. Reaching the door Jim abruptly stopped. Only one aircraft occupied this huge space. "That's it," he said, pointing at a large, T-tailed aircraft sitting high on its landing gear in the hangar.

"See anyone?" Eve asked.

"Nope," Jim replied.

"So how do we keep them from taking off?" Eve said.

"That's easy, just keep an eye out." Jim opened the door and was surprised at the equipment he'd missed from the window. The rear of the hangar had a hip wall, approximately three feet high made of concrete blocks. Behind the little wall were engine test stands, several cylinders of various gases used in welding and two bright red barrels mounted on a tall stand, a long black fuel hose hung on the front of the rack.

Jim snapped himself back to the present and quickly trotted across the hangar. A moment later he reached the nose of the airplane and knelt on one knee. Fishing in his pants pocket he found a bright red and chrome pocket knife. Suddenly a voice barked, "Hey! What are you doing?" Alex Tolovek stood in the doorway to the men's room on the opposite side of the hangar. Jim turned in the direction of the sound in time to see Tolovek pull a ball peen hammer from a tool box. Tolovek's brother Dan Hubble and his partner Thomas Langley had to be around someplace. Deciding not to stick around and find out where Jim yelled "Run Eve!" and sprinted toward the lobby door.

Alex began running toward Jim. It was too late, Jim's head start was too big. Seeing that he couldn't catch Jim before the lobby door safely closed behind him Alex bounced on his right leg and hurled the hammer like a javelin thrower. The iron missile struck Jim just below the base of his neck, stunning him and knocking him to the floor. Before Jim could clear his head Alex was on him. Picking Jim up with his left hand Tolovek twice crashed his fist into Jim's face. Then he threw Jim to the floor bouncing his head off the concrete. Jim groaned and passed out.

An enraged Tolovek now turned his attention to Eve. She screamed and fled back to the lobby of the terminal. Exiting the hallway to the terminal lobby she turned right and stopped in horror. Bonnie was gone and the phone cradle was empty! Eve glanced at the lobby windows and remembered the Land Rover in the parking lot. In an instant she asked herself if it was possible to reach the SUV before Alex caught her. The answer was immediate, it didn't matter. The keys were in Jim's pocket.

Desperately Eve searched the room. She could hear the door crash open. Her eyes fell on the golf clubs. She reached for the driver, thought better of it and pulled the nine iron. Eve took her position next to the corner of the hallway and waited.

Silence. Alex had stopped. He was being careful, sensing a trap. Eve sucked in a deep breath and flattened her back against the wall. Timing was everything. Swing too early and Alex would see the club coming, swing too late and she wouldn't generate the power needed to truly hurt the man. Eve tried to listen for his footsteps, but his soft soled shoes were too quiet. She fought down the urge to just peek around the corner. She wanted to run, just run.

Suddenly, from the corner of her eye she noticed movement. She turned her head and studied the empty room. Nothing. Then she noticed the popcorn maker! The lower panel was a flat piece with the words POPCORN 10 CENTS painted in red and gold. But the panel itself was chrome and shiny as a mirror. He was close, she could see him carefully placing one foot softly in front of the other. Now she could hear his breathing. He took another step. He was just feet away. She watched the popcorn maker, concentrating on the man's reflection. She needed him to take two more steps. Her grip on the club tightened. She had the nine iron at her shoulder like a baseball bat. One more glance at the reflection...wait, a half second more.

She swung the club with all her might. The timing was perfect, her assailant was in mid-stride. The club struck Alex's face with a satisfying crunch. The force of the blow lifted him off his feet. His eyes widened, then glazed. Eve pulled the club back for a second swing, but it wasn't necessary. Alex's eyes rolled back, two teeth fell to the floor, his knees buckled and Tolovek collapsed.

Chapter 31

Dan Hubble and Thomas Langley exited the rest room locked in conversation. They slowly crossed the hangar and walked under the fourteen foot tail of the King Air 350. Langley was proud of this airplane and loved to fly it. He was explaining the automated navigation system to Hubble when they heard Jim's groan. They turned to the sound just in time to see the lobby door open. Eve burst through the door on a dead run. She took three steps then stopped. Fifteen feet in front of her lay her husband. Her two enemies stood an equal distance past him. For a long moment no one moved. Then Langley said, "You must be Mrs. Crenshaw?"

Not bothering to answer, Eve wheeled and raced back through the hallway door. This time she remembered the deadbolt. She grabbed the door as she flew past, using the handle as a brake. Once clear she turned and slammed the door shut, flicking the lock shut just as a pair of large hands crashed into the glass. The door didn't budge and Eve found herself staring through a wire mesh lined window at a now very close and very dangerous Dan Hubble. Terrified she backed away from the window. Hubble didn't move. She reached the end of the hallway without turning around, nearly tripping over Alex's still unconscious body in the process. Hubble's face filled the door window. He looked positively evil as he spotted his brother laying on the floor. Behind Hubble, Eve could hear Thomas Langley shouting. She strained to understand what he was saying, but the sound was muffled by the thick door. Hubble turned and hurried away.

Fear now gripped Eve, she was alone, Jim was hurt and...in there, with them. Suddenly she realized where Hubble was going, the lobby flight line door! Forcing herself to act, to not just sit down and give up, she began to run to the lobby door. As she ran she watched for any sign of Hubble or Langley through the large glass walls. Just as she had guessed, Hubble rounded the hangar corner on a dead run, sprinting toward the lobby entrance. She lost the race. He reached the door first and began to push his way inside. A smile erupted across his now sinister face.

Desperation propelled her forward, she had to close that door or lose everything. Hubble had the door open a few inches and was about to step through, but Eve didn't stop. Her shoulder crashed into the heavy safety glass door. Hubble wasn't able to resist a basic law of physics. Eve's mass was multiplied by her momentum. The blow was too much for the man, his body was propelled back just a few feet. It provided all the time she needed. Before he could regain his balance she had the door closed and quickly flipped the lock.

Hubble glared at her for a moment, mouthed a curse and walked back to the hangar. As she watched the man retreat Eve heaved a sigh of relief. It was short lived. The same thing could happen on the street side door. She turned and sprinted to that side of the building. She flipped the silver deadbolt shut then peered through the small six inch window at eye height. Thomas Langley was in the parking lot headed to the Dutch Aviation door. Eve suppressed a scream and retreated to the front desk. She had completely sealed herself inside the building.

Her hands were shaking, her head seemed to be swimming, and she was hyperventilating. "Be calm, think this through," she chanted to herself. Gradually her breathing settled, her hands stopped their terrible shaking; she began to regain control.

Now Eve could truly see the room. She examined everything, slowly taking stock and developing a plan. First things first, Alex Tolovek had to be dealt with. On the corner table, next to the cheesy foyer couch stood a ceramic reading lamp. She picked it up and slammed the lamp to the floor, shattering the glass base. Then she began to pull the electrical wire free. It wouldn't budge. This wasn't as easy as on T.V. Eve hurried to the counter and began searching for a knife or scissors. Instead she found a length of rope the airport used to tie down airplanes. This was even better.

Eve returned to the still unmoving Alex Tolovek. She kicked him once in the ribs, he didn't flinch. Satisfied, she began to wrap the rope around one wrist, then the other. "Left over right, right over left," she sang as she finished the square knot. Living on a farm did have its advantages she thought. Then she took another length of rope and did the same to his feet. The man seemed to be out cold, but she didn't want to risk his waking up and attacking her from behind.

Now Eve examined the glass walls at the front of the building. They allowed a complete view of everything moving on the runway and ramp. At the far end of the ramp, some three hundred yards away, she could see the desk girl, Bonnie, unhooking a small yellow tractor which Dutch Aviation used as an aircraft tug, from a Cessna Citation business jet. The girl let the tow bar rest on the concrete then returned to her seat on the tractor. At last, help was on its way. The girl could call the tower or security or someone with her radio!

Eve watched as Bonnie manipulated some control. The tug didn't move. Bonnie stepped off the tug and kicked the tire. Then she unwrapped a set of jumper cables from the rear of the tug. Lifting the seat she hooked them to the battery and began walking toward the hangar she had just pulled the jet from. Eve moaned, this wasn't good, Bonnie wasn't coming back to Dutch Aviation for a while.

Closer Eve could see the hangar containing the Metapalm King Air. The hangar doors were partially open. Satisfied that she was safe for the moment, but disappointed that Bonnie wasn't returning anytime soon, she returned to Alex Tolovek. He was still out cold but breathing heavily. She wondered if he would vomit, people with blows to the head did that. She rolled Tolovek to his side, something she had read should be done with concussion victims. It was said to prevent drowning in their own vomit if they did. She wasn't sure but did it anyway. As she rolled the man over his jacket fell open. A plastic bag had been stuffed into Tolovek's jacket pocket. She pulled the bag out and felt a rush of adrenaline. She had it, the bag contained the cell phone and the Sarah's decoy journal!

Eve grabbed the bag and stood. They had fought and fought hard for this, but now Jim was beaten and trapped. 'They' were no longer a 'they', she was on her own. Eve walked to the hangar door. Hubble and Langley were standing next to the steps leading into the King Air. They had moved Jim. Now he was kneeling on the floor between them. He looked shaken, blood stained his shirt from a cut on his cheek. His face was pale and his head seemed to sit like an unsteady rock on the top of a mountain. She watched as he slumped forward, putting his hands out to the floor, hanging his head low.

She leaned her back against the wall. "Think Eve, now what?" she whispered. She struggled to find a way to rescue her husband. It was impossible. Another glance through the glass. They were two big men, she didn't have a chance. She rolled the bag in her hands as she watched the men in the hangar. They wanted the journal, she wanted Jim. A trade was obvious. Pushing herself off the wall she peered into the hangar. It was her only chance, trade the journal for Jim.

Then Eve began to think about the cell phone. Jim had specifically asked Sarah Cox to provide smart phones. Sarah had bought each of them a new phone. Jim had then downloaded a recording app he said would capture conversations while the phone appeared to be off. He had spent twenty minutes showing both Sarah and Eve how to use the program.

Eve thought about Sarah, she had said something. The memory was lost, gone in the constant rush of adrenaline and fear of the last several hours. Now she needed that memory. She closed her eyes, tried to relax, to let the scene play out in her mind's eye. Sarah had said, what? She nearly had it...Sarah had said that it had worked! She had it, she had recorded something that cleared Jim and Eve. "...but he took it." Eve glanced at the phone in her hand. "It" was the cell phone, it had to be. "It" was this cell phone.

One feature Eve especially liked about her own cell phone was the ability to synchronize her pictures wirelessly. Whenever Jim took a picture around the farm or she took a picture at school they could easily transfer it from one phone to another. Now she would use that feature again.

She took a seat on the leather couch and pulled a new smart phone from her back pocket. She thought about simply calling the police now, then rejected the idea. The airplane would take off, they would be gone and maybe take Jim with them long before the police could get here. She had to get Jim before that happened.

She opened the recording application on Sarah's phone and played the recording. A door in the distance, then voices, then a few bangs, then more voices. Something was odd here, there were no dead spaces. Was this really the recording she needed? She slid her finger across the application start page and opened the settings. Sarah had set the application to record only when a voice activated the microphone. Brilliant!

It was distant, like the recording had been made with a microphone in a bag, which of course it had, but it caught everything. Eve opened the synchronize application on her phone. A moment later she had copied the recording to her own phone. She switched to the recording app on her phone and tapped the 'play' arrow. Alex Tolovek's voice barked from her phone. She had copied the file properly.

Now she had to make a deal. This was the dangerous part, this was where one mistake could cost her dearly. She crossed the lobby, she knew that opening the door was a huge risk, but what choice did she have? She stopped and checked Tolovek. He lay on the floor, still breathing deeply as if sound asleep. She pushed one eyelid back and was greeted with an enlarged pupil, he was alive but definitely unconscious. Glad she hadn't killed the man she stood, spotted the golf bag and decided to stuff her phone in one of the many pockets. If this went wrong maybe someone would find the recording and clear their name.

Standing at the doorway she studied the inside of the hangar through the glass. It seemed as if the two men were preparing to fly the King Air. Langley was bent over one of the main landing gear struts, Hubble stood over a still kneeling Jim. She fought back the fear which threatened to paralyze her. If they took off with Jim in the airplane...they could go anywhere, do anything to him. She refused to think about it. Eve steeled herself then opened the door. "HEY!" she yelled as loud as she could. Langley and Hubble both turned to her. "I've got the journal. I'll give you the journal and never mention this to anyone if you give me Jim."

Langley ducked under the fuselage and stood up. Hubble immediately began to sprint toward her. Athletic for such a big man, Hubble grabbed the hammer, which Tolovek had thrown at Jim, in mid-stride and raced at her. Eve ducked back into the hallway, flipping the deadbolt and backing away from the door. Hubble smashed the hammer into the glass. A circular spider's web appeared, some small pieces flew away from the window landing at Eve's feet, but the safety glass and wire mesh held. Hubble was still on the other side.

Langley grabbed Hubble's arm and whirled him around.

She could see his face, it was red and angry. He shouted something she didn't catch. Hubble, equally as angry, turned and walked a few steps away. Now Langley stood next to the window. "Alright Mrs. Crenshaw," he called. "You want your husband. I need that journal. Open the door and hand me the book and we'll call it a day."

Eve shook her head, "I'm not stupid! No deal," she yelled back. "Help Jim to the door. Then walk to the far side of the hangar. I'll slide the baggie to you as soon as Jim is on my side of the door."

Langley's glare was physical, piercing and cold. Eve held her ground. Finally the man simply turned and walked to the far side of the hangar. Hubble fell in beside him. "This was too much," Langley thought. He glanced sideways at the big, dumb forest ranger. Things had gone south since Tolovek had enlisted the man's help, now he was stuck with him and Alex wasn't around to keep the idiot under control, an already lacking effort, Thomas thought. There had to be a way to clean up the entire problem. Langley turned and faced the door, now on the opposite side of the King Air. He studied the woman peering through the smashed spider web cracked glass.

Langley watched her for several seconds. She and her husband had to go. They knew too much, they understood what he was doing and why. It was enough to bring his company down and him along with it. Then he glanced at Hubble; he had to rid himself of this lumbering oaf too.

"Dan, c'mer," he whispered. Hubble moved closer. "Look, we're in trouble here. We need that journal. And, we need those two gone." He glanced at Hubble to ensure he caught the meaning. Hubble's smile seemed to fade.

"Look, I've done enough of that. Roughing 'em up a bit I can handle but, well...that's a bit far." Dan Hubble, for all the evil he'd participated in these past few days was not a natural killer.

"Dan, those two know about the girl. They know about the cop. They know about the journal. Dan, do I have to paint a picture?"

Hubble shrank into himself. For a moment he studied the sky outside the partially open hangar door. He seemed to be looking for an escape. "But all we have to do is get away from them, get some time and we'll be living in South America on some beach with no extradition. It's perfect. We don't need to...we don't need to do that."

"You don't get it Dan. We need the journal. But there's more, a lot more. Once we have the journal we need to produce the drug, then we need to test, then have the drug approved, then we need to market it, it goes on and on. It's a long process Dan. This doesn't just happen, we're not going to see any cash for three or four years. And Dan, "Hubble's eyes had returned to the distant horizon. "Dan. Listen to me Dan, we can't do any of that from South America or Thailand or someplace like that. We've got to be here. Got it Dan? We've got to be here working the process."

Hubble's stare shifted to Langley. "Alex said all we needed to do was to get you the journal. I got it, I gave it to you. I want my money now," he reached out and put a hand on Langley's shoulder and squeezed. Langley flinched.

"Dan, I don't have it. She's got it." He pointed at the lobby door.

"That's your problem. I did what I was asked." Hubble insisted, but Thomas could sense the man's rebellion was over.

"How much did Alex tell you I'd give him?"

"Seven million, and we're splitting it two ways," Hubble said quickly.

Langley let his eyes wander around the hangar. "We need to get the plane out of here, get it ready to take off then do it, hop in and go."

"Seven mill." Before he could finish Langley jumped in,

"I know, I heard you. And the deal was three."

"Five."

"The deal was three."

"Four."

"Three."

Hubble looked at the geek in front of him. His hand still rested on Thomas' shoulder. He squeezed again, "Four."

Another reason to get rid of Dan, he knew too much and he was greedy. "Alright, four," Langley said, "Now, look over there. See those fuel tanks," Langley nodded toward two red fifty-five gallon drums mounted atop a seven foot high, four-leg support. "I'll get the hangar doors open. You go around and shove a wrench or something into the door handles and lock them shut from the outside. Got that?"

"Yeah, I got it," Hubble was getting tired of this stuffed shirt ass-hole.

"Good, when you're done with that get back here. Use the gas in those tanks and splash it around on the walls. Close the hangar doors and torch the place."

Hubble thought about the idea. "How do we get the plane out?

Langley looked at the man, "Out? What do you mean out?"

"We're still taking the plane right?"

"Yeah, so?"

"Well, no one is going to tow it out when the place is burning like a candle." Hubble mused.

"Good point Dan," Langley was surprised it was this easy. All he had to do was open the hangar doors, get inside the airplane and go. Oh that sounded good. It had a flair to it. He liked the idea, but it wouldn't work. He needed to silence Dan Hubble as much as he needed to silence the Crenshaws.

"Normally we pull it out with the tug, but that girl is on the other side of the airport. I'll taxi the airplane out. Then you torch the place."

"When do I get my money?" Hubble demanded.

"As soon as we get to my office in Chicago, now c'mon Dan we've got work to do."

Jim lay on the concrete floor of the hangar and watched Dan walk away from Langley. His head throbbed and he was still a bit dizzy, but he could feel his strength returning.

Hubble walked out of the front of the hangar. Several minutes later he returned. "It's done," he yelled, then he went to the back of the hangar.

From inside Dutch Aviation's lobby Eve had watched as Hubble had pushed a triangular piece of wood into the handles of the glass doors opening to the airport ramp. For a moment she didn't realize what the man was doing, then it was clear, he had locked her in! She turned and raced to the street side door, but it too was wedged shut. Bordering on panic she pounded and pulled on the doors, but they wouldn't move. She ran to the hallway and looked into hangar. Hubble was going to the rear of the hangar but she couldn't see what he was doing.

For a moment Hubble examined the fuel stand used by the unknown engine mechanic. Dan took down the first fuel nozzle and proceeded to wedge a rolled up red shop rag into the handle and began spraying 100 octane low-lead aviation gasoline on the rear wall of the building. The difficulty of the task surprised him, he hadn't realized the fuel was not pumped, simply a gravity feed system used for small amounts. The hose wasn't very long and Dan quickly tired of spreading fuel over the same ten feet of the wall and laid the hose on the floor of the hangar.

Next, Dan then went to the other tank, this one marked with the words "Jet A" and began the same process. He pulled several rags from a bucket then wedged the second nozzle open and laid it too on the floor of the hangar. Quickly the hangar began to fill with the fumes of aviation fuel.

Jim didn't move. The two men still assumed he was semi-conscious and no longer a threat. Desperately Jim searched for a way of stopping Hubble then Langley. There was none, he lay on the cold floor of the hangar and, try as he might, Jim could not think of a way to end this madness.

Chapter 32

While Dan had been spraying fuel around the rear of the hangar Thomas Langley had succeeded in opening the hangar doors. With a quick glance to the rear of the building Langley had unlatched the door of the King Air 350 and swung the structure downward, revealing built-in steps to the interior of the aircraft. Once inside Langley flipped a switch and pulled the cable "safety rail" attached to the door. The hydraulically powered door swung up and shut, Langley pulled the locking lever shut and smiled. He would be in Chicago in less than an hour and his company would soon be cranking out the most valuable drug in the history of mankind.

Langley took a few steps to the cockpit of the big twin. He pulled his left leg up and over the center control console, then his right and sat down on the pilot's sheepskin seat pad. He removed a chart from a side pocket then quickly ran a basic check: "Master on, hydraulic pressure up, fuel pumps on, igniters on, props forward, flaps set, brakes set, radios set." The checklist, albeit abbreviated, was complete.

Hubble, finished with the fuel, now realized that Langley had disappeared. He sprinted to the front of the hangar and looked up and down the vast concrete ramp. The Dutch Aviation tug had been started and was now slowly pulling a large business jet toward him, but Thomas Langley was nowhere to be seen. He turned and stepped back inside the hangar, and spotted Langley's head in the pilot's window. The bastard was going to leave him!

Hubble desperately looked for a way to stop his, now former, partner when the pilot's side window slid to the rear. "Dan, torch this place, hurry up!"

"Open the door!" Hubble demanded.

"I can't start the engines if the door is open," Langley lied.

He hadn't thought of that, probably some safety switch. Hubble nodded, then jogged to the back of the hangar. Suddenly the roar of a turboprop engine filled the hangar, the prop blast causing tool boxes and assorted debris to slide across the polished hangar floor and through the gas pooled around the tanks. A second later the second engine erupted and what seemed to be a small tornado filled the hangar.

Dan momentarily steadied himself against the railing, then made a quick search of the tool chest near the acetylene tanks. He quickly found what he knew was there, a flint striker. The small tool used to ignite the flame for the torch. Another quick search and he pulled a shop towel from the cabinet and soaked one end on the fuel covered floor. Then he wrapped the towel around a wrench he'd picked up from the same tool chest. It only took one quick squeeze of the striker, a shower of sparks landed on the towel and it burst into flames. Dan backed up, remembered to check for fuel around his feet and threw the flaming wrench into the pool of aviation fuel.

The explosion was more than he had expected. A loud "wooph" and a wave of heat swept over him. In seconds the rear of the hangar was covered in flames. The prop blast increased, the added oxygen fueling the flames. He turned to see the King Air slowly creeping forward, its nose already out of the hangar. Hubble began to run. He had only taken a few steps when he realized the aircraft door was still shut. He sprinted the final fifteen feet and found himself pounding on the now closed and latched aircraft door. The airplane continued to roll forward. Dan fought the tornadic blast of the turboprop's blades. The airplane began to turn, slowly at first then faster. Hubble scrambled to keep up. Anger then fear began to gnaw at Hubble. If Langley left him here then he surely was going to spend the rest of his life in prison. Running alongside the plane Hubble pounded on the fuselage.

Suddenly a squeal as the airplane's brake pads bit into their respective discs. Then, much to Dan's surprise and relief, the prop blast lessened. The King Air stopped rolling and rocked back on its haunches. A moment passed and the door cracked open, then let down. Hubble grabbed the safety cable intent on running up the steps. He glanced upward and saw Langley framed in the opening, "Close the damned hangar doors. Make sure that Crenshaw isn't going anywhere then get your ass in here, quit screwing around!" Langley shouted.

Hubble stopped. He hadn't thought about the doors. He didn't want to kill again, but he was in too deep. Now he was embarrassed as well as angry. There was nothing for it, he was trapped. He needed to get on this plane and it wasn't going anywhere until the Crenshaw's were dealt with. Hubble hurried back to the hangar. The heat was more intense, his exposed arms and face felt like a bad summer sunburn. Just inside the hangar, next to the door he had recently smashed with a hammer, was a large yellow switch box labeled "Hangar Doors". He held his left arm to shield his face and eyes from the heat. The underside of his arm seemed to have been dipped in molten lava. Dan reached the switch box and pulled the handle down. A motor began to whine and the large hangar doors began to creep together. Then he turned to deal with Jim.

Except there was no Jim. Dan's surprise would have been comical if the situation were different and there had been anyone to see it. Hubble quickly scanned the interior of the hangar. His prey was not there, Jim Crenshaw was gone. Suddenly, from the rear of the hangar one of the two fuel barrels erupted. Flaming shards of metal screamed across the hangar, clanging off walls and showering the hangar with fiery debris. The fireball itself was intense, catching Dan's shirt and pants on fire. He fought panic and scanned the hangar. In the corner an empty mop bucket and mop stood guard next to a rack of aircraft tow bars. Dan grabbed the mop and began beating his flaming legs. The flames went out and he began flipping the mop over his shoulders to kill the flames on his back. A few screams later and he'd succeeded in extinguishing his shirt. The pain on his back was intense, bile swirled in the back of his throat.

The second barrel blew, again showering the hangar with flaming debris, this time none of it landing on Dan. He'd had enough, the doors were coming together, the heat was intense, fear now drove Dan Hubble. He sprinted for the gap between the steadily advancing hangar doors and ran for the airplane. The steps were still down and Dan didn't pause as he raced to the interior of the King Air, safe at last.

Chapter 33

I

Jim had moved to the far front corner of the hangar when Hubble began spreading aircraft fuel across the hangar's rear wall. He knew what was coming and that it was only going to get worse. The gap between the hangar door and the wall had been sufficient to allow him to squeeze through. The timing allowed Jim to watch Hubble run up the stairs of the King Air only to turn around and disappear inside the hangar. This had been Jim's chance. He removed a red pocket knife from his pants pocket and sprinted to the belly of the aircraft. Two quick thrusts and a satisfying hiss of air exploded from the nose wheel. Jim smiled and moved to the main gear. The hissing sounds were quickly overwhelmed by the roar of flames from the hangar. Jim couldn't enjoy this little victory. A loud explosion and the frosted windows at the top of the hangar doors began to glow Florida orange. Jim could only think of Eve, the last time he had seen her she was in that building. If she were still there... Jim shook his head, he couldn't, he wouldn't allow himself to think about that now.

He sprinted to the corner of Dutch Aviation. What he saw terrified and enraged him. Bright yellow aircraft chalks had been jammed into the door handles locking them from the outside. A cable or wire had been wrapped around the entire makeshift lock. He didn't stop, it would take too long to clear this mess, Hubble or Langley would surely see him. He continued to the parking lot side of the structure.

In the seconds it took to reach the back of the building the heat seemed to double. He sprinted to the weather entrance, burst through the outer door and slammed his shoulder into the main building door. The door exploded open under Jim's weight and he found himself in the foyer. He crossed the space and came to the Dutch Aviation lobby door. A large wrench had been pushed through the door handles and a small cable had been wrapped around the wrench and handles alike. The heat in the foyer was increasing and Jim began worrying about the condition of the lobby on the other side of...the...damned...locked...and cabled door. He wanted to scream Eve's name but knew it wouldn't do any good, he had to focus. He pulled on the wrench, but it was too hot. His fingers couldn't hold the hot metal. Frantically he searched the foyer for something, anything to help shield his hands from the heat. There was nothing.

II

Thomas Langley was a happy man. He'd done it and he was about to go flying. What more could he ask for? He pushed the red button centered on the top of the left side of the control yoke and announced, "Ford ground, King Air 97 Pop has the numbers and would like to taxi to the active." The ground controller smiled, for once someone told him they had listened to the automated airport information before calling him. "97 Pop, taxi to 26 Right via Foxtrot then Juliet," he shot back.

"97 Pop," Langley acknowledged. He pushed the throttles forward and the King Air began to roll. They crossed the ramp, turned onto the Foxtrot taxiway and began the long taxi to the end of the runway. Suddenly a loud thumping sound could be felt more than heard reverberating through the cabin. "What the hell is that?" Hubble shouted.

"I...I don't know," Langley was as confused as Hubble. He pulled the right engine throttle back to idle. No change in the noise. He pushed it back then pulled the left engine throttle. No change. Then it hit him. There was something wrong with the nose gear. The nose was lower. They had a flat tire!

At that moment Langley's headphones crackled: "97 Pop, Ford ground."

Langley knew what they were going to say before he answered the call, "Go ahead ground."

"97 Pop it appears you have sparks coming from your nose gear, say intentions."

Fear began to settle into Langley's gut. He wasn't going to get away from here. He would have to answer questions, the police would soon be involved, everything would come out. Langley did a quick review, could he take off with a flat nose gear? He pushed the throttles further forward, the thumping became a grind. The landing gear dug into the concrete. They now acted more like brakes than wheels. It wouldn't work, the airplane wasn't going to get up the speed to lift the nose wheel off the ground.

III

Now more angry than scared Jim stripped off his shirt and wrapped it around his hands. Finally he was able to untangle the rat's nest 'knot' that Hubble had used to tie the doors together. Then he pulled the wrench out of the handles and carefully swung the left door toward him. The heat was intense but not unbearable. The walls were keeping the flames away but it was obvious the building was coming down, and probably sooner rather than later. On the airport side he thought he could faintly hear sirens. A loud popping noise exploded on his right, the metal wall had buckled and a blast of hot air filled the lobby.

Then he spotted...it couldn't be. Jim stopped. For the briefest moment he couldn't move. A body. It had to be a body. It had to be Eve, she was lying next to the lobby counter, a large coat covering her from head to toe. She had used the coat to shield herself from the heat. It hadn't worked, she wasn't moving. He raced to the body, braced himself and ripped the coat off. An unconscious Alex Tolovek lay on the floor. Jim was now nearly insane with panic. He stood and yelled her name, "Eve, where are you?" The sound of his voice was nearly drowned out by the roar of the fire. He tried again.

Suddenly, from where he couldn't tell came a thin voice, "I'm right here!" She was close, but he couldn't find the direction of the sound.

Smoke now filled the lobby, he struggled to maintain his bearings. Over there it was brighter, the glass in the front, airport side. That way was death, the doors were locked from the outside. The foyer was...where? He struggled to keep his bearings in the smoke and the heat. He turned. She yelled again, "JIM, I'm right..." He didn't hear the rest, but it was close, then he had it. He leaned over the counter and there she was.

Eve lay on the floor, a heavy leather coat over her torso, a heavy rain suit wrapped around her legs. "Let's get out of here!" Jim shouted. Eve struggled to her feet, Jim grabbed her with both arms and pulled her over the counter. He hugged her hard and shouted over the roar of the fire, "We've got to go, now!" Jim pointed in the direction of the foyer and began pulling her along.

She stopped and pulled his arm, "JIM, JIM, we've got to take him!" She pointed at Tolovek.

"Too late, we've got to get out of here!"

"Jim we have to. I knocked him out, he's hurt bad. It's murder if we don't, get him please!" Her mouth was next to his ear and she was shouting to be heard. Jim didn't argue, it was too hot, too dangerous.

"Stay right here! Don't move." He bent down and pulled Tolovek to a seated position. Quickly he positioned himself behind the man, crouched and slid his arms under Tolovek's. Jim now straightened up, grabbed Tolovek's right hand, bent slightly and slid the killer onto his shoulder in a classic 'fireman's carry'.

The smoke was now too thick to see. Jim had to rely on his memory of the lobby layout. "Grab my belt, don't get separated!" he shouted. He didn't hear Eve's response but felt her hand grip his belt. They began to edge their way across the lobby floor. At last they reached the door and hurried down the smoke filled hallway. The outer door opened and Jim spotted a brightness in the smoke, the foyer's glass wall. He picked up his pace just a bit. "We're almost there Eve, hang on," he cried. She had a firm grip on Jim's belt but was coughing badly. He hoped she would last the final ten feet. If she didn't poor Tolovek would roast here in Dutch Aviation, it would be an easy choice to toss him aside and pick Eve up.

Jim didn't have to make the choice. A moment later the foyer door appeared, he pushed open the heavy metal door then entered the weather entrance. The heat was too intense, Jim could feel his flesh starting to roast, he could only imagine what Eve was feeling. In desperation he began to run, imploring Eve not to let go of his belt. A few steps later Jim crashed into the flimsy wooden outer door. Their momentum carried them several feet into the parking lot and they collapsed on the ground. Eve wrapped her arms around his shoulders, "Oh thank God," she gasped. Then Eve went into a coughing fit that seemed to last an eternity.

After several minutes Jim said, "I've got to make two phone calls." He quickly did a web search on Eve's cell phone, found the number for the airport control tower and hit "Call". A man answered on the second ring. "Gerald R. Ford tower, Connor speaking."

"Mr. Connor, you have a King Air 350 about to take off. The men on that plane set the fire in the Dutch Aviation hangar. And, they're murderers." Jim disconnected the phone without waiting for a response. The second call lasted only a few seconds, then Jim and Eve walked across the parking lot and into the woods to wait for Sarah Cox.

Chapter 34

Sarah Cox pushed a button on her cell phone and activated the speaker phone function. "My lawyers tell me you shouldn't have anything to worry about. They'll formalize the deal with the DA and have the judge sign it just to be safe."

The tin voice of Eve Crenshaw, her joy and relief evident answered back, "Boy, that's a great! I could see us in court for years. Thank you so much."

"I was just worried there would always be some suspicion. That we would never be sure they believed us," Jim added.

Sarah smiled, happy to have her company's prospects on the mend with a new antiviral drug in development. "Well, you saved Alex after all he did. And, catching Thomas and that man, Hubble, certainly helped. By the way, I'm told that Hubble has confessed to everything. Thomas is trying to hold out for a deal of some sort, but it won't be long. Eventually he will tell the whole story. And, the truth of the matter is that you were framed. That's already coming out. They know it, the judge knows it, it's just lawyers getting their billing hours up." Sarah smiled again, "I can't tell you how happy I am that you're all right."

"We're fine Sarah. Being able to get back to camping on the river without some goons trying to kill us is a big help though I must admit!" Eve said with a laugh.

"Sarah, thanks for all your help. Things wouldn't have turned out this well if we hadn't been able to count on you," Jim said.

"My pleasure. Had to do it. Once I found out what was going on in my own company no less and by people I trusted! Amazing, absolutely amazing." Sarah was still in shock that

Paula Pelitier had betrayed her. Poor Paula, she was looking at a very long jail term.

"Thanks again Sarah," Eve said.

"Stay in touch you two, have fun in the woods," Sarah smiled and hit the disconnect button.

Eve turned her phone off, sat back in her folding chair, took a sip of her coffee and smiled at her husband, "Jim, I'm thinking we've got about an hour before I start dinner."

"Great! Should be a few hex hatching on the river. Call me when it's ready." Jim grabbed his fly rod, fishing vest and waders. Eve watched him as he happily trundled off in the direction of the river. Then she smiled and shook her head, "Not what I had in mind Jim...not at all what I had in mind."

THE END

About the Author

HJ Gaudreau is a retired Air Force Colonel. He currently lives in Michigan with his wife Eve and beagle puppy, Agatha. They have one son, whom they are hoping moves to Michigan someday soon!

ENJOY THE FOLLOWING
SAMPLES OF THE CRENSHAWS'
OTHER GREAT ADVENTURES

BETRAYAL IN THE LOUVRE

and

THE COLLINGWOOD LEGACY

Learn more about the facts and history of this and other

books by HJ Gaudreau at: **www.hjgaudreau.com**

A simple trip to an antique show leads to a fight for their life

Jim and Eve Crenshaw live on a small farm in mid-Michigan. It's a peaceful life. But when they find an ivory tube containing one of the four pieces of French Royal Regalia they are propelled into a world of international conspiracy, priceless antiquities, and ruthless killers.

Marie Antoinette's heart breaks as her oldest son is ripped from her arms.

A WWI doughboy is caught in the horror of war. Chased by Europe's most dangerous killers, only Jim's cunning and Eve's bravery can save them. Fast paced, non-stop suspense pushes this story through the French Revolution, World War One, Montreal, Paris and the French countryside.

HJ Gaudreau

Betrayal
in the Louvre

Prologue

The notice that would forever change their lives was not found in a local, big city newspaper; rather it was in a weekly crier called the "Michigan Voice". That Eve saw it here, was a bit of a surprise. They rarely, if ever picked up the Voice. But for some reason fate intervened, and Jim had grabbed it as he left the town's only hardware store. Now, sitting on the back porch, drinking her coffee, waiting for Jim to finish in the barn, Eve thumbed through the only reading material available. And there it was, third page, lower left. "Antique Show and Charity Auction Returns to Detroit." Jim, more than Eve, enjoyed the show. Rarely could they afford the items for sale; this was not a "clean out the garage" kind of antique show. This show was hosted by some of the country's finest auction houses.

They didn't attend as buyers. Jim was a collector of arcane bits of trivia and simply found the auction to be a treasure trove of "interesting stuff". Suddenly, the baying of a beagle could be heard behind the equipment shed, a gray ghost raced around the building and headed for the pasture. Molly had picked up the scent and was close behind the rabbit. Jim stepped from the barn, slid the door shut and walked to the house. "Your antique auction is next week." She said as he climbed the porch steps. Jim washed his hands at the outdoor sink then sat in a deep wicker chair next to his wife.

"Great! That thing is always so interesting. And this year I've got something I want to take."

Eve started to laugh, "You really are a nerd. You know

that don't you?"

Jim just grinned. "What do you want to sell?"

"Well, I'm not really sure. Remember that stuff my great grandfather brought back from World War One? I'm hoping someone at the show will recognize it and be able to tell me a little bit more."

"Like if we've been hauling junk around the world for the past thirty years or not?" Eve asked in a gentle dig.

"Well, yeah," he grinned. "In any case, I thought this was a good chance to have it appraised. At least someone might be able to tell me what it is. And if not, maybe the Tigers are playing." "I knew there was more to this than an antique auction! C'mon, call your dog and let's go in. I'm hungry."

Chapter 1
Paris
3 June 1789

General Nicolas Luckner was out of bed before the man, for a man it surely was, on the other side of the door pounded a second time. In a moment he had a brace of .60 caliber holster pistols in his hands and was standing, naked, back to the wall, next to the door. The woman in the bed felt a wave of fear wash over her. The wave crested, then, human nature what it is, she admired the view.

From outside the door a young man's voice called "Mon General, it is urgent."

Luckner recognized the voice of his new adjutant and relaxed. The man, boy really, had been with him for only the past two weeks. This was the first time he'd been to the General's room after their morning drill. Luckner opened the door and let the man-boy in. The adjutant instinctively began a salute, saw the General was naked and attempted to look away. He turned his right shoulder to the General and found himself facing a young, naked redhaired woman sitting cross-legged on the bed. His surprise evident he involuntarily took a step backward whereupon he collided with the General. Shaken he spun around to meet the now angry glare of the man he feared more than anything in this life and, he was convinced, the next as well.

He stammered once, cleared his throat and before the General had finished inhaling in preparation for what surely would be one of history's great tongue-lashings he managed to stammer out the news he had been sent to deliver. "Sir, ah...Col DeAubry asked that...you have... you are supposed to..." The Adjutant's young eyes couldn't overcome the powerful draw of the woman's naked body. Like a bee to honey his eyes, without command, turned to her. The woman caught the glance, and vixen that she was, instantly decided to toy with the man-boy. She went into an exaggerated yawn, stretching her arms over her head and thrusting her bare breasts at the Adjutant. Then, like a cherry on top of a banana split, she smiled. The Adjutant's slim hold on his composure cracked.

The breach only lasted a moment as a thick hand slapped him on his left ear. The General stared down a long pointed nose, suppressed a smile and waited. The young officer regained his composure, stiffened, looked directly at the General and said, "Sir, Col DeAubry has asked that I relay a message."

"Well?" General Luckner's expression was stern, as befit a General. He was enjoying this little game. The man-boy tried again "The King has summoned you."

Luckner's brain instantly went to full attention. "For what purpose? When and where? These things should have been said already." Luckner did not suffer fools gladly, the game was over, the humor gone. The young man was now angering the General. Had he never seen a naked woman before?

"Le château de Versailles. Immediately."

"Tell the Colonel 'thank you' and I shall be with him in five minutes." Luckner said. The Adjutant, from sheer habit, saluted, stole another glance at the naked woman and fled the room. The General closed the door behind him. "No, he probably hasn't," he thought. Then his mind snapped back to the summons.

It was time, he was sure of it. This was necessary. There had been enough of patience, negotiations, maneuvering, politics and talk, talk, talk. Now, he was going to be told to round up the rabble and stuff them into the Bastille like so much sausage. Or, better yet, he'd put them to the sword tonight.

He began to assemble his uniform. In a few short minutes he was dressed, except for the boots. He could not find his boot hooks. His frustration grew as he looked under the bed, under the rug, behind the door...then he remembered. Reaching into the pile of woman's clothing on the floor he found them. The woman smiled at him. In a moment his boots had been pulled on and he was out the door.

Outside the tavern, Col DeAubry sat comfortably astride his horse, his attention focused on a hard piece of bread and moldy cheese which constituted his breakfast. A tall, rather lanky man, DeAubry had been born to a shoe cobbler. He had run from his apprenticeship at the first chance. At the age of twelve he'd taken a job as an assistant to a farrier and developed considerable expertise with horses. Five years later the man who had become more a father than employer was killed when a horse with an abscessed foot kicked him in the head. DeAubry found himself without means, a great deal of expertise in horses and a perfect fit for the cavalry.

The Colonel was known as a calm, sensible officer who could make things happen. He'd been with the General his entire career. Except of course for the three years he'd spent, at Luckner's insistence, with Rochambeau. He had survived a fever in the West Indies and distinguished himself on more than one occasion while fighting the British in their war with the American colonialists. His study and knowledge of siege warfare had been particularly useful in the later part of that campaign.

Under Luckner's sponsorship he'd risen to an almost unheard of rank for a man so low born. He was a trusted second to the General and the men feared and respected DeAubry as much as they feared and respected the General.

A few moments after DeAubry received the message a smartly dressed, fully alert General Nicolas Luckner exploded from the tavern's front door and mounted the horse held by the Adjutant. DeAubry relayed what little information he had, took up his position on the General's left and they began the short ride to the château de Versailles.

It was mid-afternoon, a light rain fell from a gray sky. The rain was welcome in Luckner's mind. It kept the rabble in their houses and it washed the sewage and animal droppings from the streets.

As they approached Le Potager du Roi the General noticed several handbills tacked to the trees outside of the royal garden's tall fence. Before he could pull one from its posting he spotted several men running across the road into the buildings and fields to his right. Instinctively his hand went to his pistol and he surveyed the doors, windows, alleys and bushes along his route. He wished he'd taken an escort; two men and a man-child would not do. He was not afraid of these traitorous fools, but he did not wish to be delayed. He would speak to DeAubry later about this.

Not knowing what the handbills were all about but feeling they may play a part in the upcoming meeting with the

King he stopped, dismounted and ripped one from the trunk of a large oak tree. The Colonel did the same.

DeAubry was shocked by what he read, the author accused the Queen of being a lesbian and whore. "More attacks on the Queen's reputation." DeAubry muttered as he shook his head.

Luckner read the paper in his hand. It railed against the King's treasurer Monsieur de Barentin, incompetent government and the King's intelligence. He snarled, crumpled the paper and tossed it to the ground.

Other bills peppered the trees and buildings for the next several hundred yards. They walked their horses for a few moments, silently reading the posters. DeAubry examined the fields and buildings. A boy appeared from behind a cottage. He yelled something and threw a rotten apple in their direction. The apple landed well short.

What were these people about? There had been a time, not so long ago when the French military had faced down the British across the globe. People had looked at him with pride. Now? Well, now things were different weren't they? DeAubry couldn't put his finger on it, something was happening. He was looked at with contempt, sometimes hate. He didn't understand it, he didn't know what it was, but he knew change was coming. And, from all he had seen, it wasn't change for the better. Luckner was mounting his horse. The rain was thicker now; the sky seemed a darker shade of gray.

Settling into the saddle the General pulled his collar up against the wind and the rain. He pulled his sword, indicated to the Adjutant to do the same, then leaning toward the still dismounted DeAubry he said. "Have as many men as possible, with good horses, at the palace in an hour. I suspect we're going to be busy tonight."

Luckner then turned his horse in the direction of the château, kicked the animal with his heels and cantered away. DeAubry would do his best, but horses were becoming scarce.

Chapter 2

"The Detroit Antiques Show is the biggest in the mid-west and I'm not going to miss it. Who knows, we could have something worth bizzillions of dollars." Herman James Crenshaw, retired Air Force Colonel, now proud co-owner with his wife of a sixty acre corn farm called from the attic of his cottage styled log home.

"Hey, do you know where that box of my great grandfather's stuff is?" The sound of boxes being moved and old furniture banging could clearly be heard above Eve Crenshaw's head. "Damn!....." More thumping of boxes. "Eve could you bring up a flashlight please? I forgot to turn on the light."

She stood at the bottom of the attic ladder, face turned up to the dark void overhead and smiled. "Yes Jim, I'll get you a flashlight." Eve walked into the kitchen and retrieved one from the pantry. "Hon, here's the flashlight."

She climbed the ladder, flicking on the light switch next to the attic door pulling a cobweb from her shoulder length honey auburn hair. Light filled the room, making the flashlight superfluous. "Did you find it?" She asked, doing her best to suppress a grin and failing.

"No, but I did find that lamp you bought in North Dakota." They both laughed. It was the worst lamp they'd ever seen. They bought the lamp to use as a gift in their squadron's dirty Santa Christmas gift exchange; the object of which was to find the ugliest, funniest gift possible.

Unfortunately, Jim had received orders before the party and they'd spent that Christmas moving into another house at another Air Force base. Now, here they were nearly thirty years later, retired from the Air Force and they still had it. She laughed at the absurdity of the thing. Jim smiled at his wife, he loved how her golden eyes sparkled when she laughed.

"Hey, here it is!" Jim triumphantly held up a wooden Boraxo soapbox. He sat the box on the floor, knelt beside it and opened the top. Inside was a mess kit, with his Great grandfather's name crudely etched onto the back of the pan. Jim held up the mess kit, showed it to Eve, still standing on the ladder, and then placed it on the attic floor. Next he held up a cigarette lighter with "Ardennes 1918 – Crenshaw" carved into the side. "Can you believe these things were used in the mud and trenches of World War One? It's amazing."

Jim was an unabashed history nut. In rapid succession the lighter was followed by a knife, a badly aged book with a faded cover, a handful of uniform decorations, none of which Jim recognized, a patch with a red arrow pierced by a small line and a dirty light coffee brown coloured tube with dirty brass ends.

"What's that?" Eve asked.

"I don't know," said Jim "but this is what I've been looking for. I've been wondering about this thing since we found it when we went through Mom's stuff. I'm betting it's a map case, maybe German. I'm hoping someone can tell me at the show. Maybe it was used to carry something like a unit flag or maybe it was a spacer of some sort."

"Let's open it and see what's inside."

"I've tried. I can't unscrew the damn thing and these lids don't pop off. I'm afraid of breaking it if I put too much pressure on it." Jim replied. Studying the tube for a moment Jim looked at Eve and said, "It just seems like it's pretty well made, it's a quality piece; but what it is, I'm totally blank on. I've tried looking in museums and on-line and I've never seen anything remotely like it. So, this is my last hope at solving the great Crenshaw mystery."

"Well, let's hope the mystery is solved then," she said.

They examined the tube. It seemed fairly stained and dirty. It had some markings on the side, but they couldn't make out what they were. The ends were metal and appeared as if they would polish nicely.

"This thing's filthy. I'll get a couple of rags and some soap and water." Eve started for the workbench.

"No, no, we can't do that. They say you shouldn't clean an antique; it makes it less valuable. We better wait. I want an expert to see this thing."

"Jim, that's nuts."

"No it's not, any expert will tell you that."

"Name one."

"That fat guy on TV, he says that all the time." Jim began to grin.

"You're making that up...but okay." She looked at Jim and smiled back. "Just wrap that thing up before you put it on my car's carpet."

"Okay, okay, you've got a deal," Jim said as he began putting the various items on the attic floor back in the box.

"That's all you're taking? It's a forty dollar ticket! We've got to take more than just that," she exclaimed.

"Well, I've got a couple of tools that I could get rid of. And, we could take this lamp," Jim smiled.

"The lamp? No, that's special." Eve laughed and backed down the ladder.

HJ GAUDREAU

NOVELS ARE AVAILABLE AT:

www.hjgaudreau.com

&

AMAZON.COM

Learn more about the facts and history of this and

other books by HJ Gaudreau at

www.hjgaudreau.com

ENJOY THE FOLLOWING
SAMPLES OF THE CRENSHAWS'
FIRST GREAT ADVENTURES

BETRAYAL IN THE LOUVRE

and

THE COLLINGWOOD LEGACY

Learn more about the facts and history of this and other

books by HJ Gaudreau at: **www.hjgaudreau.com**

THE COLLINGWOOD LEGACY

Only the treasure in an old smuggler's boat can save a rags to riches business

Financial ruin turns a psychopath into a kidnapper and murderer

Jim races to keep Eve from being dumped in the middle of Lake Michigan

Please enjoy the following sample of HJ Gaudreau's next thriller

Chapter 1

Detroit, September 1931

Anna Lademan ran an iron along the length of a man's long sleeve shirt. Not satisfied with the result she set the iron on its end and picked up a tall glass bottle with a yellow Vernor's label and a cork sprinkler head. She gave the bottle a shake and scattered small droplets of water along the sleeve. Again taking up her iron she finished the sleeve, placed the shirt on a hanger, and hung it next to a dozen similar shirts. After a quick glance at the remaining baskets of laundry she placed her hands on her hips, bent backward, chin to the ceiling and sighed. At five cents a shirt she could not afford to rest, but she had earned a quick stretch.

Anna then took a woman's floral dress from her basket and began to spread it on her ironing board. She did this with a bit of nostalgia. Her wedding dress had been a pretty flowered dress like this one. They had met in late winter, 1916. Her husband Abell had been a big man, with a full head of red hair and a broad back. He was also a romantic; he loved flowers and the spring. He had insisted they marry when the earth was new, crops were in the ground, and flowers were blooming. So, in the spring of 1918, two weeks after Anna turned nineteen they married. He died the next November.

She always thought that ironic, so many people were celebrating the end of the Great War, and her husband, who had fought in it hadn't been there. Abell had gone off to war in January 1917. By the February of 1918 he was home, one leg left behind in France, but home. She had her man and they would be all right. Then came the Spanish flu. Abell left in the morning for his job at the post office, that night he came home with a cough, by evening he couldn't stand, and he died before morning. The speed of his death had always troubled Anna. She hadn't had time to tell him how much he meant to her, about their unborn child, to make plans. He hadn't seen his boy, didn't know how much his son looked like him; never tussled his hair. Anna's eyes began to tear.

In what seemed like the Almighty's ploy to drag her from the depths of depression a crash sounded from the small living room behind her. An instant later Anna's pride and joy, her son Ezra, exploded into the kitchen.

"David told me he needs help selling newspapers today," the boy announced.

There had been another murder; one of the Licavoli Squad had been gunned down by the Purple Gang. The Times had run an 'extra' edition.

"He said I'd get two cents for every paper I sold."
"How much does David get?" Anna asked with a knowing smile.

"He keeps three cents. He said it's because he's the official representative of the Times and he's responsible. Come on Ma, I can get us a half bushel of apples if I sell twenty-five papers."

Anna smiled a mother's smile and nodded at her boy. "Give me a kiss," she said and Ezra was out the door.

The fall of 1931 was cold and rainy. Today was no exception. David Puginwitz stood outside the Collingwood Manor apartment building and called to the pedestrians on either side of the street. In the last hour he had sold only five newspapers, and the day was turning old. David pulled his collar up and shoved his hands deeper into his pockets. It worked for a moment, but the strap of his newspaper bag slid off his small shoulder and the bag fell to the wet sidewalk.

Worried the newspapers would be ruined, David uttered a curse he'd learned from his father, removed his hands from his coat pockets and hiked the strap back to his shoulder. He then blew on his clenched fists and jammed them back into his pockets. If he hunched his shoulder the bag held its position. Sadly, to David's never ending annoyance, the moment he relaxed his shoulder it fell to the sidewalk and the process was repeated.

As David pulled the newspaper bag to his shoulder for what seemed the fiftieth time he heard his friend Ezra's voice. The two boys greeted each other and immediately fell into a detailed discussion of their mutual obsession, the Detroit Tigers. David was a master of recalling the details of each of the summer's games. And, what he didn't remember he could invent. Ezra was a walking almanac of baseball statistics. Today, the conversation quickly turned to how bad this season had been and which players their team needed to replace. After a few minutes of baseball David pulled the newspaper bag from his shoulder and handed it to Ezra.

"I'm going inside to get warm. Don't let the bag get wet. I can't sell a wet newspaper."

David got all of two steps when Ezra suddenly exclaimed, "I almost forgot! Look what I've got!"

With that, Ezra pulled a tin from his coat pocket and opened it. Inside lay a small stack of baseball trading cards; several packs of cigarettes lay on top of the cards, candy wrapped in foil peeked from between cards. Ezra put the newspaper bag on the sidewalk, causing David to grimace and handed one of the cigarette packs to David.

David examined the pack of Sweet Caporal cigarettes. "What do I want with these? I don't smoke. And I ain't startin' now. Ma says it makes your teeth fall out."

"Geeze, I know that. But, turn it over," Ezra said with a proud grin.

David did as he was told. To his delight on the back of the package was the prettiest Ty Cobb trading card he'd ever seen. "Holy smokes! This is great!" he explained. All thoughts of a warm stove disappeared. Immediately David began offering combinations of his cards in trade for one of the new Ty Cobb cards. A brief argument over the value of various cards, new cards versus old cards, gum cards versus dry goods cards, a round of potential deals in which both boys tried to dump hated Yankee players on the other and soon a deal was struck. A few minutes later David was examining his new card when the possibility that Ezra had stolen the cigarettes crossed his mind.

"Where'd you get the cigarette packs Ezra?" David said with newly found suspicion. "If you lifted them and my Ma finds out..."

"I didn't steal nothin'!" Ezra then began to explain how Mr. Kacrozowski left two cartons of cigarettes and four shirts at his house. He was coming to the part about how a drunken Mr. Kaczorowski tried to grab his mother, and what she had called Mr. Kacrozowski when she hit him on the head with a frying pan, when a new, black four-door Chrysler coasted to a stop in front of the building. Instinctively, both boys ceased their chatter.

The front passenger door opened and a man with a dark gray tweed overcoat stepped to the curb. He took a moment to study the street. His glance passed over the boys, then both sides of the street in each direction. Finally, he studied the windows of the nearby buildings. Satisfied, he nodded in the direction of the car. Two men climbed out of the back seat. One reflexively skimmed his hand over his hip and said, "I didn't bring my gun."

The other glanced at him, "I told ya, ya don't bring guns to a meeting like this." Walking around to the trunk of the car he removed a brown briefcase. The three men gathered on the curb. The driver shut off the engine, got out and walked around the front of the car. As if on command the three men, in matching strides, approached the steps to the building. Their shoes making a rhythmic 'smack...smack...smack' on the wet concrete as they approached the boys. The driver hurried around the car and ran to catch up.

Ezra knew something about the street. These guys were going to take his baseball cards and maybe shake down

David for his paper money. Realizing it was too late to slip the tin back in his pocket he pushed it to the bottom of the newspaper bag. Then he stepped behind David.

The three men swept past the two boys without looking at them. The driver, now only a step or two behind, turned and flipped a silver dollar in their direction. "You kids! Keep an eye on my car," he snarled. Ezra tried to catch the coin and missed. The man stopped. The coin rang off the step and rolled to the sidewalk.

"C'mon Sol!" one barked, and the men entered the apartment building.

Chapter 2

Harry Keywell stood silently at the window of Collingwood Manor, apartment 211 and watched the street. After ten minutes he finally said, "They're here."

Irving Milberg and Ray Bernstein both joined Harry at the window. Harry Fleisher remained sitting on the couch.

"I don't have any argument with Sol," Irving said.

"I don't want a witness," Harry replied.

"Look, Sol's all right. We leave him alone," Ray announced.

Fleisher stood up, "You sure about that Ray? I hope Sol doesn't bite us on the ass."

A moment later Keywell answered the door. Joe Lebowitz, Hymie Paul and Izzy 'The Rat' Sutker walked in. An awkward silence filled the room. Finally Bernstein broke the tension. "Boys, take a seat," he said and pointed to an oversized couch and easy chair.

Ray's eyes focused on the briefcase. Maybe this would go alright. Harry turned on Izzy Sutker, "I think we all know what this is about," he said.

"Sure Harry, we know we owe you some money..."

"not just some, you owe us a lot of money Izzy."

"You know we're good for it" Sutker continued.

"I've heard that before," Ray said from across the room. "You've promised, and you've promised. You came to us and asked for a loan and I gave it to you. It makes me look like a fool. But the worst thing is that you idiots went and tried to cut us out of the business. Then you guys had the moxie to ask for another loan..."

"And we damned well gave it to you," Milberg cut in. Ray glanced at Milberg, then continued, "Now you're telling us you need more time. We already gave you more time. After all that, you tell us you can't pay."

"What is this?" Harry demanded.

Hymie Paul concentrated on Harry's every move. He glanced at Milberg and Bernstein then his partners Izzy Sutker and Joe Lebowitz. Finally he said, "I think we can work something out." He patted the case. "I've got half of your money right here. It'll take us a little time, but we should have the rest of the money to you in three months."

Keywell erupted, "Half? You come here with half? What the hell do you think this is?"

Almost imperceptibly Ray shook his head no.

Fleisher put his hands out as if to pat the air. "Boys, let's all be calm. Look, let's not get worked up about this. I've got some cold beer in the basement. I'll go get us some and we'll work out some terms." The decision had been made. Ray, Irv and Harry Keywell all glanced at each other.

"Yeah, I think you're right," Ray said.

Fleisher walked out into the hall and headed for the street. The car would be idling in back in three minutes.

"We need it all," Irv said a moment later.

Harry Keywell moved to the next window, his hand slipped inside his jacket and gripped his pistol.

"Look, we ain't got that much, we're lucky to have this," Hymie's throat had tightened; his voice was almost a squeal.

Irv grinned, "I don't think you understand. We employ you, we give you a good territory, and you knock over our runs, you don't pay your debts, you steal from us!"

Irv's voice was getting louder, he took a breath then very slowly he said, "We...need...our...money...NOW." His fist slammed onto the table.

Lebowitz glanced at his two partners. "Look, Irv, I understand. We'll get you the rest. But it will take time, we'll need a month."

Milberg looked at Keywell and shrugged, "Seems like an awful long time don't you think?"

Keywell pulled his gun, "Times up."

David stooped to pick up the silver dollar. Ezra had failed to catch it when Sol had tossed the coin. "Those guys look like gangsters, Ezra. We've got real life gangsters right here!"

Ezra was staring at the door where the men had disappeared. David sat down on the wet step, Ezra joined him. Still shaken neither boy said anything. After a few moments Ezra stood up and announced, "I'm going home."

"What! You can't leave. Neither can I. That guy gave us a dollar to watch his car. That's a lot of money. If we leave he'll come back and get us. We have to stay right here." David was older and so he must be smarter. Ezra sat back on the step.

"I think those guys were the Purple Gang," David said a few minutes later. "There was a story about them in the paper last week. I saw their picture. They're famous."

Suddenly a series of pops could be heard from a long distance away. Both boys jumped to their feet, eyes searching the street as they turned a slow circle. Another round of gunfire and this time the two friends could identify the location of the sound, as one they turned and looked to the second floor. A moment later the building's front door burst open and the driver of the car ran out carrying a brown briefcase. Taking the stairs two at a time he collided with Ezra and David knocking the boys over and falling to the sidewalk. The case flew from his hand scattering several bundles of cash on the sidewalk. The case slid across the sidewalk and under the big car.

"What the...," David cried. Ezra slid across the sidewalk and came to rest against the Chrysler.

"Gimme that," Sol Levine shouted at Ezra as he jumped to his feet. Sol grabbed the newspaper bag and pulled. The boy was jerked forward and fell to the sidewalk, landing on the side of his face with a yell. Sol dragged the bag from the boy's grasp. Then he scooped up the bundles of cash laying on the sidewalk and stuffed them into the bag. After a quick glance at the door of the building he ran to the Chrysler. In a moment the engine roared and the car was turning the corner onto Grand Boulevard.

Seconds later three men tumbled from the door of the apartment building, each man carrying a pistol. They ran down the stairs, past Ezra and David and into the center of the street. The three men turned in circles looking for the car. It was too late. One man spotted the briefcase laying on the curb. He picked it up, looked inside then threw it back on the street.

"The little shit! He took it all!" the man yelled.

"Ray, I'm gonna kill that little S.O.B.," another whispered.

The three men then walked back into the building. It was as if David and Ezra were invisible. Ezra dabbed his bloody nose and began to cry.

HJ GAUDREAU

NOVELS ARE AVAILABLE AT:

www.hjgaudreau.com

&

AMAZON.COM

Learn more about the facts and history of this and other books by HJ Gaudreau at

www.hjgaudreau.com